TEMPEST

KRIS MICHAELS

CHAPTER 1

T*hree years ago:*

"Mother, please, this isn't necessary." The limo slowed, but the draped interior prevented Pilar Grantham from knowing exactly where they were other than somewhere in New York City.

Regina Grantham didn't bother to look up from her laptop. "Your inappropriate inquiries into my business dealings must be addressed, and do not call me that." The car stopped, and Regina finally looked up and pulled the curtain back a fraction of an inch.

Fine. She drew a deep breath and tried again. "Regina, you sent me to law school for a reason.

My questions could eliminate potential problems for you. Working with insider information will eventually land you in prison." Her mother's business was laced with questionable actions in the limited areas she'd been allowed to see.

Regina examined her with cold disinterest. "*I* tell you what to do and when to do it. You work on the projects *I* send you. No others. You will not deviate from my instructions, and we will not have this conversation again. To emphasize my point, you will experience, first-hand, how I gain information." She flicked her finger toward the door. "Accompany the man waiting for you. Do not make a scene, Pilar. You bear my last name and you will act accordingly."

She held her mother's stare for as long as she could before she dropped it. Regina sighed and turned back to her laptop. "Go."

She slipped out of the car and gazed up at a dilapidated building. The man waiting ushered her into a huge bustling, warehouse, moving at a clipped pace so she had to mind her step in the heels she wore. The brute's hand gripped her arm, tugging her toward the elevator. She ripped away from his grasp. "Stop! I am Regina Grantham's daughter and I will be treated as such." She yanked her thin cotton top over her camisole and lifted her chin daring the man to say anything she could use against him. The titan sneered but retracted his hand. She sneered back at him. They understood each other. That was the power of her mother's name. People knew who she was, and no one wanted to make the woman mad. No one, herself included, however she'd pushed too far this time. God, she knew it when she opened her mouth. She knew Regina would be upset, but this little demonstration... it was over the top, even for an absolute control freak like Regina.

They went down an elevator in silence and wound through a maze of junk before she was led down a tunnel. She tripped in the darkness, the man clutched her arm in a painful grip. Once upright she jerked her arm from his grip. She glared at him. He motioned with his hand and they continued. Her mother's barbarian opened another steel door with a series of taps on a keypad.

Seriously, what was underground that was so important? Regina's secret vault of nefarious informants? Perhaps it was a tree that grew insider information. Or a magic wand...

The putrid stench slapped her first. She covered her nose and mouth with her hand. Tears stung the back of her eyes. A citrusy chemical astringent covered the undeniable smell of rancid body odor and... oh hell, she had no idea. "What in God's name died down here?"

The man chuckled and tipped his head to the left. She shook her head. "Thanks, but no thanks."

The goon pointed down the hall and slammed the door behind her locking them both in the stench-filled confines. She glanced from the door to him. A skin-prickling sense of dread crept across her arms and neck. This, whatever this was, wasn't good. She threw back her shoulders and spoke through her hands which still covered her mouth and nose, "Fine, let's get this over with." She gagged and coughed as they headed down the hall. The floors, walls and ceiling were steel now, unlike the tunnel they'd traveled down. She was forced to take five or six to every one of the behemoth's steps. Being five-foot-nothing sucked sometimes.

She scurried to keep up with Mr. Mountain, but stutter stepped when she noticed the doors in this hall. All steel with bars up top and a single slat in the door. Prison. The word shot around her brain and ricocheted into ridiculous and terrifying thoughts. Surely her mother wasn't putting her in prison. The guard, yes, he was a guard, stopped in front of one of the doors and withdrew a set of keys.

"What are you doing?" She started to back up. Whatever was inside that room could stay in there.

"She wants you to see this." His accent was one she couldn't place, Slavic perhaps. He reached out and snagged her arm.

"Let me go!" The door opened and she was pushed into a dark hole. The door slammed in her face. She grabbed at it and then flipped around praying nothing was going to attack her from the darkness. Fluorescent lights flicked on and blinded her for a moment. She jerked right and left bouncing her attention from point to point.

Sink. Toilet. Bed.

"Oh, my God!" She took a step toward the cot in the corner of the room. "Oh, dear merciful heavens." A person was on the bed. She covered her mouth, but this time not because of the stench, but because she was going to puke. They put her into a cell with a dead person!

The huddled form moaned and tried to turn, only to gasp in pain. No, not dead! She darted across the small room. Shaking like a leaf, she moved to touch his shoulder. "What can I do to help?"

The form was nothing but skin and bones. Bruises covered his body. There was a wound on his leg that was caked with blood. God, he needed to be cleaned so infection... but dear Lord, infection was the least of this man's worries. She leaned over him and shifted the ripped scrubs bottoms covering the man's fragile frame. He flinched away from her. "I promise I won't hurt you."

She whispered the words as her eyes flew around the little cell. She ran back to the door and pounded on it. "I need medical supplies. Get me medical supplies or I'll tell her you touched me and made me touch you!"

The small door at the top of the metal bars opened. She backed up so she could see him. "Shut up."

"Bring the supplies or I'll make sure she thinks you attacked me." Pilar pulled at the neck of her shirt, ripping it. She scratched at her face, desperate for the damn fool to believe her.

The man's eyes widened. "Wait." He shut the little window and she heard him move away from the door.

She scurried back to the cot. She tugged off her shirt, shredded the cotton fabric, and moved to the stainless-steel sink bolted to the wall. The water stayed on only as long as she depressed the plunger on the faucet. It took time to wet a larger patch of the material, clog the drain and fill the sink with water. It was a slow tedious process. The water, bloodied by cleaning his wounds, needed to be emptied many times.

The door opened and a white case was thrust in her direction.

She grabbed it and demanded, "Give me your shirt." Her camisole wasn't going to be warm enough to wrap around the injured man.

"Go to hell."

"Then I'll meet you there! Because she'll send you before she sends me," she hissed and held out her hand in expectation. The man growled but his shirt came off and was tossed in her face. She snatched it, spun and dropped to the floor by the cot. The door to the cell slammed shut. "Look. Here we go." She broke open the seal on the first aid kit and examined the contents. "Damn it. I'm sorry, but the only thing for pain is acetaminophen." She dug through the contents and found a small cup. Two pills went into the bottom of the cup and she poured water over the top to soften them. The drink was going to taste like shit, but maybe it would help him.

The man's eyes opened. No white was visible in either sclera. Red filled around the gold- flecked green of his eyes. She shook her head. How could anyone do this to another person?

"What happened? Who did this to you?" She carefully reached and pushed back his hair. It was filthy with sweat and blood. The dark brown strands were long. So damn long. At least a foot in length if not longer. It rested on his thin shoulders and fell down his back. Each vertebrae of his back-bone punched through bruised skin.

"Why are you here?" The words were low and came from bloody, broken lips.

"Here. It won't help much, but I have some pain killers." She grabbed the cup, but he closed his eyes and turned away from her.

"Why are you here?" His body shook against the bare mattress.

"I'm being taught a lesson." *Be anything other than her marionette and you'll end up like this, Pilar.* Lesson learned. She picked up the guard's shirt. "Here." She draped it over his shoulder and wished she had a blanket.

"By who?"

"My mother," she hissed and closed her eyes.

The sickness in her gut rolled and pitched at the thought her mother orchestrated this evil.

"Explain." He shivered against the mattress.

"I will. May I lie down beside you? It might help to keep you warm." The man didn't answer, either he'd passed out or he didn't care. She put the cup on the side of the sink and carefully slid onto the pallet. She spooned behind him and carefully put an arm around his gaunt waist. The groan he released may have been from the pain of her gentle jostle of his position, or perhaps relief from whatever warmth her body provided.

The lights clicked off leaving the cell in complete darkness. A small slice of light filtered in from under the cell door. "Motion activated." The man's faint whisper reached her.

"Are they watching you? Cameras?" That she'd given aid to the person Regina was trying to extract information from wouldn't help her cause, not that she gave a damn about her mother right now.

"No. No camera, no mic." He gripped the shirt and pulled it closer to his shoulder. "Thank you."

She swallowed hard, trying to stop the tears which welled in her eyes. His gratitude for simple human kindness sliced her heart.

"Why is she doing this to you?"

He jolted a bit. "She?"

"My mother."

"She?"

The question had to have been asked for reassurance. "Yes, my mother."

There was silence for several long moments. The man's shaking subsided a bit. "Tell me about her."

"Why?"

"I want to know who is doing this to me." She heard a small hitch in his voice and somehow knew he was crying, although his shoulders barely moved. This man was broken. She kept close to him, willing her warmth into his too thin body. She spoke soft words of comfort, of promises she couldn't keep, telling him everything would be okay.

He whispered hoarsely, "Name?"

"My name is Pilar. What is your name?"

There was no movement except the shallow in and out of his chest as he breathed. She thought he'd fallen asleep, but eventually he answered, "I no longer have one." The man drew a deep breath and relaxed slightly into her. Moments turned into minutes, that lengthened into hours, and she held him because it was all she could do. Finally, he stirred.

She helped him off the bed and watched as he willed himself to remain standing and shuffle to the sink to brush his teeth with the tail of the new shirt. Only his jutting hip bones held up the cotton scrub bottoms he wore. His body hunched as if the effort to straighten his spine was too much.

"You need food." She marched to the door and pounded on it. The man spun; his body braced against the sink.

The guard threw open the window. "What now?"

"I want food." She crossed her arms and stared at the goon on the other side.

"It's coming. I'll open the door for you to exit when it arrives."

"Exit?" What in the hell was he talking about?

"No food for him." The goon tossed his chin toward the man.

"Wrong answer. You will bring my food to me, in here. Do we need to go over what will happen if you don't?" She ran her fingers across her camisole straps. "I mean, you've already torn my shirt to shreds."

"Fucking bitch."

She smiled at the man. "Just like my mother. Remember it, and you'll survive."

The man's eyes narrowed, and the flap slammed shut.

"You shouldn't anger them." The man shuffled back across the floor to the bed and lay down slowly.

"They're terrified of my mother."

"Who is she?" The man groaned the question as he turned onto his side to talk to her.

She lowered her eyes to her hands. *Wasn't that the question of the decade.* "I don't know. Not really. I'm not sure I ever knew her." She moved to the cot and sat on the floor, so they were eye to eye.

"Why are you here?"

"Punishment, I guess. I asked too many questions and wouldn't let it drop." Pilar shook her head and stared at the edge of the cot.

"What kind of questions?"

Pilar stared at him. The man's bruised face and bloody eyes scored her soul in ways she couldn't fathom. She was her mother's attorney. The law required that she keep her secrets, yet somehow, she knew this man wouldn't live long enough to repeat anything she'd said. "I wanted to know where she got the information she was using. At the time I had access to her stock market accounts. I was supposed to be learning about her wealth and how it was managed. I saw her sell massive amounts of stock only to have the same stock tank two days later. Of course, she funneled the ownership through countless shell companies so it wouldn't trigger FCC investigations."

"She's powerful?"

Pilar shrugged and then nodded. "Yeah."

"She wants you to follow her path." The man's eyes closed. "Regretful."

"Her path? No. She has my future planned and expects me to be the marionette on the end of her golden strings. I want nothing to do with her or her companies." Pilar jumped when the door clanked. A tray was shoved through the space in the bars. She scurried to the door and caught it before it fell.

She took it to the cot. "When was the last time you've eaten?"

The man opened his eyes. "Time is hard to gauge here. A while. They give me enough to survive."

"Okay, then we might need to take this easy." She reached for the cup with the over-the-counter pain killers dissolved in the bottom. "Drink this first and then we can work on getting some of this food into you." She motioned to the tray which held a sandwich, a bag of chips, and a carton of milk.

"No. It's yours."

"I'm always trying to lose ten pounds. You need this more than I do." She handed him the cup and watched him sip the small amount of water until it was gone. "Okay. We start with bread. If it stays down, we can move on to the other stuff."

She took the cup back and examined a triangle of bread before she tore off a small bit. "I have no idea if I'm doing this right, but I watched a movie once that said if you were starving, you needed to slowly reintroduce food."

He took the small piece from her and placed it in his mouth. "Would you leave if you could?"

Pilar glanced from the bread she held to the man. "Here or her?"

"Both."

"Here? No. Not until I know you are okay. Her? Yes, absolutely yes." Pilar sighed and tore off another small piece, handing it to the man. "What did you do? Who put you in here?"

"I don't know. My captors ask for information I don't have."

"Can I help?"

The man's eyes slid to hers. "How can I trust you?"

Pilar blinked at him and then whispered, "You think I'm one of them?" He continued to stare at her, and she handed him another small piece of bread. "I would never allow this. Never."

"Words."

"What can I do? She twisted and glanced at the door. "How do I prove to you I don't want or agree with any of this?"

He remained silent until he'd eaten both pieces of bread and the cheese slice. Finally he drew a stuttering breath and said, "There is a way to help. I know where I'm being taken."

CHAPTER 2

P *resent day:*

Jason King's glower stared back at Doctor Jeremiah Wheeler from the computer screen of his desk in Hollister, South Dakota. "It's time to make the call, Remi. Are you giving him a Go or not?"

The CEO of Guardian Security could be intimidating, but Jason's resting bitch face wasn't going to change this conversation. "He's been through a significant trauma. Years of abuse, both mental and physical. Tempest is lucky to be alive."

"That's a given. Physically he's been cleared. Hell, he's running circles around our training cadre at the Rose. My concern is for his mental health."

"As is mine." Remi sighed.

Jason leaned forward. "Doc, is he cleared or not?"

"I have my doubts."

"About what specifically?"

"He's hell bent on revenge."

Jason made a noise in his throat. "Wouldn't you be?"

Ah, now *that* was an emotional response. Remi narrowed his eyes. "No. Would you?"

His boss shook his head and sighed. "You're not psychoanalyzing me, Doc. What else do you have?"

"I think he still hasn't told us everything. Especially during the time close to his rescue. He claims he can't remember some of the last months."

"Did you talk to Maliki? Physically, the man was near death's door. Is it a stretch to think he couldn't remember everything?"

"No, but you asked for my opinion, and I'm giving it to you. He's fixated on those last months and guarding them."

"From what?"

"Me, you, everybody. The woman who helped him is the key, I'm certain."

"He hasn't disclosed much information about her."

"No."

Jason tapped his pen against the desk, deep in thought. Remi waited for the next question. Jason leaned forward. "Is he a threat to her?"

"God, no. I think, to a degree, he's idolized her."

"For helping him escape from hell? I probably would have done the same thing. Bottom line. Is he a threat to himself or others?"

Remi chuckled as he shook his head. "Define others."

Jason rolled his eyes. "People not coded."

"He's absolutely a threat to the people who held him. I don't doubt for a second he's going to do everything in his power to go after them."

Jason smiled. "Then there are no concerns on our part. We want him to go after them."

Remi blinked at the screen. "Are you serious?"

"He has the motivation and drive to reach the people who have been eluding us for years. Yes, I'm serious. We'll assist him in his endeavors to find and eliminate them." Jason leaned back in his chair.

"And if they are in the United States?"

"Above your need to know, Remi."

"Ah." Put firmly in his place he glanced down at

the files he'd accrued while treating the operative he knew as Tempest. No other name had been given, nor did he ask for it. The man had worked damn hard on his physical and mental rehabilitation. Could he release him? Yes. The question was, should he? Putting the man back in the environment where he was captured in the first place was fraught with problems, triggers, and memories. But Tempest had told him point blank he wanted to return to his previous life, that he felt he was needed in his profession. The organization had been willing to wait years for the man to recover. Tempest must be one hell of an assassin. He shifted his eyes to the screen. "May I ask a question?"

"Ask. I don't guarantee an answer."

"What is his... methodology?"

"Well..." Jason leaned forward and steepled his fingertips. "He makes statements."

Remi stared at the screen. *Statements.* So, Tempest's assassinations were more than likely violent, noisy, and intended to be noticed, unlike those whose work was meant to be innocuous. That didn't really mesh with the quiet, contained man he'd worked with. Everything about Tempest was measured and calm, but the operational end of the man's work was not his concern. His mental health was, and even though he had a gut feeling Tempest was hiding things, there was no reason to hold him longer. He sighed and nodded his head.

"I have a couple follow up sessions, but yes, unless something drastic comes up during our last appointments, I will clear him—with reservations. He's been doing this work long enough. It is my recommendation he should change positions and retire from this line of work, but I have nothing clinically to stop him from returning if he chooses to do so."

"I'll inform Fury. Archangel out."

The screen went black, and Remi leaned back in his chair and stared at the years of notes. It was time to let the man go.

Tempest once again examined the vista he'd memorized long ago. He'd stared at this portion of the Arizona desert every evening for almost three years. His routine varied minimally, as necessitated by the weather or in the beginning, his health. Tonight would be the last night he'd gaze upon the purple and pink vista. Dr. Wheeler had finally given him a 'Go' on his Go/No Go evaluation. A small smirk tilted the corner of his lips. He had immediate plans, and they didn't include accepting a mission from Guardian. At least not any that would divert him from his primary objectives.

Her footsteps were as familiar as the vista as she approached the small cottage he'd lived in for almost three years. The Rose was mostly underground, but after his confinement he only went into the underground labyrinth when it was necessary. He heard the familiar pant and smiled slightly. Liberty was by her side, as always. The German Shepherd preferred to be out at night, and with the heat during the day, he couldn't blame her.

"Hey, sorry we're late, but Libby got the scent of a rabbit or something, and we walked forever. Did you move already?" Eve McDade sat down in the chair across from him. He chuckled as she leaned forward, saw his rook and murmured, "You did. Damn it."

"You left your queen in jeopardy. One should always protect the queen." Tempest had been beating Eve at chess for the last year, although she'd vastly improved during the course of their evening sessions.

She leaned forward and studied the board. "I'm going to be in check soon."

Three moves to checkmate, two if she made a mistake and moved the bishop. "It would appear you are correct."

Eve groaned and flopped back into her rocker. "One of these days, my friend, I'm going to win, and when I do, I'm going to make you eat your superior attitude."

Tempest chuckled. *Friend.* Strange, but he considered her one, too. An unlikely pair to be sure. When Eve had moved to the complex, she'd shunned all things to do with his profession. He'd watched her epic meltdown when he was rescued and heard about her ultimatum to Thanatos. Over the years he'd watched her grow up and mellow out. No longer was she the naive woman who had surfaced at the Rose about the time he had started to take an interest in living again.

"What occupied your day?" She pushed the decking and set her rocker in motion. Her eyes had returned to the chess board, and she studied the squares and pieces.

"PT and sparring in the morning, a doctor's appointment in the afternoon."

She stopped rocking. "Is everything okay?"

He nodded. "Routine appointments."

"Dolan said you were kicking his ass during training runs, and no one can beat you on the mats. You should be happy. He's a man who prides himself in being the best at everything he does."

"He is no longer the best because he won't train in the tactics and skills he needs to maintain his proficiency without your approval."

Eve sighed. "I know. We've been talking a lot. In here, in my head, I know what he used to do saved countless lives. I *know* it. I'm working on it. Dolan promises me he doesn't miss that life, but I know keeping him from being *able* to go if he wants to leave is wrong."

Tempest absorbed the statement and turned it around and around in his mind. Since his captivity, taking his time to decode and decipher intent and sincerity had become the norm for him—perhaps due to the intensive psychological therapy he'd gone through since he'd resurfaced.

No. His internalization of others' words and meanings allowed him to strip *his* emotion from his responses. The words he uttered needed to be congruent with what would allow him to complete *his* goals. He had two missions to perform, and he'd be damned if a misplaced comment would sideline him from dispatching his objectives.

He glanced at his *friend*. She studied the board intently. The metamorphosis of the woman since she'd arrived paralleled his. She'd grown up and he'd grown older. She'd learned to understand her husband's life, and he'd learned to understand what happened in his past affected his future. She wanted nothing but to love her man, and he wanted... two things and only two things —to free Pilar and to eliminate the three Fates thereby destroying Stratus. He stared across the darkness.

"You've changed. So has your man."

Eve leaned forward. The tactic was one she employed when she wanted him to look at her. A tick of a smile twitched at the corner of his lip as he glanced at her for a moment. Only then did she ask, "What do you mean?"

"He's happy here. Content and settled. He wasn't before you."

She drew a ragged breath. "Thank you. You don't know how hard it was to come here and draw a line in the sand, to tell him what *I* needed to make our relationship work. The doctor warned me some people would call me selfish or self-centered, but it wasn't why I asked him to walk away from his past."

"Then why did you?"

"Well, I guess it was so we both could get to *this* place. The point where logically I know he'll go again if one of you is in jeopardy or he believes his skills are needed. Doctor Wheeler worked with both of us, and because Dolan agreed to step away from it when he did, we were able to walk down this path together. I was so ignorant. Arrogant even, but he never gave up on me."

"He loves you."

"And I love him." She reached down and shifted the pawn forward one block. It was the best move in an impossible position. "What are you going to do now? Scuttlebutt downstairs is that you've been cleared to work."

"Ah." He chuckled and moved his knight, taking the pawn. "Check." He smiled at her groan. "I have some people I want to reacquaint myself with."

"Yeah? Anyone special?" The tease in her voice danced on the night air.

"Special is a vague adjective." He arched a brow as she moved her king to the right one space. "You're still in check."

"Damn it." She slid the piece back and flipped

her gaze up to him for a second. "Okay smarty, are you going to visit a woman?"

"Indeed." *Four women to be precise.* Numbers One, Two and Three, but before he paid each of those women a deadly visit, he would find the one female who was the reason he was rescued.

"What's her name?" Eve's face split in a wide smile. She was a child in a woman's body sometimes.

Savior, comfort, peace, deliverer, strength, beauty all the words fit her, yet none were enough to describe what she'd been for him. "Her name is Pilar."

"Pilar? A very interesting name... unless, is it a code name?" Eve's smile wavered a bit.

"No. It's her given name." Or it was the name she'd given him when she'd held his hand.

"How do you know her?"

"She was the one who had access to a computer and watched for a message. She memorized what to say and how to phrase it in order to respond to the query your husband sent. She answered it. I didn't." This was the skimmed down version of the truth he'd told his handlers. The real depth of what she'd done for him would never be spoken. Pilar was the reason he'd clung to life as long as he had.

Eve leaned back in her rocker. "I've heard portions of Dolan's side of the story. I never asked myself how you answered his email. Lord knows you were in no condition to find or gain access to a computer when we arrived."

He arched an eyebrow at her, and she rolled her eyes.

"I know. Dolan did what he had to do. I see it, *now*. But put yourself in my shoes for two minutes. You know about my past. Mentally at *that* point in my life, I wasn't ready to see or understand *anything* that happened that day. I couldn't pick it apart and examine it for a long time."

"Yet your man stayed with you."

"He did, and I'll stand by him as he does what he has to do. I hope he'll never be in the position to take a mission, but if he does, I'll be here when he comes home, and I'll love him as hard as I know how because that's what he's given me. Unconditional love." She reached forward and tipped the king, dropping him to the board. "Two moves and I'm in mate, no matter what I do. I must bore you to tears."

Tempest chuckled. "To be honest, you're a slow learner."

She gaped at him before she laughed, "But, I *can* be taught."

"This is true."

"Will you be leaving soon?" Eve stood and whistled for Liberty who'd sniffed herself out into the desert.

He nodded. "Very soon. There is one more conversation I need to have before I leave."

"Well then, I'll say farewell because I don't want this to be goodbye." She walked to him and dropped a kiss on his cheek. "We can play chess online."

He shook his head as she dropped off the porch and waited for her dog to return. "I'll contact you when I can."

"You better or I'll have Dolan come find you and kick your ass."

"He'll need help."

"I'll send the freaking cavalry after you if I have to. Don't make me prove it." She waved and walked back to the clinic and the elevator which would take her and Liberty into the underground training facility.

Tempest waited for several long seconds before he spoke quietly. "Would you like a transcript of the conversation?" He heard low chuckles from one side of the porch and a crunch of gravel from the other.

Fury dropped into the rocking chair vacated by Eve and glanced at the chessboard as Thanatos settled into a relaxed lean against the front post of the porch. He removed three fat cigars and passed one to each of them. The clippers followed, with a gold-cased lighter making the same path. Thanatos puffed his cigar to life last and blew a stream of smoke. "What's the plan?"

Tempest puffed on his Cuban. Damn, it had been forever since he'd allowed himself the indulgence. "I'm going to leave."

"No shit." Fury's disdain for his answer hinged on the end of his voice the way the ashes hung on the end of his cigar. "Be specific."

"I need to find her. I believe her to be as much of a prisoner as I was." He knew Fury had read his transcripts with the doctor. Hell, he wouldn't be surprised if Thanatos, as Fury's second here at the complex, had read them, too.

"Do you know where to start?" Thanatos hiked himself up to sit on the porch rail.

"I do."

Fury puffed a bit before he remarked, "You're not alone in this."

He pushed his rocker a bit and enjoyed the cigar and the companionship before he answered. "Everyone is alone in life... and in death." The memory of Pilar's hand stroking his cheek as he suffered flitted through his mind. "If you're lucky, you find someone to walk beside you." He took a puff on his cigar. "I've never been lucky."

Fury snorted. "Damn good thing you're not counting on luck. Check in with Anubis. The new protocols are in effect."

"Ah, yes, the collar and leash."

There were teams specifically trained and dispatched to the last known location of those who did not report in on time. No longer would Shadows be without support. After he was recovered and had reported the events that had transpired, it had been a logical step to ensure Guardian's assets could access support immediately. Archangel had stipulated teams locate to a Shadow's general position for support. Check in was every twenty-four hours. Period. One minute late and the teams would be dispatched to go in and extract the Shadow. Logistically sound for retaining assets, but it put restrictions on people who should be able to act independent of control.

"Asset protection." Thanatos tapped his ashes into his hand.

He puffed his cigar and flicked his ashes onto the deck, sliding his foot on top of them to ensure there was no spark left. "Irritating and restrictive."

"Necessary," Fury added.

"Tell me you would have agreed to such limitations." Tempest rolled his head and stared at the original Shadow.

Fury shook his head. "No, but I worked in a different world at a different time. Now there are ways to check in that won't compromise position or concealment."

"And if the enemy should learn these methods?" Tempest stared at the red tip of his cigar.

Fury shrugged. "Then we move to the next method. Nothing is forever. Tech changes, we change."

Which was true, yet he couldn't help wondering... "Have you considered the Shadows may be moving toward obsolescence?"

"As long as there are monsters upon the earth, and innocents without hope, people like us will always be needed." Fury tapped his ashes onto the porch.

"I'm going after them." Tempest cleared his

throat. "After I find her, I'm going after them." There was no need to define who 'them' was. Stratus and the Fates were his. He'd survived their version of hell, and he'd earned the right to send them to Satan's depths, permanently.

"How will you find them? Guardian with all its vast resources haven't been able to locate them." Thanatos extended his arms wide. "I know where you're coming from, remember I made a vow about my parents' killers. It became an obsession which nearly ruined my career and my life. Besides, Shadows aren't sanctioned to work in the States."

"True. True." He puffed on his cigar again. Guardian might not know how to find them, but he believed he had a lead. First, however, he had to locate Pilar. He prayed she'd done as he'd asked, and stayed safe until he could come for her. Tempest pushed his boot on the boards and set his rocker going again. It had been so long, she probably thought he was dead. Did she continue to rebel? Had her mother's desires become hers as well? The questions chased themselves around his mind.

They smoked together in a quiet, comfortable silence until the cigars came to an end. Thanatos slid from the rail and extended his hand. "I will miss you, and so will Eve."

"Take care, my friend."

"Always. I'm here if you need me as long as you need me." They shook, and Thanatos tugged him in for a hard hug before the man headed back to the clinic entrance of the facility.

Fury spoke, low and quiet, "No bullshit, there are no doctors around, are you okay?"

Tempest rocked in his chair and thought about the question. He'd probably never again be the man he had been, but he was as well as he could be. He had a future which consisted of ensuring the woman who saved him was well and happy and then tracking down and killing every member of Stratus he could find. Hopefully, the trail would lead to the Fates. No, he wasn't okay. Okay wasn't a word in his vocabulary at this time. He stared at the stars and said, "I'm... changed."

"Who wouldn't be." Fury rocked for a bit longer. "Wheeler gave you a Go, with reservations. He thinks you've been doing the job too long. He'd rather you transfer or retire."

"Not fucking likely." Those bastards were his, whether or not his employer agreed.

A low evil chuckle rolled from the man next to

him. "Unfinished business. One hell of a motivator."

"You would know."

"I would. I also knew when to walk away."

"I have *that* line set in stone. There is no grand plan here. It is simple. I take care of the woman who helped me, and I go after those who held me."

"Stratus and the Fates."

Fury put into words the targets he held in his mind. Hearing it from another's lips firmed the concrete determination to eliminate the evil they represented. It was useless to deny facts.

"Yes."

"For the record, I don't agree with Dr. Wheeler. I know what motivates people like us. I know where duty ends and personal vengeance starts, and I'm confident you know it, too. I don't believe you'll blur the lines--too much." Fury stood up and extended his hand. Tempest gripped it firmly. "Thanatos does not have the need to know, but the Fates *have* been coded. If you find them when you dismantle Stratus, take them down regardless of locality. If you need assistance, you know where I am. Whatever it takes."

Fury dropped off the porch and walked into the night. Tempest rose, leaned against the front porch post and stared into the gathering darkness. "As long as it takes," he whispered to the stars in the heavens.

There was a saying... revenge was a dish best served cold. He'd waited for almost three years, and Fury's parting comments had released the ties that bound him. It appeared today was a very cold day in hell, and the storm held at bay had been released. It was time to become the real Tempest again.

CHAPTER 3

Pilar Grantham sat quietly as she waited for Regina to finish. The determined jut of her mother's chin and sharp angled cut of her dark hair enhanced her mother's cold hazel eyes. Once again it struck her that she bore no resemblance to her mother. Absolutely none. She had sandy blonde hair, blue eyes and where her mother was stately and incredibly thin, she was smaller in stature, some would say petite, though she disagreed. No matter how much she worked out and watched what she ate, her form held more curve than the haute couture purchased for her was designed to contain. She wasn't exactly over-weight, more curvy than overly plump, but she'd never be svelte like Regina.

She leaned back into the chair and stared through the massive window. The panoramic view of the Atlantic Ocean was a priceless piece of art, framed by the hand carved crown molding which wreathed the thick, hurricane-resistant glass. Regina's presence in Florida was surprising. Her mother disdained heat and humidity which made the trek from the white marble inlaid corridors of her Upper East Side New York office a rarity. Her preference was for airconditioned hallways, minimum people, and maximum efficiency. On the surface, Regina Grantham ran a multi-national conglomerate and was a powerful woman, but she'd witnessed a side of her mother that chilled her to the bone.

Her mother sighed. "I am once again at a loss for what to do with you."

Pilar waited. Asking what Regina meant by the comment would only garner her scorn. It was a lesson she'd learned as a child, so she waited.

"It was my intent to have you join me in my business endeavors, not fight me at every turn."

Ah. Now she understood. "I'm *your* lawyer. You retain me to ensure you don't go to jail. The money was obtained through questionable channels. Once again there was no documentation indicating the decedent wanted to assign their fortune to you. I understand financial institutions are not authorized to go looking for heirs but removing all the funds from the accounts without the family's knowledge or consent is unconscionable."

Her mother shrugged. "The fact we have transferred the funds without FDIC inquiry should alleviate any concern."

"Actually, it concerns me more. Fortunately, I have the good sense not to ask how the feat was accomplished. If you continue in this fashion you *will be* sued, and the way those assets were obtained will come out. The warning I sent to you falls in the prudent and required category." She'd been placed in charge of the 'non-profit' foundation after she'd graduated law school. A proving ground, Regina had called it. What it proved to be was a massive front for laundering money stolen by sleight of hand and fabricated paperwork.

"The money's origin does not matter. As you are well aware, none of the families have brought a case against me. They never will. Your degree was obtained so you could take your place at my right hand, not to bring inconsequential minutia to my attention. By now you should understand your role and the requirements I have for you." Regina angled her chin and glared at her. "Or would you rather I show you exactly how I ensure there will be no claim against me?"

"As your lawyer I *can't* know, and as your daughter, I'd rather you didn't." The memory of her time comforting the man her mother had tortured still caused nightmares. *Where was he now? Had she helped? Had he died or had he escaped?* She'd never ask Regina. Her mother would consider her concern for the man a weakness, and she'd learned never to show a weakness. Her mother's strict code of decorum was harsh and uncompromising. She knew not to deviate.

Regina leaned back in her white leather chair and steepled her fingers. "This streak of morality you insist on displaying needs to be eliminated. You were given the position as my lawyer to give you experience and to learn the company's machinations at a basic level. At this point in your life, I had intended to bring you into the fold *before* we launched you politically. Unfortunately, this latest occurrence of moral turpitude has reinforced my hesitation. My dilemma is what to do with you if you continue to fight me at every turn."

Pilar stared back at the woman across from her. "Easy, conduct yourself and your business legally."

Regina tilted a sculptured eyebrow. "Do you honestly believe it would be as simple as changing my business plan?"

Pilar folded her hands over her lap and mimicked her mother's arched brow. "It *is* that simple. Honestly Regina, you and I never agree, on anything, but I would never make the mistake of misjudging the power you wield. I'm sure you could... remove anything which gets in your way. I am smart enough to never put myself in such a position. Especially after seeing the results of your displeasure."

Regina cocked her head in confusion. "Displeasure?" She blinked several times. "You're referencing the cur in the cell, how many years ago? Two?"

"Almost three." Pilar answered honestly and inwardly cringed. By knowing the time elapsed, she'd just armed Regina with the knowledge the time in the cell with one of her victims still haunted her.

"Indeed." Regina's phone chirped and she snapped an irritated glance at it. "That wasn't an example of my displeasure. No, he had information I needed. There was no emotion involved in the process of breaking him. With you, however, there is a significant attachment. One I must admit I was blissfully unaware of until the question of what to do with you if you don't start complying became paramount."

"So, what will you do with me, Regina?" Her stomach rolled with nerves she couldn't let her mother see.

"For now, you'll continue as I've outlined. Your campaign manager will be here this afternoon."

"Ah, well, now I understand why you're in Florida." She wanted nothing to do with the mayoral campaign. Politics, her major in her baccalaureate program, held little interest for her, especially after she'd realized politicians were puppets of special interest groups or political backers, such as her mother.

Her mother leaned back in her chair and studied her. "You will run for the office, and you will win. This insignificant platform will launch you into the state political system. You are going to be the first female President of the United States."

"Do my desires mean nothing to you?" It was an observation she'd made many times before, but never voiced.

A slight crease formed between Regina's eyebrows. "Why would they? Your life has been destined for this." Her mother's shoulder moved in an elegant shrug. "The keys to the world are at your feet. Don't imitate a swine and trample them."

"Swine? Hardly *Mother*." She accented the word as Regina hated the term.

"Please, go amuse yourself until our campaign manager arrives. You will leave this ungrateful attitude outside the door when you return, or I will remind you what I do to those who don't appreciate my... gifts."

"Gifts? Planning my life and giving me no input is a gift?"

Regina raised her hand in a regal gesture. "Look at what you have. A private beach, a mansion and staff to provide for your every whim. Really Pilar, are you so ungrateful?"

"No. I appreciate everything you've given me, especially the superior education you've provided." Unfortunately, the education she referred to wasn't the expensive schools she attended. She was thankful her mother had shown her the type of person she never wanted to become. She was grateful for the time she'd spent with a man who was broken and suffering, but who'd still found the determination to oppose his death. She was eternally gratified she'd been able to send the message she'd memorized.

Regina stared at her for a moment and nodded. "I believe you, and that is why I'm at a figurative crossroad. It is a dilemma I haven't faced before. I find I *want* you to succeed and to embrace the life you will have. An interesting conundrum, this effect of being emotionally involved." Regina shook her head as if to dislodge the troubling thought and picked up her cell phone. "Close the door after you."

Regina's assistant, a small mousy man, entered through a side door. He carried his ever-present tablet and took up his place by the wall playing statue until her mother needed him. She'd never heard the man speak above a soft whisper, but he'd been at Regina's side for as long as she could remember.

The door closed solidly. She drew a breath and waited. The distinct click of the electronic lock sounded behind her. The stroll from her mother's wing of the mansion to hers took several minutes. She sank into a chaise lounge and stared through another ornately framed window at the thunderstorm approaching the shore. An appropriate metaphor. There was a storm heading her way, and the squall had been brewing as long as she could remember. In the last three years it had gathered strength.

Fat raindrops hit the window, blurring the view of the pounding surf. Palm fronds whipped in the wind, and lightning flashed in the distance. A typical afternoon storm. She reached for her laptop and opened the browser. In a practiced act, she moved the cursor from social media accounts to email, looked at clothing, makeup, and then started a game, leaving all the tabs open. She opened a browser and clicked the email account, signed in, and glanced at the draft folder, something she did about once a month or so, probably because she hoped the man had lived.

The inbox was empty as usual but... A shot of fear and delight struck her when she looked at the draft folder and saw the number out to the side. **1.** Oh, dear merciful heavens, a message after all this time. There could only be one person who would leave a message. *Him.* The man who'd been so kind, even in his pain. She clicked on the folder and opened the message.

>*I'm coming for you.*

Her racing heartbeat thundered, obliterating the natural sounds of the storm outside. The man *had* lived. In those short hours together, they'd made promises, and sworn a fealty which only the desperate and inconsolable could give each other. When her mother had seen fit to release her, she'd held up her side of the agreement by checking the email account every day. When the message he'd hoped for came, she replied as he'd taught her. He'd lived, and he was obviously trying to fulfil his promise.

Dare she hope she could be removed from her mother's span of influence and control? She sucked her bottom lip in and worried it with her teeth as she sightlessly stared through the window. Only a person who was confined by the will of another or by physical restraints could know the *fear* the prospect of real hope instilled into one's soul.

How? How had he survived? It had been almost two months from the time she'd been forced to leave him in the cell to the time someone had sent an email. She'd given up hope that he'd lived. Thirty-three months and... twelve days.

In that time, things had changed. *She'd* changed. The weekend she'd been shown how her mother gathered information, she'd discovered her mother commanded a maleficence of heinous quantities. It centered with her mother but ran through others who conducted business with Regina. The path she chose to walk after that weekend had been jagged and almost impossible to navigate, but she'd taken a page from her mother's script and for the most part pantomimed the woman, draping herself in a cloak of normalcy. Unfortunately, there were times she cracked, bristled under the armor she'd put in place, and goaded her mother. Times like today.

The main issue she needed to solve was how to get the information she'd accumulated to someone who could do something with it without revealing her as the source. The elemental question was what organization was strong enough to go up against the empire Regina controlled? Her only option was to keep compiling the information, watch for an opportunity, and find a way to make her mother pay for the multitude of sins she'd discovered.

Her rescuer was walking into a maelstrom, and she needed to warn him away. But how? At the time they'd met, she'd had only myopic glimpses of Regina's corrupt world.

In reality, her concern about betraying her oath to the court was minimal. What Regina would do if she discovered Pilar had betrayed her formed the basis of her sleepless nights. The darkness in her mother terrified her. The risk of betraying Regina was one she couldn't take until she found an entity impervious to Regina's money and power. She was caught in her mother's poison laced web of corruption, intimidation and death. Why hadn't she seen it before she'd been shoved into the cell with him? Well, the blindfold had fallen from her eyes. She saw *everything* now.

Her mother needed to be stopped, and yes, brought to justice. Was *he* strong enough to go up against the empire Regina controlled? *No.* No single person would be able to take on the staggering organization Regina had amassed. If she'd only known three years ago, she'd have told the man to forget her. She stared sightlessly out the window. She had to warn him away, but how could she get word to him? She closed her eyes. She desperately wanted to see him. To make sure he was okay, to know that he'd recovered.

A flash of lightning and an immediate sizzling clap of thunder startled her out of her thoughts. The power flickered and then went out. She waited for the emergency generator to kick on. It took a while, but the lights flickered to life. The clouds darkened the sky and the din of rolling thunder echoed the somberness of her memories. *He* was coming, and she would see him. If only once to warn him away.

She deleted his draft and closed the tab before systematically closing down the rest of the tabs and clearing her browser history. It wouldn't matter if someone with a computer forensics background looked into her actions, they'd know what website she'd gone to, but she wasn't going to make it easy for just anyone to determine where she'd been.

In the darkness of the afternoon storm, she drew a deep breath and smiled. The day after she'd sent the message, her mother'd had a meltdown. Well, what constituted a meltdown for Regina. It made sense now. The message she'd sent worked. He'd escaped.

His friends had moved quickly. It had to be why her mother had been irate. Cold, calculating, reserved Regina had shocked everyone in her New York offices that day. Her mother was *never* loud. Never spoke above a flat calm tone. A lift of an eyebrow or a muscle twitch around her eyes were effusive gestures for Regina.

"What?" The threat in her mother's screech sent a

wave of gooseflesh crashing across her skin, and she was two offices down. She made no pretense about walking to Regina's door and eavesdropping on the unprecedented outburst. "Repeat what you just said," her mother hissed. The fury banked behind the words was a living thing.

Whoever was on the other end of the phone call was in jeopardy of losing their life—or worse. She'd seen first-hand what her mother was capable of doing to another human. It had only been two months since she'd been with the man in the cell. Two months of waking up from horrible dreams and worrying about someone she'd no doubt never see again.

"You will find who aided him. You know what to do when you discover who it was." The words were almost shouted before a longer pause. Her mother paced back and forth behind her desk. Her assistant noticed her, strode toward the office door, and closed it. The door rested in the jamb not an inch from her nose. The metallic click of the electronic lock engaging was the last thing she'd heard from Regina's side of the door for over two hours.

Of course, her mother's outrage sent shivers of apprehension through her and the rest of the office workers. She'd assumed the results from her message sent the day before to be the motivation for the woman's rant. Could they link her to the man's escape? Was there a way to connect the message she'd typed and then deleted from the draft message box to her?

That day, she'd been terrified of discovery. Now, years later, her greatest fear was becoming her mother—a creature immune to simple human kindnesses. How long until she decided the end justified any means?

She closed her eyes and calmed herself. If Regina had taught her anything, she'd taught her to live with the decisions she made. The lesson her mother provided so well almost three years ago had ripped away the last vestiges of doubt as to Regina's character. She'd thought of a hundred ways to report her mother and had even tried to contact the police in New York. The police had laughed at her. She'd had no idea where the man was *currently* being held. She'd had the address to which he would be taken, but the man had made her swear she wouldn't tell anyone the address unless someone made contact via the dead drop. If his captors knew the address had been compromised, they'd change it, and he'd lose any chance of rescue.

So, with the information she could release, she'd contacted the police and of course Regina had denied everything, shrouding her concerns in doubt and ridicule. Her punishment for trying to report the man being held had been immediate. She'd been shunned for over a year. Her mother's intense anger at her attempt to help the man had resulted in a tightly fisted net of people inserted into her life to watch her and report back to Regina. The illusion of freedom was there, but from the moment she'd called the police in New York, she'd had zero freedom. She was, for a lack of a better term, hostage to her mother's decrees.

As she stared at the storm, she contemplated once again making the move to aid someone, but this time the someone she would assist would be herself. Lord knew she'd seen enough to understand her mother's ethics were... nonexistent. She would have to release the irrefutable proof she had acquired. But to whom and how? And the cost... Would it be worth it? No, when she acted this time, she would find a way to get the information to someone with a chance to succeed with any action taken. Yet the question still remained, how could she stop Regina? Her silent meditation and the storm outside raged on as she stared into the swirling rain.

CHAPTER 4

The packed, wet sand held him as he ran along the surf. The mansions to his left adjacent to Florida's A1A highway claimed the ocean view. His stride didn't lessen as he approached the residence he'd been observing for the last week. The white tiled roof gleamed under the south Florida sun. Minimalistic landscaping and stark white block walls rose three stories above the ocean front beach in a monolithic abomination of modern architecture. *This* was the address she'd recited to him moments before she'd left his cell.

Imaginary ants crawled under his skin as he jogged past the mansion. The woman who had been, at a minimum, aware of his captivity, owned the house, and the daughter who'd freed him resided in those confines. His careful pace faltered as memories threatened to escape the fenced off place in his mind where he'd forced them to live. Carefully he counted his strides and glanced toward the mansion. The expanses of glass placed him in full view of the occupants, but there was no way Pilar would recognize him now.

He ran on as his mind worked on a thousand different points of information and filtered through obvious concerns. Would she trust him? Did she still want to escape? If she did, how fit was she? Would she be able to run on the beach far and fast enough? If not, what was his secondary exit route? Tertiary? What happened if she wasn't in the residence? Did he risk making contact again? The draft he'd placed in the email account two weeks ago had disappeared. Had she checked or had she betrayed him? Would she give him information about her mother once she was free? If she hadn't betrayed him, then how far would he go to gain the information he needed to climb to the top of Stratus and locate the Fates? It could be her mother had little to no connection to the organization, but the coincidences were too stark. She *had* to know someone in Stratus. Someone in Stratus had to have approved her daughter's punishment and placement in his cell.

There were many questions and few answers. He wasn't ready to make contact with her yet, and he wasn't going to rush the prep work. He was... rusty. The skills he'd refined to a surgically sharp edge had dulled. Granted, his physical fitness was the best it had ever been. The training regimen at the Rose was second to none. His exposure to the Arizona sun had deepened the naturally dark complexion of his skin. He fit in on the Florida beach. In fact, he'd been raised not too far from here. A lifetime ago. But somehow, he'd fucked up in Tahiti. Somehow, he'd been made, and the fuckers who took him were a step ahead of him. *How?* The question remained unanswered and gnawed at him, giving doubt in his skills a place to reside.

He slowed his pace when he reached the public beach where he'd parked. The run past the house just before sunup and the return run as the sun rose into the sky had given him a first-hand view of the grounds facing the beach. The windows on the north side of the house were opaque when he ran past after sunup, but clear when he'd jogged by earlier. He needed to obtain the blueprints for the house, which had proven difficult. The plans filed with the city weren't this house. An administration oversight perhaps? Possibly, but it didn't seem likely.

His gut told him Pilar's mother was involved with Stratus. Perhaps, if he was lucky, the woman held some sway at a management level. Regardless of her position, there would be information to be gathered, and from the data collected he'd be a step closer to the top of Stratus. During his captivity he'd vowed to take the organization down. It was a vow he wouldn't fail in executing no matter if it took the remainder of his life. Thankfully his objective and Guardian's aligned. He rolled his shoulders in a shrug. There would have been a parting of the ways if his organization had tried to prohibit his actions.

He walked off his five-mile run and headed past the dunes toward the parking lot. His watch vibrated on his wrist. *Annoying*. He opened the SUV and grabbed a bottle of water, downing it all. Tossing the bottle into the passenger side floor-board, he got into the vehicle, started it, and drove onto A1A to take one more look at the front of the estate. His watch vibrated again. He rolled his eyes, swiped the face of his phone, and keyed in the number.

"Operator Two Seven Four."

"Sunset Operative Six."

"Standby Sunset Operative Six." The woman's voice had never changed. He honestly wondered if Guardian had some leading-edge tech—artificial intelligence or some other new age system.

"You don't have to call in." Anubis' voice held a hint of humor.

"Yeah, I know, but I figured if you wanted me to check in at this ungodly hour, I'm going to make sure your ass is up, too."

Anubis chuckled. "I've been up. Physical training starts at four-thirty."

"I didn't realize you needed to get up early to ride a stationary bike, or are you logging miles on a treadmill this week?"

"Ha-ha, fuck you very much. You want to know how fit I am, come on up here, and I'd be happy to take you down and humble your ass."

"It would take more than you, my friend." Tempest smiled because he knew he was right. His past gave him an edge. One he wouldn't be losing. Not again. Not ever.

"In your dreams. Do you need our assistance?"

Tempest narrowed his eyes and flicked a quick look at the phone. "No."

"You don't have to go at this alone."

"This?" As far as he was aware, only he and Fury knew his objective was Stratus and the Fates. He'd been checking in with Anubis daily, so obviously the man knew he was active, but...

Anubis made a noise akin to a snort. "Fury briefed me."

"And who else?"

"Don't know and don't care. As your primary point of contact I needed to know. Fury isn't loose lipped."

Tempest barked a laugh. That was a mental picture––Fury gossiping. "I concur, he isn't. I don't require help."

"We *can* provide assistance."

"In the form of?" Tempest eyed the eight-foot-high wall and ornate black wrought iron gate of the mansion he'd targeted as he passed. The security booth outside the gate was manned. A different guard than earlier. Shift change had happened while he was on his run. Another data point gathered.

"Intelligence, surveillance tech, equipment, and if necessary, manpower."

"Thank you." He appreciated the offer, but this one was his and only his. He'd already made calls, lined up materials, found people to use without their knowledge. This was personal.

"That was the nicest 'fuck-off' I've received today."

"I'd say you need better friends."

"Nah, those I have have proven I can count on them, and I want them to know they can count on me."

"Noted. If I find myself in need of assistance, I'll reach out." Being stupid wasn't one of his faults. He knew when he needed an assist, but he wasn't going to call it in to make himself comfortable. Unease made a person aware, and he needed to be very aware.

"As a reminder, we have a team in the area. There is also an asset nearby. Just in case."

Tempest's eyes shot toward the phone. "Asset?"

"Mmm... a member of our branch of the business."

"And you think this member would be of assistance?"

"He has skill sets."

"Well if I need to make a statement, I'll reach out. Until that time, keep him clear. If I determine someone is following me..." He let the statement go. His meaning was clear.

"Understood. Do me a favor, use your tech to check in tomorrow. It's Saturday and my daughter is staying at a friend's. Momma and Daddy are having quality time."

Tempest's head whipped toward the phone. "Learning you were married was... surprising."

"I'm damned lucky, and I acknowledge that fact daily. I'm married to a woman too good for me, and we have a precocious daughter who can wrap me around her finger."

He knew about Thanatos, Bengal, Fury and Moriah being married because they'd been to the Complex. Damn, had everyone gone soft while he was... away? "Seems as if everyone is entwined now."

There was a pause before Anubis replied, "Asp found his woman in Colombia; Lycos is married and has a son. Lycos also took Demos' job."

Tempest nodded and drove into a random apartment complex parking lot, pulled into the first slot available, and checked his six, making sure he wasn't followed. He put the car into park but left the air conditioner going. He'd spent three years without it in the Arizona desert. It was a luxury he was going to enjoy while he could. "I knew he'd taken over for Demos. So, all of you are removed from active status?"

"No. Asp, Moriah and Smoke are active. Asp and Moriah are more selective as to what assignments they will take. Lycos has taken recruitment but rarely leaves his mountain other than to procure candidates. Bengal is out, but he helps me manage activities and smooths coordination with the D.C. entities. But mainly he keeps his wife from working herself to death and handles her section's personnel. I am on reserve should I be needed."

"Who is in the field?"

"Smoke, Reaper, Maximus, Phoenix, Harbinger, Centurion... and many more you don't know."

"They were so damn young. Well, except for Smoke."

"And now *they* are the elite."

"Damn, ages a person, doesn't it? We're old."

"Speak for yourself," Anubis chastised, laughing a reply. "Besides, you know the saying. People in our profession don't grow old. They die or they walk into the light."

"Death and I are well acquainted. A transition to either ending will come, or it won't. I'll use the tech to contact you from now on unless I need assistance."

"Whatever it takes, my friend."

"For as long as it takes." Disconnected, he stared at the cars in front of him. Death or the light. In actuality, he'd resigned himself to death until he'd met her. She was the one who'd kept him going those last days. Those short hours of warmth and whispered promises could have meant nothing to her, but to him, they ordained his continued existence. He'd given up. Stratus had won. They'd broken him, and he had nothing left to fight for, until her.

"How did you do it?" The psychiatrist's face peered at him from the monitor. He rather liked Remi. He'd peg the guy as a biker, not a shrink.

He arched an eyebrow. "Do what?"

"Survive. Mentally what did you do to stay... present."

Tempest leaned back in his chair and twirled the rubber band he'd found on the desk as he thought of his answer. "At first I built a house."

"What kind of house?"

"Just a house. I dug the foundation and poured it. Next was the framing. Board by board. I pounded each nail, sanded, scraped, sawed, painted, ran the electricity, the plumbing."

"You did this when?"

"After the sessions. During the months they forgot about me." He'd disclosed all the hows of the torture sessions to the good doctor. He also knew of the starvation and the neglect. There was no need to drag the baggage out and repack it. They'd gone through those sessions and the aftermath in detail.

"What happened when you finished the house?" Remi leaned in as if his answer would be intriguing.

"I added a room, built a porch and started on the garage."

"Was there ever a time you felt like giving up?"

"Many."

"Was there ever a time you gave up?"

Tempest caught the rubber band and leaned his elbows on the desk. He stretched the band in his fingers and nodded.

"Tell me."

"I thought she was a dream at first. She was so gentle." He chuffed a humorless laugh. "God I must have been rank, but she... washed me, cared for the worst of my wounds and then she slid behind me on the cot and..." It was the first time he could remember being warm in... an eternity.

"And?"

"She held me and gave me a shirt to wear. I was so fucking cold."

"What else did she do?"

"She talked to me." It had been forever since someone had talked to him. Interrogation, screaming slurs, inflicting pain and taunting, yes. Human conversation? No. She'd spoken as if he mattered... and the simple tactic had shattered him.

"How?"

Tempest felt tears form but he'd be damned if he'd allow those emotions to be seen. Remi Wheeler had seen tears before. No doubt he'd witnessed tears of frustration, of pain, of suffering, but these tears were not for anyone to see. His emotions and his thoughts of Pilar were sacred to him. "Kindly."

He closed his eyes and dropped his head. She'd wrapped her arm around his waist and held him. Beaten, starved and nearly dead, she'd held him like he mattered. As if he was someone. His strength in that moment flowed from her gentle nature. He cried then, too, although like today, there were no outward tears. She whispered soothing words, none he could recall, but she allowed him her strength when he had *none, when he'd given up. That gift had been precious.*

"What happened then?"

He glanced at the monitor. "Nothing and everything."

CHAPTER 5

Pilar dressed carefully and checked her makeup. The Chanel business suit, Louboutin heels, Louis Vuitton briefcase, and purse were her armor. She glanced one more time at her hair. The French twist was easy to maintain and professional, keeping the length of her curly blonde hair tamed during the workday.

The consultation with the campaign manager had morphed into a marathon meeting which included a video conference with a PR specialist, and an election expert. She sat silent while her mother orchestrated a flurry of activity with minimum word count. A surreal afternoon. Her life being molded and shaped with zero input from her. No one spoke to her. The reality her mother had put this machine into motion long ago marched itself into the meeting and sat down beside her, silently chiding her for not realizing sooner her life wasn't her own. If she hadn't been there, it wouldn't have mattered. She was a game piece to be moved as her mother saw fit. Which was the story of her life. Do what Regina says, when she tells you, and don't screw up.

She strode to the front of the manse. The butler, Henry, opened the door for her and her driver, Cody, opened the Bentley's door. She spent less than thirty seconds in the humid Florida weather before she was ensconced in leather and comforted by air which was cooled and circulated. She leaned back in the corner of the seat and waited for Cody to trot around the front of the vehicle and get into the driver's seat.

"We aren't going to the office, Cody. Take me to the 15th Circuit Law Library."

"Yes ma'am." His professional reply, as always floated back to her.

She'd use the computers at the library to contact the man and warn him. She wouldn't use her computer again, out of an abundance of caution. She'd check out some continuing legal education videos as a cover. It would take her a few minutes and even though she suspected Cody was reporting on her movements, he wouldn't find her detour nor the time it took to obtain the CLE from the staff out of the norm.

She called up her phone and looked up the website for the 15th Circuit Law Library. There was a title she could rent which would convince her mother she was attempting to execute her wishes. The DVD, *42nd Annual Local Government Law in Florida,* would work nicely. With her upcoming campaign, the topic would be appropriate should her mother's minions backtrack her actions. She didn't think they would, but she wasn't going to drop her guard. Not now.

The drive up I-95 took thirty minutes. She waited for Cody to pull to the front of the building and trot around the hood to open her door. "Will you be requiring assistance, ma'am?"

Surprised at the question she narrowed her eyes and stared at the chauffeur. Channeling her mother's superior attitude, she asked, "Have you earned a law degree? Have you passed the bar here in Florida?" She sounded exactly like Regina, and the realization repulsed her.

Her driver blinked in surprise and shook his head. "No ma'am."

"Then no, I do not require your assistance." She strode across the walk and ground her teeth together. She marched in and moved directly to one of the few vacant computers where she accessed the internet with the law center's log in. She called up the law center's website before she accessed the email account. Words she'd trimmed down and rehearsed in her mind were quickly typed.

> Drago's Deli. 12:15.

She hit send, closed both open tabs, stood up, and made her way to the desk. "I'd like a copy of *the 42nd Annual Local Government Law in Florida* CLE please."

"One moment." The librarian accessed her computer and then moved to a small filing cabinet to retrieve the DVD. "Ms. Grantham, I'll charge this to your account."

"That would be fine. Thank you." She took the DVD and carried it from the building. Cody opened the door for her, shut her in, and jogged around the car again. He parked in front of her office building thirty minutes later. She purposefully left the DVD on the seat as she exited.

"Damn it. Cody, would you please get the DVD for me?" She pointed to the seat. The man bent in and had ample time to read the cover and even open the jewel case to ensure the DVD was real. She took it from him and dropped it into her bag. "Be here at six."

"Yes ma'am." Cody shut the door and she headed inside.

"Carol, what do we have today?"

Her paralegal's head popped up from behind her computer. "Two meetings this morning. A family member of one of the donors from... March of this year. That's at 10:00 a.m. and then the pro bono case at 11:00 a.m."

Her mother had deemed it a good idea for her to take on pro bono cases about two years ago. Criminal law. Not her forte, but the cases which arrived on her doorstep were hand-picked. Obvious cases of misconduct, ignorance, or neglect on the part of the city and a firm foundation to go after a mayor who ran a city which couldn't get things right. Her mother's detail work in action.

"All right. This afternoon?"

"Nothing until 2:00 p.m. Quarterly video meeting with the rest of the corporate lawyers. Mary said her boss was in a hell of a mood, so there will be someone getting ripped to shreds.

Remember everything so you can tell me." Carol waggled her eyebrows up and down and smiled widely. If she wasn't absolutely certain Carol's loyalty lay with Regina, she could like the woman.

"As long as it isn't about me, I'll take copious notes."

"It would never be you. No one would take on Regina Grantham, and putting you on the spot is putting her on the same square. *That* fool hasn't been born yet."

She flashed an insincere smile and grabbed her messages before she walked to her office. Unfortunately, *that* fool had been born thirty years ago. *She* was going to take on her mother, hopefully with help, if she could find it, but if she had to go it alone, she would.

The meeting with the lawyer representing the now bereft family member of one of the 'donors' who'd had his entire fortune routed to the Grantham-Hughes Foundation ended with the promise of lawsuits and investigations. They'd been threatened before, yet nothing had ever gotten to court.

Carol picked up several slips of pink paper. "Your messages."

"Yeah, thanks. Hey, I need you to do me a favor.

Make sure I'm not disturbed. I have CLE I need to catch up on."

"Do you want me to interrupt if the discovery on the Rayford claim comes in?"

"I'll grab it after I come back from lunch. I'm going to try to slog away at these local government lectures and get them done."

"All right. I'll hold the discovery with the information on your next pro bono case." Carol nodded to a thin folder in her out box.

"That's a pro bono file? When was it referred?"

"The day before yesterday."

"Okay. You'll probably have to do some leg work on this one. Sorry, in advance."

"No worries, I like job security," Carol said absently and focused on her computer.

Pilar went into her office and scanned the messages. Nothing important, as usual. She started her computer and shoved one of the DVDs into the slot, turning the sound off, but putting her earbuds in. If Carol walked in, her secretary would assume she was listening to the lectures even though she wasn't.

She grabbed her day planner and started leafing back through the calendar. Carol hated the fact she kept a paper planner, probably because she couldn't control what went into it. The planner stayed with her always. She wrote in shorthand and no one could decipher her writing. There were twenty-seven 'donations' which she'd been part of since she became her mother's lawyer. Twenty-seven families who'd lost everything when the head of the family died.

Last year she'd started backtracking and compiling *how* the people died. Vehicle and pedestrian accidents, suicides, three breaking and enterings, and several accidental electrocutions. Not one of the 'donors' passed from natural causes. It didn't take a rocket scientist to determine these people were being killed. With the absolute lack of follow through from the families after they threatened court action, she suspected even more foul play. The names and contact numbers were all logged. She had to find a way to contact them and determine if her beliefs held a grain of truth. Her gut told her they did.

She'd transcribed last year's notes in this binder. The planner started in July and the effort tallied up to fifty plus handwritten pages. She had substantial evidence. Embezzlement was a slam dunk. Intimidation and witness tampering? Yeah, those were almost guaranteed, but there was a darker truth which ran through the threads of these cases. She leafed through her notes and shook her head. She needed to ascertain what her next step was going to be.

"Let's talk about expectations." Remi Wheeler glanced up from the papers in his folder. The doctor traveled to Arizona once a quarter now to conduct sessions in person. He was two months early. Obviously, this was his evaluation. The one he'd been waiting for.

"Yours or mine?" Tempest's eyes rose, and he pegged the doctor with a stare.

"Both. We'll start with yours. What exactly do you expect to happen when you've been given a Go?"

He leaned back in his chair. He knew exactly what he wanted to happen. The question was, did he tell his shrink the truth, knowing it would be relayed back to the people in charge? He shrugged and kept his mouth shut while he worked through the scenario in his head. To be honest, it really didn't matter if Guardian approved of his plans. He was going to track down the people who'd held him and kill them.

"When you give me a Go, I'm going after the Fates."

"What if Guardian doesn't want you to?" The doctor

leaned back in his chair and crossed his legs. The heavy soled combat boots he wore were another anomaly which made up the biker-slash-doctor. Doc Wheeler was nervous today. The pen in his hand clicked in a repetitive sound which shattered the silence of the room.

He leaned forward, elbows on his knees and stared at the doctor and then intentionally moved his gaze to the pen. The doctor froze his thumb on the downward strike. He brought the pen up and looked at it before he set it down on the side table next to his chair. "My apologies."

He stared at the doctor. "Why are you nervous?"

Remi drew a large breath and released it before he answered. "I'd like to approve you, to give you a Go, because you've worked so damn hard to get this far."

He stared at the doctor for a few moments. "I can't fathom an instance where Guardian would disapprove of my endeavors. These people are the rarest form of evil. According to what I've learned, they are coordinating worldwide efforts to subvert political leaders and gain profit and power to forward their end goals."

"And what are their end goals?"

"I don't know. I'll be sure to ask someone before I remove them from the equation."

"Is it simple for you? Killing?"

"Simple?" He leaned back in his chair and let his

eyes drift toward the window to the desert beyond. "No. Taking a life is never easy."

"Then why do you do it?" Remi uncrossed his legs and leaned forward.

He let the question spin for a moment before he answered, "Have you ever wondered what the world would look like if the abominations who exist among us aren't controlled?"

His doctor shook his head as he spoke, "No."

Tempest smiled. "The reason you haven't is because they aren't allowed to impact your life."

"Have they impacted yours, before you came to work for Guardian?"

"You know the answer to that question. You've read my file."

Remi shrugged, "Humor me."

"Yes."

"How?"

"I was drugged at a party and kidnapped at the age of nineteen. When I came to, I was in a cage."

"And?"

"You want the gory details? They are in my file."

"I want to hear you say it."

"Fine. They revealed the plans they had for me and the others they had taken. When they transferred us, I was able to escape and free two others. The two girls

weren't fast enough. They were retaken. When the police finally believed me, they found the girls. They'd been killed after they'd been assaulted. The cops arrested me."

"Why?"

"Because I had a long record by that time. No supervision and cheap drugs." He shrugged.

"How did you get out of the situation?"

"Demos."

"I thought he only recruited killers?"

"He does."

"Who did you kill?"

"Does it matter?"

"Yes."

"The man who killed my mother."

"Why did you kill him?"

"He'd walked on the charges, and he'd killed again."

"How did Demos know you'd killed him?"

"The cops had charged me, but the fire had compromised all the evidence."

"Fire?"

He chuckled. "I like to make big statements."

"And you still do, for Guardian." Doctor Wheeler nodded.

"I don't care how I kill the people in Stratus or how I get to and kill each of the Fates. Silently dead is still

dead. I'm accomplished in many aspects of my specialty."

"So, if Guardian was to say no?"

"I guess I'd cross that bridge if I came to it, Doc." He wasn't going to make it to a bridge. There was no way Guardian wouldn't allow him to take down Stratus. "What are your expectations?"

His doctor met his questioning gaze. "I expect I'll give you a Go. Physically, you're ready."

"Ah. But you're still concerned about my mental strength."

"God, no. You've survived an experience which would have crumbled others with less mental stamina."

"Then what concerns you?"

"The people who knew you before have indicated the person you are now isn't the person you were before the incident."

"No. Shit." He shook his head. "Doc, I've changed. I'm not that man. My reasons for continuing in my line of work have shifted. I'm no longer a blunt instrument used to make a statement to the rest of the world. I have a very specific skill set and a need for vengeance. My need aligns with my employer's goals. I'll be the Shetland in their dog and pony show, and I'll perform exactly the way they tell me to perform."

"And if your goals and Guardian's ever diverge?"

"Again, a bridge I'll cross if I ever get to it."

Doctor Wheeler leaned forward. "Would you kill without a target being coded?"

"To protect myself or others, yes."

Wheeler stared at him for several long minutes, and he held the gaze. Finally, the man nodded. "You've got your Go. I hope you take care of yourself."

He stood and extended his hand. "I will."

Tempest stared at the mass of humanity. Drago's was a huge deli in the middle of an ocean of office buildings. People packed the area to the point of overcrowding, making it almost impossible for anyone to overhear a conversation. Pilar had chosen well.

He made his way through the line while looking for her. It had been almost three years, but those beautiful features had been etched in his mind. Sandwich, chips and drink purchased, he turned and made another survey of the area. There were a multitude of blondes, but none were Pilar. He weaved through the tables heading back to the furthermost seating area before he saw her at the very back at a table by herself.

His faltering steps could be attributed to the

crowd and the jumble of tables, but his pause was due to the woman herself. She was everything he remembered and so much more. He forced his eyes from her when all he wanted to do was stare. A lump formed in his throat. He turned away from where she was sitting.

My God. His heart hammered in his chest faster than when he'd completed his physical fitness test at the Rose. The grip he had on the damn tray was the only thing keeping his hands from shaking. *Fucking hell, man up.* With grit and determination, he stood calmly and looked around the seating area. His emotional response contained; he sent another searching look across the filled tables. He meandered and weaved through the tables before he stopped by hers, turning to peer at the sea of people as if he was looking for a seat.

"Are you looking for a seat?" That voice. Husky with a hint of velvet. He closed his eyes for a moment before he turned around.

Her eyes widened but she schooled her features quickly. "Please, I'm almost done." She pointed to the vacant chair across from her.

He sat down and proceeded to unwrap his food. "Thank you." He looked at her and ducked his eyes again. "For everything."

She picked up her drink and swirled it in her hand, taking a final sip. "I'm glad you're alive. Under my tray." She stood and slung her purse onto her shoulder before she weaved through the crowd.

There was half a sandwich left on her tray which gave him plausible deniability when the harried busgirl tried to clear the tray. "My friend will be back."

The woman headed to another table without so much as a pause. His back to the wall, he slowly ate his food as he watched the crowd. There were a few people who could be watching him. He made a show of pulling his phone from his pocket and instead of reading he used the camera to capture pictures of the three men and one woman who didn't sit well with him. His training had taught him to trust those feelings. Two of the men left together. Quick glances at their watches sent them scurrying. The woman gave him lingering, appraising, glances. He wasn't going to dismiss her... yet. The third man finally stood and waved toward the front of the deli, his cheap suit jacket hiking up as he waved. Ah... a gold shield. A police officer. His demeanor was what had tweaked him about the man. He glanced back toward the woman in time to see her empty her tray and make her way from the building, the sway of her hips turning heads as she departed.

He finished his food and waited as the multitude started to thin. There was nothing out of the ordinary, nothing which caught his attention or raised concern. He finally stood, palmed the envelope from under Pilar's tray, and exited the deli.

The office buildings which had emptied to fill the restaurant once again became millstones and the afternoon work hours commenced. Warm breezes fanned palm fronds in the courtyard. Tempest shoved his hand in his pocket and covered the envelope. He headed back to his safe house. It took two hours via a circular route, including a stop at the grocery store and a filling station to make sure he wasn't being trailed.

The amount of traffic was insane. When he'd grown up in the area, Federal Highway and A1A were quiet stretches of road meandering between the cities along the coast. Now, condominiums sprouted up in the medians between the highways' lanes. Those spaces used to hold gas stations, small donut shops, and believe it or not, grass. Grass was missing from this portion of the world, at least the land west of A1A. Everything close to the beach was built up. The mega-rich had snagged the ocean front property. The rich had purchased the land on both sides of the intercoastal waterway and the middle class and poorer residents had been pushed west, past I-95 into the sweltering heat which didn't benefit from a coastal breeze.

He drove down a small road off of A1A and made his way back to a 1960's ranch style house at the end of the street. He keyed his remote and waited for the garage door to open before he drove in and shut the door behind him. Once the door was down, he retrieved the letter.

CHAPTER 6

Drawing a deep breath, he opened the envelope, tugged out a single page, and read the words inscribed by hand.

I was shocked when you contacted me. I feared you had died. I absolve you of any oath you've sworn. I wanted to aid you, and I hope in some small way I did. I can never change what she did to you. You have no idea how much I wished I could.

Circumstances are different since we last met. I am more certain of the concerns I spoke of during those hours. Do not endanger yourself for me. You are free and my heart rejoices for you. Someday perhaps we shall both be free and meet again. Until then, live well.

Pilar

Tempest read the note again and then a third time. No, he would not let her face the complications of her life alone. He was alive because of her, and he'd make sure she was able to live a life she *wanted* to live. He exited the SUV and grabbed the sacks of groceries from the cab. He stopped when he noticed the alarm to his house had been placed in passive mode. He placed the groceries on the floor and slipped to the side of the garage where he extracted a gun from the underside of a shelving unit.

Soundlessly, he opened the door and stepped into the old house. He rounded the corner and pointed his .45 at the center of a man's chest.

"About time you came in the damn house."

"For fuck's sake, Smoke, I could have killed you." A movement to his left dropped him to the ground in a crouch. His weapon trained on the man behind him.

"Yo, yo! Not a target, dude. He's my partner. If you kill him, Fury will kill you, and then I'll have to kill Fury, and *then* shit will get messy." Smoke laughed and walked in front of his weapon, taking the bullseye off his partner. "You're pretty fucking touchy. Why are you so jumpy, my man?"

"Why the hell do you think, asshole? Why are you in my safe house?" He stood, still eyeing the smaller man. "Who are you?"

Smoke responded, "Sage Browning, this is someone I've known most of my adult life. What are you calling yourself these days?"

"Pissed." Tempest stood and glared at Smoke. The motherfucker damn near got himself and his partner capped. Fucking idiot.

"Not a good moniker, dude. You need something more manly." Smoke snorted and dropped onto the couch. "I'm here because Sage and I were in the Keys visiting friends, and after we left, we needed a place to chill. Figured I'd use your house for a couple days, except I found your shit in my bedroom--"

Wait, what? "Your bedroom?"

"Well you *did* say I could use this place whenever I needed to. I really didn't need to, but you've got a great view of the intercoastal, and it's peaceful." Smoke ran his hands through his hair. He was wearing it longer and he'd lightened it.

He took his finger off the weapon's trigger and

eyed his old... friend. "Stay the fuck out of my room. There are three other bedrooms."

"Yeah, but they're small, and they have to share a bathroom." Smoke shrugged. "Sue me, I made myself at home. Not like you've been down here in years."

He snarled at his friend. Literally, snarled. "Thanks for the reminder, dickweed."

"Like you need one? Hey, let's go out for dinner. The Banana Boat up in Boynton Beach has some fantastic Mahi Mahi."

"Can't. I need to do some research." He glanced at Browning. "How do you put up with him?"

The man's fingers and hands flew in American Sign Language. "I ignore him. If you don't, he'll drive you crazy."

Smoke fired back at the guy, "You can't ignore me; I'm special."

He glanced from the Sage to Smoke looking for an explanation for the ASL.

"Sage here has an issue with stuttering caused by a TBI he suffered while serving in the Marines. Nothing that incapacitates him, but it's easier for him to communicate this way."

Tempest extended his hand. "Pleasure."

Browning gripped his hand for a moment before he signed, "Likewise."

"What research do you have to do? We're on down time and bored to fucking tears. Tried to get our friend in the Keys to go deep sea fishing with us, but he's doing another gig for Homeland, so the trip was for nothing."

"I need to break into a mansion off of A1A tonight."

Smoke clapped his hands together and rubbed them excitedly. "Excellent. Where are the schematics?"

He shrugged. "Don't have any. There was nothing in the public databases and the recorded deed for the place also seems to have disappeared."

"Oh, *that* kind of place. Okay then, I'm assuming you've done a drive by?" Smoke rubbed his hands together.

"Yes, I did." He headed back into the garage and picked up the plastic bags with his dinner inside and placed them on the kitchen counter. "Manned gate house, twelve-foot brick walls around the front and sides of the compound, open access from the beach. The windows have opaque capacity which leads me to assume cutting edge tech." He'd planned on countermanding the alarm system, but unless he knew what type of alarm they used, he could fuck it up.

"Tough. Well, how long do you need to get inside?"

He shrugged. "I can preposition at the water's edge, but the run to the house and the time to pick the locks or find a way in? Roughly a minute, maybe a few seconds longer."

Smoke narrowed his eyes and glanced at Browning. "Feel like taking down a substation tonight?"

Browning rolled his eyes and drew an exaggerated breath. Smoke ignored his partner and pinned him with a sharp gaze. "If they have an emergency generator, they'd still have to clear all the alarms which a power failure would cause. Even if the alarms are hooked into an uninterrupted power supply, the outage would fuck with them. You could get in, lock the door and do what you need to do, but once in and the generator is running, you'd be on your own. If they have the interior alarmed, you'd be screwed."

"There are occupants and staff. They won't have the interior alarmed."

"Except maybe the opaque window area." Browning sighed loudly, tipped his chin toward

Smoke and then signed, "Why do you always end up blowing shit up?"

Smoke looked at Browning and gaped. "*Because it's fun!*" He pointed to Browning and then looked at Tempest. "He does have a point, though. The asshole." Smoke shoved the smaller man, and they both cracked up laughing.

The easiness between the two men was remarkable. He crossed his arms over his chest giving Smoke's plan some consideration. "How long would you need?"

"Oh... forty-five minutes or so from the time we leave here. I'll need to make a pit stop at the marina and gather a few bits and pieces. Taking out a substation is easy. Hop the fence, nuke the middle breakers which will trip the outside breakers, and then boom. Lights out. The fun part will be determining which substation serves the house, but we can find it. Sage, get your computer."

Two hours later, after grilled steaks, baked potatoes and a salad Smoke had whipped up, they had a decent plan. "At sunset we leave." Tempest glanced through the large picture window which showcased the intercoastal waterway. If he were inclined to sell the house now, he could ask millions of dollars for the lot, but he enjoyed the simple little house and the neighbors who only lived in Florida four to six months out of the year.

"That works. Traffic should be light going to both locations by now." Smoke dropped his feet onto the coffee table and stretched back. He glanced around ensuring Browning had gone down the hall giving them a moment together. "So, you're back in the game?"

"I have a few personal items to accomplish, and then..." He shrugged.

Smoke tipped his chin and narrowed his eyes. "Who are you going after, and where do you need us? As long as we don't have an assignment, we can help."

He nodded his head toward the hallway. "You trust him? Implicitly?"

"Without reservation. He's saved my ass a time or two, and I've pulled his bacon from the fire, too."

"Where did you meet?"

"Guardian loaned me to Homeland for a project down in Cuba. Didn't do much except skipper a massive yacht around, but..."

"Loaned you?"

Smoke chuckled and shrugged. "I needed to lie low. A certain celebrity and I were in the same place at the same time and the paparazzi clued in when some asshole mistook me for him, snapped a picture of me, and posted it on Instagram at the exact same time someone else posted a picture of that celebrity across town. It went viral. So, bobbing around in the ocean was a great way to hide."

"Ah, so that's why the hairstyle change." He chuckled and plopped his feet up on the old coffee table, too.

"Yup. But back on topic. I trust him."

"Do you know when you're on deck?" He had a plan for a way to get Pilar alone, and it was starting to gel, but there were so many moving parts. Tonight, being the biggest.

"Not for another two weeks. There are enough teams to do a one month on, one month off rotation in our area."

He cocked his head and asked, even though he had a gut feeling he knew the answer, "Where is your area?"

"The Southeast, baby!" Smoke laughed when he rolled his eyes and groaned. "That's what you get for letting me in the house. An almost permanent houseguest. At least until I can find something this sweet." They watched a sixty-foot yacht cruise down the intercoastal. "Damn, that's the life, isn't it?"

"I'm sure you could afford something similar. Why are you still in the game?"

Smoke stared out the window. "I actually own something similar. A bit bigger. It is moored in a rented slip about ten minutes away. We Ubered here. And to answer your question, I don't know man, just not the right time yet. Sometimes you have to wait until everything settles into place, you know?"

He nodded. Hell yeah, he knew exactly what Smoke was getting at. He had no reason to leave the game if Pilar... He shook his head. He couldn't let his imagination about what was between them run amuck. He shot his friend a look and asked, "Is there someone for you?"

He shook his head. "Not really, but there's always a hope, you know?"

Yeah, hope was a double-edged sword, and it was a sharp motherfucker. It could protect you or kill you depending on what you based your hope on. "I do."

"So, before Sage comes back, are you Tempest or..." Smoke left the question hanging.

He cleared his throat before he said the name he'd almost forgotten, "Luke. Luke Wagner." Of course, Smoke had no way of knowing the name wasn't an alias, which was as it should be.

"Cool. Is it okay if we crash here after we do that little job? Unless you have a problem with us being here? We can drop you near your mark and then head to the substation, blow it up, and then come back to get you. Using your truck of course."

It made sense, and he sure as fuck wasn't going to kick them out after they did him a favor. "Of course. As long as you get the hell out of my room you can suit yourself." He got up and stretched. The sun had just about set and he needed to change.

Smoke's laugh followed him down the hallway. "I always do!"

CHAPTER 7

Pilar settled into the corner of the lounger she adored and listened to a classical music YouTube channel. The strains of Mozart's *Piano Sonata Number 11* filled the room while she stared through the window at the gathering darkness. The waves were no longer distinguishable in the distance, only visible when they broke on the beach. However, she wasn't seeing the scenery but rather thinking about the man she'd seen today. He was breathtaking. The voice and those eyes were the only thing which echoed a familiarity. Everything else about him had changed.

She hadn't been sure it was him at first. He was healthy and robust, nothing like the shell of a man she remembered. The breadth of his shoulders under the worn t-shirt and the long, tan, muscled, legs and tight ass which filled his board shorts were remarkable. His hair had been trimmed, but it was still rather long and windblown. The sun had obviously kissed not only his skin, but his hair as well, shading it with golden highlights which matched the gold flecks in his eyes. Eyes that had haunted her for the last three years. He was *alive*. She closed her eyes and said yet another prayer of thanksgiving for his survival.

She refocused on the darkness outside the window. The man she met today dwarfed her memory, eclipsed her dreams and surpassed her wildest desires. She shook her head and examined her nails. *Fat lot of good any of it did.* Those desires fed fruitless fantasies which would never materialize. She'd cut the man loose from his vow today, and she'd never see him again. She couldn't be responsible for him being taken by her mother again. When she compared what she'd known about her mother then and the knowledge she held now? She'd been a fool, a child throwing a tantrum, and her mother had given her a time out. But the man in the cell had given her purpose, and the information she'd compiled could easily land her in a cell or, more likely, a grave.

The strains of *Für Elise* filled the air one moment, and the next, the room fell into silent darkness. Pilar rose from the lounger and peered through the window, straining to see if the neighbors had power. The silence and complete darkness of the area meant another power outage. The generators would be flickering on as soon as the security guard out front made it to the shed and flipped the breaker. The manual switching could take time, depending on how familiar the guard was with the system start-up. She'd weathered tropical storms and Category One and Two hurricanes in this house. Power outages were nothing new.

The benefit of living in one space for years was you knew where the furniture was and could make it into the bathroom even in the dark. *Damn it!* "Shit, shit, shit!"

She dropped onto the arm of the couch and grabbed her foot. She'd jammed her little toe against the coffee table. "Man, I think I broke it." She ran her hand along the side of her foot. Yep, the toe was pointed out, not up like the other four. "Great. How am I going to wear heels now?"

She'd experienced this level of hell before when she'd broken the little toe of her *other* foot while attending college. It had hurt for weeks, even in tennis shoes. There was nothing to do but... She slid her hand along the side of her foot and pushed the toe back into place. The sharp pain was nothing like the initial break had been. Maybe because she'd maxed out her pain receptors. She wiped at her tears and groaned. She wasn't taking a step further until the guard at the front of the house turned the damn electricity on. She needed to tape it and ice it. Elevate it, too.

What was the acronym? RICE? *Damn.* R... rest, out of the question. Next was I... ice, yeah, yeah, except she had to get up and walk to get it and excuse the French, but fuck that. C... *oh, man what the hell was C for?* Whatever, she'd figure it out later. E was elevation. Okay she could do two of the four. "As soon as the lights come back on!" she screamed to the ceiling, as if anyone was going to hear her.

She was a klutz. Leave it to her to break her toe in the middle of a blackout. She dropped her head to her knee and held her foot. The throb of her heartbeat swelled and centered itself at the base of her little toe. Oh, this was bad. She had a full calendar tomorrow and Friday. Well, she'd have to tell Carol to reschedule, at least until

Monday. By then she should be able to walk. *Maybe*.

The lights flickered back on, and she glanced down at her foot. A dark green and blue bruise had formed on the side of her foot and stretched to the base of her toe, already swollen to twice the size it should be. Perfect. Just... *perfect*. "I'd like to kick the ass of whoever caused the damn blackout."

"That would be me."

Pilar spun and lost her balance, crashing down onto the coffee table, which tipped sending her to the ground. She popped back up and shoved the damn table away from her. The man, *her* man was next to her, his hand on her forearm. "Are you all right?"

"All right? No, I'm not all right! I have a broken toe and... how did you get in here?" She pushed back and sucked in a gasp when her wrist crumpled under her. "Oh, damn it."

"Hold still." The man... *her* man's arms tightened, and the muscles of his chest bulged as he moved the mahogany table to the side. With a single motion, his arms burrowed under her and lifted her from the floor. She clutched at his neck and shoulders and hissed when she moved her injured wrist. With a gentleness at odds with his massive physique, he lowered her to the couch. "Let's see the damage."

His scent, a wonderful combination of soap and male musk filled her pained inhale. "I'm fine."

She wasn't, not by a long shot, but her injuries weren't what was important. He held her wrist in his hand and examined it. His fingertips carefully moved her joint. She hissed when he trailed his fingers down the side of her arm. "No obvious breaks. Probably a strain or sprain from bracing yourself when you fell." He trailed his fingers across the back of her hand when he lowered it.

"How did you get in here? How did you get past security?" She glanced at the door to her living quarters. It was shut and a high back chair was wedged under the knob. She turned and hissed at him. "Are you insane? Do you know what she'll do if it's reported you're here?"

He reached for her ankle and stopped short of touching her. "Who's going to report it? You?"

"No!" She glanced at the door, although why was beyond her. Nobody came in her rooms when she was home. *Ever.* The butler was in his quarters this time of the night. The maid was here only during the day, and the chef came in every other day to prepare the meals she ate, which was why she still needed to lose ten pounds.

"What happened here?" His big hands cupped and supported her ankle. He turned her leg to examine the side of her foot and her swelling toe—now the size of her big toe. "I think you may have broken it."

"I did. It was sticking straight out. I pushed it back in place. Stop diverting and answer the question. *Why. Are. You. Here?*"

He lowered her foot and sat back on his heels. He stared at her for a moment. She shivered at the intensity of those gold-flecked green eyes. "I made a vow."

"I absolved you of your pledge." She shook her head. "Look, you have to go."

"Why, did your mother come back?"

"No... wait, how did you know she was here?" Using her good hand, she pushed herself up into a sitting rather than lounging position.

He rose from the floor and headed to the back of the room. "I've been watching. Is the bathroom back here?"

"Ahh... yes. Wait, how long have you been watching? Why have you been watching?"

The light in the hall came on. "About two

weeks. Medical kit?"

"Top cabinet above the vanity." She shot her foot a pissed off glare and dropped back onto the cushion of the lounger. She opened her eyes and stared at the hallway. "You still didn't say why."

She heard him rustling around in her bathroom and then his footsteps coming back to the sitting room. "I've been watching to make sure you weren't in danger and to ensure you aren't being followed."

"Followed? No, she's planted enough people in my life. I don't need to be followed. She dictates my schedule, my appointments, and my life in general."

"People such as?" He moved the coffee table and placed the white plastic medical kit down.

She blew a lungful of air. "The butler, the chauffeur, my legal assistant, security, which by the way, how did you get past him?"

"I came up from the beach when the power went out." He opened the case and removed a beige elastic bandage.

"Oh." He supported her wrist and started to wrap it. "Wait, how did you know there was going to be a power outage?"

He glanced up at her and smiled. Her breath

caught in her chest. He was devastatingly hand-some. "Planning the outage helps."

"You?" She glanced toward the window. "How?"

"A substation may have exploded... probably more than was necessary." He rolled his eyes and smiled before he turned his attention back to her wrist.

"You blew up a substation?" He finished the wrap and secured it with two of those stupid little claw-like fasteners. "Thank you. It feels better."

"No, *I* didn't blow up a substation. Ice?"

"Behind the bar." He rose from where he'd been and headed to her well stocked private bar. "Pour me a brandy while you're there, please. No wait. Would you please pour me a bourbon? A really big bourbon." She was having a bourbon day. Definitely a... *Oh, wow...* His black jeans hugged his thick thighs and tight ass. Broad shoulders and arms which had supported her without any problem veed to a narrow waist. Every part of him she could see seemed to be formed from roped muscles, as defined as if they'd been chiseled from stone. He made the turn to walk behind the bar, and she snapped her gaze away from his body. What were they talking about? Oh right, the substation. "Then how do you know it blew up?"

He chuckled as he worked behind the bar. "Let's call it a trade secret." He opened several cabinets under the bar. "That will work."

What? What will work? She pushed up with her good hand, trying to see over the lip of the bar. "What are you doing? And what kind a trade blows things up?"

"I'm making an ice pack for your foot." He waved a bag as he leaned back to look under the bar. "Several trades utilize demolitions. Do you ever stop asking questions?" He disappeared behind the bar.

"No, I'm a lawyer. It's what I do. I can't think of even one occupation which uses explosives."

"You're sheltered, then. Woodford Reserve or Maker's Mark?"

"I am not sheltered. Maker's Mark, and name three."

"Only three? The military, oil well riggers, and civil engineers." He rounded the bar with two glasses and the ice bag in his hand. He put the bag and one glass on the table and handed her the other glass. "Be right back."

She watched him walk away and shook her head. The health and vibrancy of the man in her rooms now was nothing like the skeletal ghost she remembered. He came back with a hand towel and wrapped the ice bag in the towel before gently positioning the ice around her abused little toe. "Please, tell me why you're here."

He sat down on the coffee table and grabbed his bourbon. "Three years ago, you saved my life."

"I wish I could have done more." She shifted her eyes from him to the drink in her hand.

He reached forward and tipped up her chin. The warmth of his fingers sent a shiver through her cold, stressed body. He took her bourbon and set it on the table.

"You saved me. Not the email you sent, although, yes, it initiated my rescue, but you gave me the will to keep going. I'd given up."

"Why did she do that to you? What is your name? Why did you come here?" She gripped his wrist with her good hand and stared into his eyes. "Who are you?"

Tempest let his hand fall from her beautiful face but intertwined his fingers with hers. The way her small hand fit inside his was imprinted on his mind. The softness of her skin compared to his rougher work-hardened hands provided a demarcation between her life and his. A difference he couldn't deny. Not any longer. He stared at her ivory colored skin against his tanned darker complexion. "All very good questions, and I will answer them, but first *I* need information."

She extended her injured hand and carefully touched his cheek. "Tell me your name first."

His gaze traveled to those blue eyes. She stared up at him, and he was powerless to do anything but smile. Just as he remembered her. Wide-eyed curiosity melded with innocence, but he could sense the inner iron of her indomitable will. The beauty he remembered and yet she'd changed, too. There was a resolve, a hardness which hadn't been there three years ago. "My name is Luke. Luke Wagner."

She smiled and dropped her hand slowly. "Nice to meet you. Now tell me why you lost your mind and came back into chum-riddled, shark infested waters?"

He smiled at her. "I can see why you're a good lawyer."

She raised her eyebrows. "Faulty logic. Being tenacious does not make me a good lawyer."

He shook his head. "No, but being tenacious, smart and a survivor does."

"Survivor?" The question drifted between them. "The term doesn't fit me or my situation."

"I disagree. Your mother is putting you in an impossible position. Your note indicated things had gotten worse?"

She closed her eyes and slowly shook her head. "I can't discuss it."

"Because of your ethics, not hers."

"I gave my oath." She gave a humorless laugh. "I'm not as good as you'd like to believe. If I could find a way to get the information I know about her to an agency that could act on it without implicating me as a source, I'd dump everything on them and watch as she landed in jail. Unfortunately, if she goes down, I will too. I know too much. I've been *told* too much, *seen* too much, to be considered innocent, and that's as she wants it."

He leaned forward. "What if I told you I'm part of an agency that could help?"

She snorted a laugh. "Right. The FBI, NSA, CIA or even Homeland couldn't make such a guarantee, and if you'd been one of those organization's assets, all hell would have rained down on her as soon as you gave your statement."

"Ah, faulty logic, counselor." He chuckled at the frown and narrowed glare she sent his way. "I am attached to an organization which is building a case against not only your mother, but others in a larger organization. My employer wants me to return to you in the hope you'd be willing to help us build a case and gain information against the people your mother works for."

Her eyes blinked several times, and he watched as she processed the information. "My mother doesn't work *for* anyone."

"We believe she does. We believe she has vital information which links several... layers of criminal activity together." The thought of using her to get to her mother and perhaps squeeze the woman for information on the upper level of Stratus felt dirty, but he was going to be upfront with Pilar from the start. If she wouldn't help, he'd find a way to get to her mother. His personal hatred for the bastards responsible for his torture and imprisonment aside, the organization which enabled someone to do this to him, and others like him, needed to be brought down in a smoldering heap. No survivors. He'd leave nothing to grow back into the abscess carved by Stratus or the Fates.

"Who is 'we'?" Her fingers tightened around his. He glanced down at their joined hands.

"Guardian."

A sigh preceded the sudden release of tension in her small body. "Guardian Security." She closed her eyes and a tear fell down her cheek. "God, I've hoped for a way for so long. I'm having difficulty believing what you're saying is true."

"I know. Is she following you? Monitoring your activity?"

"Ah... yeah, every day, all day. Like I said, the butler, security, my driver, and my paralegal were all hired by her, so I'm assuming their loyalty is to her." She winced when she moved her foot. He reached back and repositioned the towel and ice pack on her injured toe. "Why?"

"If you were to cancel your appointments and, say, hire a charter while your toe healed, would it cause difficulties?"

"It depends on how long you want me to be gone. I can manage a week or so, maybe two, but she's got plans which include me after that point."

"Plans?" He arched an eyebrow. He'd fucking take the woman down if she was planning to hurt Pilar. One twist of her neck would finish the woman's plans for anyone.

"Oh, I'm sorry, we haven't been properly introduced. According to my mother, I'm going to be the first female President of the United States. According to the machine she's put in place, my mayoral campaign starts in three weeks." A lift of her slim shoulder spoke of a resignation he didn't like.

"I'll start the wheels in motion. Tomorrow you'll receive a call from a skipper who is contacting you about a form you filled out tonight for a charter."

"But I haven't—" He held up a finger silencing her. "I know. Please stop questioning the process. It will happen. He will call you and give you a quote for a two-week charter. You'll call your mother. Explain your accident in the dark and use whatever rationale she'll believe. The skipper will give you the name of the boat. Relay it to your mother. The cover will be solid. Bring whatever information you have on your mother. Anything you can get your hands on which may incriminate her or anyone else attached to the corporations she oversees."

Her eyes narrowed but she nodded.

"I need you to trust me, Pilar. The same way I

trusted you. I will not let anything happen to you, and your mother will be brought to justice."

She nodded and then cocked her head. "If I had a normal relationship with her, I'd be horrified at the thought of handing over information which could cause her imprisonment."

"But you don't have a normal relationship, do you?"

She shook her head. "There's no closeness. No bond of any kind. I have more fond memories of my nannies and school teachers than I do of her. But she's my mother, and you'd think I'd harbor some... reticence at plunging headfirst into providing you information to convict her."

He cupped her cheek. "The crimes she's committed are not yours to bear."

"The sins of others always affect those who try to live within the confines of decent social constructs. It's why we have a legal system. Justice needs to be blind. No favoritism or immunity can be levied, and even then, so many escape the grasp of the law. I've sworn to uphold the system. I'll be breaking that oath when I turn over confidential information. Are you sure your organization can utilize it without anyone knowing I supplied the information?"

"I'm certain." He'd seen Guardian pull a magic rabbit out of its hat so many times he had no doubt his handlers could do it again.

"Then I'll make the call after the captain contacts me tomorrow. Oh, I'm not going into work tomorrow. The thought of putting it--" she pointed to her toe underneath the ice pack "--in heels makes me want to cry."

"I take it no heels isn't an option?"

She rotated her head and blinked owlishly at him. "Mr. Wagner, I believe we need to work on your haute couture education."

"Obviously." He chuckled and raised the back of her hand to his lips. "I'll see you soon."

He stood up but she reached forward and grabbed his hand. "Wait, how are you going to get out? The alarm is running again. Did you stage another outage?"

"No. Nothing so drastic. I bypassed the alarm system at the back door, putting it into a loop. It thinks it's locked, but it's not. Instant access and departure."

"You did all that in the time the power was out?"

"Well, I admit, I didn't break and reset my little toe..."

She barked a laugh. "Go. Be safe and I'll see you soon."

He leaned down and tilted her chin placing a quick kiss to her lips. The sweetness damn near killed his willpower, but he managed to break the kiss, keeping it a promise of more rather than claiming what wasn't his. *Yet.* He stood straight and her uninjured fingers went to her lips. *To hold you until we're together again.*

He forced himself across the distance to her door, removed the chair and checked the hall before he slipped into the darkened hallway. He moved from the house and skirted the sensors that would trigger the back spotlights. Two weeks with Pilar. The thought put a smile on his face until he remembered who'd be on the boat with them. Smoke. The man was movie star handsome. Literally. Fuck him, perhaps he'd have a talk with his old 'friend' before Pilar stepped foot onto the ship.

He jogged down the beach to the parking lot where he'd meet Smoke and Browning. He had an operation to put into motion. He smiled as his feet found purchase in the hard-packed sand by the surf. Anubis was probably going to regret the offer of assistance.

CHAPTER 8

"**D**ude, you didn't take very long." Smoke greeted him as he jumped into the back of the old SUV.

"Did you have any problems?" Tempest asked as they sat in the vehicle and watched his six to make sure he wasn't followed down the beach.

"None. Man, you ought to have seen those sparks flying. It was like the world's biggest Roman candle." He elbowed Browning who snorted and shook his head.

"Is that offer to help while you're on down time still good?" Both men's heads whipped back to look at him. They looked at each other before they sent their gazes back to him. He pointed at Smoke and moved his finger between the two men. "Okay, that was weird."

"You're serious?"

"I am. I need a charter boat, a captain and crew I can trust implicitly."

"What's the scoop?" Smoke said as he started the vehicle.

"Head back to the safe house. I have a feeling we're going to need a touch of Guardian magic to make this happen."

"Th-this? Wh-what is th-this?" Browning asked.

Okay, so yeah, Browning had a stuttering problem, but it wasn't so bad he couldn't be understood. Probably more of a hindrance than anything.

"I may have stumbled onto a member of Stratus."

Smoke jerked the wheel and immediately righted his course on the road. "Are you fucking shitting me?"

"Not in the slightest."

"We need to brief Fury." Smoke said and Browning nodded in agreement.

"And I need to call in to Anubis."

Browning rolled his head and stared at

Tempest for a moment before he signed, "Shadow?"

He arched his eyebrow and stared back at the man. Browning shook his head and signed, "Please tell me you have better impulse control than this guy."

He chuckled and signed back, "Everyone has better impulse control than this guy."

Browning cracked up; his rich laughter filled the vehicle. Smoke snapped his eyes to the rearview mirror and glared into the backseat. "What? What did I miss?"

Tempest deadpanned, "Nothing. Your partner seems to think one of you has impulse control issues."

Browning whooped with laughter and slapped his leg a couple times before he pointed to Smoke. "Y-yeah...You."

Smoke batted Browning's hand away. "I don't have impulse control issues. I see something I want to do, and I do it. How is this an issue?"

"Shall we bring up the op in the Azores." Tempest tossed one of many ops Smoke had complicated because he was "having fun".

"What? No way man, I blew the boat to smithereens. There was no problem."

"Right and where were you supposed to have the boat explode?"

Smoke shrugged. "Out at sea."

"And where did it blow up?"

"The pier, but you gotta remember, they made an unscheduled change of course."

"Because the father learned you were screwing around with his daughter, and he was coming back to kill you," Tempest rebutted.

Smoke snapped his head toward his partner. "I wasn't screwing around with anyone. The daughter had the hots for me because she thought I was *him*."

Browning's chuckles diminished, and he shrugged. Tempest raised an eyebrow and met Smoke's frown in the mirror. Well then, he had called it right. Smoke was interested in his partner. Whether it was sexual or not he didn't have a clue, but Smoke explaining his actions to anyone, not brandishing them proudly, was a new wrinkle in his friend's behavior.

"Do you have secure comms on the boat?"

"Yeah. We do." Smoke's answer was clipped.

"Take us there. I'll need to brief Anubis on my suspicions, and we'll need to make a plan of action."

"Fair enough." Smoke hit the turn signal indicator and navigated his way to the harbor.

"Shit. *This* is your boat?"

"Well, technically, my baby is considered a ship. Meet my lady, the *Dark Angel*."

"Y-yacht," Browning interjected.

"Yeah, I can see that. Fuck man, how much did this thing cost?" Tempest stared at the sleek lines, darkly tinted windows, and the host of antennas and radar attachments to the... well hell, up there would be a bridge, wouldn't it?

"Oh, you know, it would be really expensive except the guy who used to own it died somehow, and what do you know? When I changed the name and country of registration it kind of became mine." Smoke shrugged. "Funny how shit happens."

"Holy hell, this is magnificent. Why the hell are you staying in my 1960's piece of shit house?" Two... no three levels on this thing. A hundred-foot-long if it was an inch.

"Well, we like this area, and when we're here, I can get some maintenance done on her."

"This is better than I could have hoped for. Get me on board this thing, we've got work to do."

Smoke led the way onto the opulent yacht. Browning headed inside, and Tempest put a hand out, stopping his friend. "Is there something between the two of you that I stepped on?"

The man ran his hands through his hair. "No, but he is special to me. I'd like him to respect me. I don't want him to think I'm a manwhore, you know what I mean? Thank God I'm not usually around people who know about my past." Smoke drew a breath and gazed into the ship's opulent living area. "Sage is one of the best people I know. He makes me want to be a better person. To bring myself up to his standard."

"Damn. Does he know how you feel?" Tempest crossed his arms over his chest. If his lesson in hell had taught him anything it was life was too fucking short not to grab what you want. He had a plan, and he was going to execute it. If destiny was a righteous bitch, he'd end up with Pilar, and with her information he'd find and take out Stratus and the fucking Fates.

"No, it isn't like that, man. There are damn good reasons for my respect and this topic is closed. Permanently." Smoke moved past him and into the now well-lit interior of the vessel. "Comms are up in the bridge. Follow me."

Tempest narrowed his eyes. It wasn't like

Smoke to be so possessive of a person. He'd attached himself to his new partner. Not like in the past. There was something between them, but it didn't appear to be sexual. Again, another first for Smoke. He trailed Smoke through the well-appointed ship and up to the bridge. By the time they'd arrived, Browning had already powered up the ship's systems. "Shut the door behind you. This room is shielded. No one is going to listen to us via electronics, and it is soundproofed so good old-fashioned snooping is out too. Who do you need first?" Smoke clicked on a sat phone line and opened the encryption keys.

Tempest sat and ran his hands through his hair. "Anubis." The man was going to be pissed. Tonight was his alone time with his woman. He glanced at his watch. Sucks to be Anubis.

Smoke keyed in the number. The phone rang twice.

"I take call duty as a favor for one night—one fucking night—and I've had three calls. Smoke, this had better be good."

He hadn't heard Bengal's voice in a while.

Smoke cleared his throat. "I've got Tempest and Sage with me."

"Authenticate Action."

"Movie. We need to go secure." Smoke placed his hand on the key.

"One second. Okay, go secure." Sat phone light changed from red to yellow to green.

"Line is secure. What do you need, Smoke, and why aren't you calling Fury?"

"First, I don't need jack shit. I'm loafing around at Tempest's safe house, and he shows up, and now I believe we've been sucked into his op. But hey, where are my manners? How have you been? How's the wife? Work okay? We should get together sometime and have a drink."

"Tempest, do me a favor and shut him up, please," Bengal's beleaguered voice begged him across the connection.

Smoke smiled at him and high-fived Browning. Clowns. Seriously, they were both teenagers in grown-ass men's bodies.

"I have a lead on a person I believe is a member of Stratus. Highly placed if my gut is leading me in the right direction."

"Stand by, Tempest." Ah, there was the Bengal he knew. Hard-assed and driven.

Smoke walked to the back wall and opened a small fridge. He extracted a water and held it up in question. He lifted his hand and the bottle sailed through the air. Smoke grabbed two more and made it back to the table where all three of them sat as people started checking in over the secure phone line.

"Thorn One on the line." Fury's growl pierced the silence.

"Alpha on."

"Dom Ops."

"Cyber."

"Archangel."

Guardian personnel chimed in before Bengal came back on the line. "We have Tempest, Smoke, and I'm assuming Browning with us."

"You are correct," Tempest acknowledged.

"Break it down for me." Archangel's gravelly voice gave the command.

"When I was held by Stratus, I had a visitor, about two months before I was released." Tempest studied his hands as he spoke. "I'm sure those with the need to know have access to my Go/No go and have been briefed on what transpired. Suffice to say, I returned to Florida to fulfill my obligation to her. I determined her mother was the one who placed her in the cell with me. She was teaching Pilar a lesson on how she acquired information."

"It never ceases to amaze me how parents can reach into the depths of depravity. What ever happened to taking care of your kids?" Tempest listened to the woman who chimed in as Cyber pop off. He'd never talked to her, but he'd lay odds the woman was Bengal's wife.

"What makes you believe the mother is Stratus?" Alpha's question went straight to the point.

"The woman in the cell with me intimidated the guard and used her mother as the threat to get him to do what she wanted."

There was silence for a moment.

"This wasn't included in your debrief folio," Fury commented.

"I was so far gone by that point I didn't know if what I remembered was real or not." Which was a bald-faced lie. He remembered every second of his time with her as if it were inscribed on his DNA. "I made contact with her and validated what I believed to be true."

"What is the mother's name?"

"Regina Grantham."

A low hum sounded across the line. "Not a name we've heard before," Dom Ops said, and he heard typing in the background.

"I got her," Cyber crowed, "She's got some kick

ass controls on her digital footprint. I mean... almost nothing is out there. I love a project. I'll crack this nut. Give me time. Her daughter... damn almost the same except for school records. Ah, smart... an attorney."

"Her mother's attorney," Tempest supplied.

"So, we aren't going to get any information from her." Exasperation filled Alpha's comment.

"No, actually she's willing to give us all the information she has on her mother as long as it doesn't come back to her. Morally, she's conflicted. She took an oath to protect the confidentiality of her client, but she's seen what her mother is doing. If we can use *anything* she gives us to find a toe-hold into Stratus, it would be a boon." Tempest willed the powers to be to listen and attend to what he was saying.

"What type of information?" Archangel queried.

"I don't know. She didn't give it to me, but I believe it is enough to pressure Grantham into talking."

"How do we get the information?" That was Dom Ops.

"I have an idea. If you approve it, we can conceal Pilar's intent to betray her mother and give Guardian time to work any information disclosed behind the scenes."

Fury's low, evil chuckle came across the line. "Let me guess. You're going to need a boat."

"A yacht actually. The one I'm on now would work well."

"What do you have in mind?" Archangel's query gave him the opening he needed. He walked them through his intentions step-by-step.

"It could work." The woman spoke again. "I can get a webpage up, and have Alonzo back up the history of the website for a solid four or five years. We can spoof the web server into believing the site has been up for years. It won't be perfect until mid-morning, but if you can hold off contacting her until then, there is no way anyone close to her will be able to ascertain the charter company hasn't existed for years. Of course, I'll have to break into the State of Florida's LLC database and load the company, show annual verifications and payments. Tax bases are Erika's specialty, and she can take care of it in the morning. No need to call her in tonight. Are we using established personas for Smoke and Browning?"

"Yeah, we've done the charter boat thing before with Homeland," Smoke responded.

"Snap, that's right. Perfect. You'll have a history established. Awesome sauce. This is entirely doable." The keyboard tapped away in the background.

"I want another asset in the area." Archangel's command cut through the connection. "From all indications, Stratus is disjointed, but they've shifted their focus from political aspirations to economic."

Tempest made a sound of disagreement. "I believe you're wrong on that point, sir. Pilar has been told she will be the first female President of the United States."

The keyboard went crazy. "But she doesn't hold any office."

"She's going to be running for mayor here. A stepping stone to a Senate seat."

"Fuck. All right." Archangel vented his frustration. "Let's get this put into motion. Alpha, Fury, get together with Anubis in the morning and determine what backup is going to be utilized. Tempest, this is out of your wheelhouse; you can exit and leave it to us."

"It will be a cold day in hell before I leave the woman who saved my life."

"Well it certainly isn't cold in hell. I know. I

train men in the bowels of Satan's sandbox every day," Fury snarked. "We'll get backup heading that way. If I know the three I have in mind, they will be lounging around on vacation, but they'll be ready."

"Copy that. I want a full briefing on all points tomorrow morning at 0900hrs. Archangel out."

"Well when you come back, you come back with a bang, don't you?" Alpha chuckled. "Fury, I have Sierra team available."

"Use them. My people are committed, but I need to alter the rotation due to Tweedledee and Tweedledum fucking up my schedule."

"I'm Dee." Smoke interjected.

"No, you're not. I'm out."

Smoke's eyebrows scrunched together. He mouthed, *"I'm Dee,"* and pointed at himself. Browning flipped him off which returned the man's smile.

"If you need anything, call the switchboard. You're now on their priority list. Whatever it takes, my friend. Alpha out."

"Thanks for the fun, you guys. I totes love having something new to do. Stay safe. Cyber out."

"And that leaves me." Bengal sighed. "I'll brief Anubis in the morning when he checks in. Make sure you're not walking into a shit storm. I'll have Cyber monitor chatter on the Darknet, but Stratus rarely leaves tracks, digital or otherwise. Check in daily."

"Ah yes, the new leash." Tempest leaned back in his seat.

"Necessary evils. It's nice to see you back in action, my friend."

"I'm not doing my job here, I'm gathering intel."

"Guardian is evolving. Shadows are no longer one dimensional."

"Ain't that the truth." Smoke waggled his eyebrows. "I have so many dimensions. Layers and layers of dimensions."

Tempest rolled his eyes. Smoke was an assassin, but he didn't fit the mold for this line of work. He wasn't a loner. He loved people, and he looked like--

"More like layers of bullshit. Bengal out."

"Damn, a guy could get a complex."

"I wonder why." Tempest leaned forward. "Can you sell the charter business if someone shows up asking questions?"

"Damn straight. We've done this before. Don't worry; we won't put your lady in jeopardy. Get her here, and we'll keep both of you off the radar so you can work. Bonus is, we get to float around South Florida, and Guardian pays for our fuel, food and drink. Ain't life sweet?" Smoke elbowed Browning.

The man chuckled and shook his head. "B-better th-than th-e al... al... -tern-native."

CHAPTER 9

"To what cosmic confluence do I owe this call?" Regina's voice rolled through the connection, modulated in the bored, bothered, and over-it condemnation which always tinged her mother's voice.

"I had a little accident last night."

"Indeed?" From her mother's bored tone, she gathered the butler had already called about her hobbling around the house this morning.

"There was a power outage, and in the dark, before the generator kicked on, I managed to break my little toe, fall over a coffee table, and sprain my wrist."

She could picture her mother rubbing her brow

during the ensuing silence. "And *why* are you calling me?"

No sympathy, no concern, no *'Oh, no! Are you all right?'* She hadn't expected an emotional response. But really, the woman hadn't even asked if she'd been to the doctor. She had, first thing this morning. Money and a private doctor made the appointment happen before 9:00 a.m. But still, her mother hadn't cared. Obviously. *Well yeah, but does she actually have emotions?* Other than an angry outburst one time, she'd never seen any.

"Notification, really. I'm cancelling my appointments for the next two weeks. I'm going to put my foot up and rest. The doctor said no heels for at least two weeks. Regardless, there's no way I can look professional for my upcoming engagements until the swelling goes down. To that end I've rented a yacht to take me out for two weeks. I'll work on those speeches you wanted me to practice and get some sun, so I look like a Floridian."

As she talked, she stared at the desktop in her mother's office, the only place she could call on the secure line her mother insisted upon. She sat down in the white leather chair and tugged open the middle drawer. Pens, paperclips in a small ornate dish, and a stack of sticky notes. She bumped the dish and spilled the paperclips. *Damn it.*

"I'll need the specifics of the vessel and the crew. I'm not letting you go alone."

"Oh, for heaven's sake, Regina. I don't need a babysitter, and as a matter of fact, I absolutely need some time alone. I haven't had a vacation in years. If you want me to come back refreshed and ready to get on with the plan you've laid out, let me go and relax for god's sake. I'm exhausted. I want to breathe fresh air, sleep in late, and putz around in the sun before I have a drink and repeat the cycle."

"Hmmm... send me the information for the charter. If it is reputable, I'll allow it."

"Send it? I don't have my computer at home. I left it at work." Which wasn't a lie. She'd left it at work on purpose so she couldn't access the dropbox and beg Luke to come see her. He'd shown up anyway. A smile spread across her face as she waited.

A long sigh came across the line. "Use my desk computer then. I'll allow access this one time."

"I'll need your password." She wiggled the mouse and watched the screen come to life.

"It is my birthday. Day-month-year and then year-month-day. You have ten minutes."

"Regina, I have a broken toe. It will take me ten minutes to get back to my room to get my phone with the charter information."

"Why do I put up with this?"

"Because I'm going to be the first female President of the United States." She put as much confidence behind the statement as she could muster.

The silence this time wasn't expected. "So, you're interested?"

"In making history? Yes, I believe I am. We'll need to discuss platforms, and I will most definitely have pet projects which you will fund."

There was a low laugh. "You're learning."

"My teacher is very, very good." Her teacher was Luke Wagner. *Not* Regina. *Never* Regina.

"You have thirty minutes."

"Thank you."

"And Pilar, I can see what you do on my system."

"Really? How cool is that?" She put the last paperclip into the small dish and shut the desk drawer. "I've got to go. I have to hobble all the way to the other side of the house."

"What a mental picture. Send the information."

"Yes ma'am." She disconnected the call and step-heeled it to the door. She might not be able to click on anything but the email server, without Regina knowing what she was doing, but she could get screenshots with her phone of what she was able to see in her mother's email.

The trip to her quarters and back left her sweaty and breathless and more than a little achy. The heel-step-hop-hip swivel she had going on jarred her poor toe with every step. She ground her teeth together and sucked it up. Lord, it was a little toe! How much more had Luke gone through? She shivered at the memory of the battered man on the cot. A broken little toe was nothing.

The captain had called her this morning. He gave her concise information which included a website with beautiful pictures of a one-hundred-foot yacht and the testimonials of several satisfied customers.

Sitting down in her mother's chair, she woke the machine. Casually, she held her phone, pretending to check the website address as her thumb depressed the camera button and took a picture of every screen that appeared on the monitor. The desktop, the internet browser, the email icon. She clicked on the icon and took a picture of the web address. She'd never seen an email server act like this one. Whatever, it was an email, how hard could it be? She hit compose and typed in her mother's name. An address appeared. She checked the name she'd typed into the search bar again to make sure she'd typed it correctly. Yes, her mother's name was spelled correctly. Just like her mother using an email address that couldn't be associated with her. Regina was one of the original cyber security supporters and having any footprint was unacceptable to her mother. Her social media accounts drove Regina crazy and her mother had forbidden any until college. What idiocy. She added a subject line and then entered the information the captain had given her this morning. Nothing more, nothing less, as she'd been instructed. She took a picture of the email screen before she sent it, backed out of the program, and logged out. In and out in less than a minute.

Now to pack and await Regina's official blessing. She stood and slid her phone into her pocket before she hobbled from the office and shut the office door behind her. Stopping outside the door, she drew a deep breath and waited for guilt or any feelings of remorse. There were none. Even the lingering fear of being disbarred and jailed for her knowledge of the crimes her mother *could* have committed, seemed less life-altering since Luke had come into her rooms last night.

Swimsuits, as in all of the ones she owned, almost filled one side of the suitcase. She had to come back with a tan so her mother didn't become suspicious. Her day planner with the printed speeches she was to memorize and the political talking points her campaign manager had emailed to her office went in next. Then several sundresses, shorts, tank tops, jeans and a couple nice tops along with assorted unmentionables filled the other side of the case. She left it open and took a small bag into the bathroom where she added her makeup, lotions, perfume, brushes, combs, scrunchies and other bits and pieces.

She hobbled from her bathroom and stilled. The butler waited at her bed, beside her suitcase. "What are you doing in my private rooms?" Her heart thundered in her chest. She narrowed her eyes at the man to keep herself from looking at her suitcase. Was there anything in there that could compromise the story she'd told her mother?

"Madam wanted to inform you your vacation has been approved."

"You could have called. The next time I find you in my private area without my permission, I *will* speak with my mother. Perhaps we'll discover who is more valuable to her future plans."

The man bowed, but his sneer wasn't concealed. He left quietly and shut the door behind him. She was certain Regina had sent him into the room to spy on her. Good Lord, the woman was paranoid. For good reason. She went to the bed and stared at her suitcase. The clothes didn't appear to have been shifted. She checked her bathroom bag and refolded a few items before she checked her day planner. Everything was there. Nothing unusual. She snapped the case closed and snatched her phone from her pocket. It took ten seconds for the phone to connect to the number which had called her this morning.

"Captain Collins."

"Yes, Captain, this is Pilar Grantham. I'd like to confirm my charter for today."

"Yes ma'am, we're fueled up and ready to go anytime you're ready to depart."

"Excellent. I'll be there within the hour."

"Yes ma'am, thank you for your business."

Hitting the end button, she called her driver.

"'Ma'am?"

"Cody, I need the car. Also, come to my rooms when you arrive. I have luggage."

"Yes ma'am. I'll be there in less than twenty minutes."

"Thank you." She disconnected and stared at the suitcases. What was she forgetting? She glanced at her foot. Shoes. Open toed sandals, flats. God, did she even have flat shoes other than the ones she wore to the doctor? She limped back into her closet and searched her shoe racks. "Well hello." She grabbed a cute, embellished pair of flip flops and one other pair of flat sandals. She shoved the sandals into an outside pouch of her bathroom bag and carefully put the flip flops on. Oh man... if she was clumsy in her bare feet, she was awkward as hell trying to walk in a flip flop. She used her arms to steady herself on anything solid and made her way to the main door of her rooms. Just as she reached it, Cody knocked. She hobbled as she backed up when opening the door. "Ma'am didn't the doctor advise you to stay off your foot?"

She blinked up. Concern lined the man's brow. "He did, and that is exactly what I'm going to do for the next two weeks."

The furrows in his forehead deepened a bit. "By traveling?"

She chuckled. "I'm going to go get on a very

nice ship and for the next two weeks do nothing but bask in the sun and keep my foot elevated."

"Very good." Cody smiled. "May I?" He asked permission to go into her rooms.

"Absolutely. The two bags on the bed."

He moved past her and picked up the luggage easily. Man, how had she ever thought he'd over-stepped yesterday. "I'll get these settled and come back to help you down the stairs and to the car."

"Thank you." She waited for him to pass her and shut her door behind her.

Good to his word, Cody met her at the top of the stairs, and she leaned on him, letting him hold the arm of her injured wrist and gripped the bannister with her good hand to ambulate down the stairs.

"You know, I believe I owe you an apology for yesterday."

"Ma'am?"

"When you asked if I needed any help. I'm not accustomed to genuine concern."

Cody opened the front door and helped her across the threshold before he closed the door and offered her his arm again. "No need, ma'am. I over-stepped." He opened the door for her and helped her into the vehicle before jogging around the black sedan and getting in the driver's seat. "Where to?"

"Palm Beach Yacht Club and Marina, pier three."

"Yes ma'am."

The throb of her toe demanded action, so she shifted in her seat, picked her leg up, and settled her foot upon the leather bench seat. She dropped her head back and closed her eyes. Sleep hadn't come last night. The heartbeat in her toe and overall shock of seeing Luke again had guaranteed that. His gold-flecked green eyes had haunted her for so long, seeing them with the whites clear of blood had shocked her. She'd tried to imagine what he would look like healthy. Normally, her suppositions ended with a verbal admonishment that he was probably dead. She drew a deep breath. She'd often wondered if he'd died at her mother's hand. Thank God he hadn't. She shook her head and reprimanded herself again. The kiss last night wasn't sexual. A press of flesh against flesh. A thank you of sorts. Probably. No, definitely. But if he wanted more... A shudder of hunger raced through her veins. Yes. The answer would be emphatically, yes.

CHAPTER 10

Tempest watched from the darkened windows of the bridge as the Bentley drove to the end of the pier. Smoke and Browning hustled from the deck, down the long pier, to the car. He stayed out of sight. Browning carried two suitcases, and Smoke strolled slowly along with Pilar as she limped down the long stretch of pier. The ship was too big to fit in a slip and was tethered to the end of the pier. If he'd been down there, he'd have picked her up and carried her to the boat.

Which was exactly what Smoke did. *Motherfucker.* Pilar scrambled to grab ahold of Smoke's shoulders. He threw back his head and laughed as he strode down the planking toward the boat. The only thing saving the son of a bitch from a major ass kicking was the talk they had last night and the fact Pilar looked about as willing to be in his arms as a feral cat. *Bet that's a blow to your self-esteem, hey bud?*

He could hear Sage down below and finally Pilar's voice. He moved to the rear of the bridge and watched as Smoke put her down on the lounger. Sage brought her what looked like a glass of wine before he grabbed another pillow and propped her foot up.

Smoke joined him on the bridge. "She's on board. Sage is bringing in the mooring lines. We'll go north and head into the Atlantic using the Lake Worth Inlet. The next closest inlet is to the south, the Boynton Inlet, but it has a fixed bridge and the tide is in. We wouldn't get under it. Too tall." Tempest stared toward the back window as Smoke talked, and the motors grumbled to life under them. "Her luggage is in the lounge. You won't be seen."

"On it." He grabbed two handheld devices, each the size of a deck of playing cards, and headed down the stairs. He flipped a switch and passed the electronic box past her small bag, careful to ensure he had complete coverage by lifting the bag and passing the box under it. He put the bag down and moved to the larger one. Two lights lit and then a third. Damn it. Her bag had a GPS tracker and an RF tracker, plus a hidden microphone. *Fuck.* They couldn't disable them without causing alarm. He laid the suitcase on its side—a prearranged signal indicating the case was bugged.

Browning walked in and stopped by the door. The man signed, "What do we have?"

Tempest answered, "GPS, RF and a recording device."

Sage looked at him and moved his hands. "Is she working with them?"

Tempest shook his head, definitively. *There was no way in hell.* He'd be in a cell again if she were. Browning nodded and exited through the lounge area toward the bridge. Undoubtedly, Sage would inform Smoke of the fun and games he'd found. He carried the luggage to Pilar's room, the one adjoining his, and settled them on the luggage rack at the foot of the bed. The recording device wasn't concerning. Whoever was on the other end could listen to Pilar change clothes and sleep all day every day. The problem was the RF tracker and

GPS. Regina Grantham was tracking her own daughter. Well, if she wanted to track a ship, no problem, he'd oblige. Carefully, he opened the suitcase and searched through... damn. Bikinis. Okay. A lot of bikinis. Damn. He picked one of the pieces up. A sky-blue scrap of fabric and strings. *Hell no*. She'd be wearing these suits around Smoke and Browning. Fuck... he needed to get a grip on this jealousy issue he'd been bumping up against. Really, he did. The fabric fluttered to the suitcase, landing among the cornucopia of colors. Out of habit, he glanced at the door and moved her day planner using his hand-held device to locate the trackers. *Smart.* They'd placed the GPS tracker in her pen. He removed the cap and slid the tracker onto the bed's duvet before he reassembled the pen and then located the RF tracker. This would be harder. He'd have to find the RF chip and then the locator. He swept the bikini-filled half of her case before he switched sides. The tracker was attached to the inside of the suitcase. It looked like a silver stud placed at the seam of the lining. It took the work of a moment to remove the transmitter. The RF chip he found was lodged in the metal casement which wrapped the seam of the suitcase when the case was closed. He used the tip of her pen to remove the tiny chip and placed it beside the tracker on the bedspread.

The microphone and recorder were clunky and installed by a moron. They dangled off the back of the suitcase's dividing webbing. He attached it more firmly and wound it through the webbing so it wouldn't fall out. *Idiots.*

Taking the GPS and the RF components, he knocked on the bridge's door. Smoke popped out and looked at what was in his hand. "How do you want to play this?"

"Are we out of the marina yet?"

"Nope."

"Stop here. Declare an engine issue or whatever else it takes, but give me a half hour."

"You got it."

Tempest went to the galley kitchen and found a resealable plastic bag and placed the electronics into it. After ensuring it was water-tight, he shoved them into his board shorts and double checked the Velcro closure was securely fastened. Careful to remain out of sight of the piers and the people who were at the yacht club's restaurant, he crept to the bow of the boat and lowered himself over the edge before dropping into the warm water of the sheltered harbor.

He filled his lungs with a deep breath before he went under. Swimming in a marina was dangerous as fuck. Some dickhead drunk could come roaring in or out at any time, but they needed a boat for Regina Grantham to track, and he knew which boat to select. All morning he'd been monitoring the loading of another luxury boat which had also been prepping for launch. It was still moored, but the crew was watching the pier, as they had when Pilar had notified them she was inbound. He made it to the ship and used the ladder at the rear of the *Ocean Queen* to take him up to the swimming platform. Crab walking across the pristinely maintained platform, he moved silently to the floating dock which had been raised in preparation for embarkation and sailing. It took less than twenty seconds to plant the chips under the seat of one of the two jet skis. His body slid into the water moments later. He surfaced about thirty seconds and a hundred feet away from the yacht, filled his lungs and dove under the water again. The burn of his lungs as he surfaced felt fucking amazing. Since he'd recovered, the need for exercise, for being free and able to move, was almost irrational.

A rope ladder flipped over the side at the bow. He glanced up and watched as Browning leaned over the ledge. He signed, "Hurry up, the harbor master is going to board us if we don't move soon."

Grabbing the rope, he stepped two rungs up before the engines fired to life, and the boat started to move. Damn, he hadn't been gone long. He flipped over the bow and glanced at the entrance to the inlet. Well hell, three boats were holding, waiting to enter. *Note to self, in the future get rid of trackers before leaving the pier.*

The sun warmed the deck, and unable to move without being detected by the incoming boats or the ones pushing off from the pier, he cupped his hands under his head and let the sun dry him. The motor of the ship droned powerfully as Smoke navigated the vessel away from the channel. Browning shuffled by and kicked his foot telling him he could move safely. Sage was sharp, and he could see why Smoke liked him as a partner. He sat up and watched as Smoke took them out of the inlet. The open ocean waves could have tossed the ship around, but with the stabilizers deployed, the ship sliced through the water with barely any sway. Smaller boats peeled away hovering closer to the shoreline. They followed the channel markers out to deep water. He did a careful 360 before he stood. A soft wind fanned his skin and gooseflesh prickled across his overheated body as he moved from the bow to the stern. The powerful motor below them and the sound of the water's rhythmic clap against the side of the ship coalesced into a quiet hum. In the shelter of the main cabin and upper floors, the wind all but ceased and formed a sheltered oasis of sun, warmth, and utter relaxation.

Pilar sat where she'd been deposited. The cool white wine had formed a sheen of condensation on the outside of the glass she held. She stared toward the wake of the boat, motionless except for the movement of her hair in the breeze. He straightened his shoulders. It was a curiosity, but whenever he thought of this woman, he wanted her to see him as more. More than the excuse of flesh he'd been when she'd been thrust into his life. More than the failure he was for being caught. More than someone to be pitied. The doc had said it was because he'd never been so vulnerable, and it was normal to want to show the woman who'd given him back his life, he was worthy of it.

Tempest shook his head. He'd give the doc credit. He'd gotten close, but his real motivation was to show Pilar he was worthy of *her*. Worthy to be in *her* life. Those considerations had caused him countless sleepless nights because he couldn't tell her until he'd completed his vendetta against the Fates. Work he couldn't dismiss, or delay, prevented him from declaring his true feelings for her. *Stupid*. He'd known her a handful of hours, although it seemed like so much more.

Regardless, *his* feelings weren't the important issue here. He'd hunt down Stratus and the Fates like the animals they were, and he was going to use her mother as a stepping stone to reach his goal. His drive to use her mother was enough to damn any future with Pilar to hell and back. She wanted her mother to be brought to justice. He didn't deal with terms such as justice. He wanted revenge. He wanted to destroy Stratus and inflict a slow torturous death upon the Fates. If pressuring Pilar's mother would advance his goals, the Fates' continued existence would be brief and agonizing.

He moved closer. "Is something wrong with the wine?"

She gasped and jerked around, spilling half of the wine on top of her and the chair. "Shit!" She moved quickly and then hissed as she stood too fast. He grabbed her arm to stabilize her. "I was so worried. I thought you weren't going to be here." She looked at him. "You're all wet."

He grinned. "So are you." The wine had turned her white shorts transparent. She wore hot pink panties.

She glanced down and groaned. "Perfect." She gave the remaining wine in her glass an evil glare.

"Let's sit over here." He pointed to the built-in couch along the side of the ship. He helped her totter to the seat and waited until she got comfortable before he sat down. He bent down and cradled her injured foot on his lap, elevating the ravaged foot and giving him an excuse to touch her.

"Where were you?" She seemed to notice her wine glass and took a sip. Her eyebrows rose, and she murmured, "This is nice."

"Inside. I didn't want anyone who might be watching to see me."

"In case I was followed."

"Exactly."

"So, what happens now?" She took another sip of her wine. "And why are you wet?"

"I took a small side excursion. Your luggage was tagged with a GPS and RF device which are no longer there, but it still has a recording device in it."

"What?" She scrambled to catch her glass when it went sideways again.

He reached for the glass and took it away from her. "The GPS and RF tracker were in your suitcase. One in the pen of your planner. One in the case itself."

"What did you do with them?"

"I planted them on another vessel which I believe is about to set sail."

She blinked at him and shook her head. "The recording device?"

"Old tech and not installed well at all."

"The butler did it."

Tempest couldn't help the chuckle and smile. "He usually does."

Her brow creased for a moment before she reached out and smacked him on the arm, but her smile made an appearance. "I'm serious. The butler came to my room this morning while I was in the bathroom. He works for my mother."

"No worries. They won't get much from it unless..." His mind dipped into darkness, but he shook his head.

"Unless what?"

"Would your mother ever blackmail you?"

"Blackmail?"

"Yes, if she couldn't get you to do what she wanted, would she blackmail you?"

Pilar grabbed her wine glass back from him and downed the remainder. She handed him the glass back and flopped back into the cushions. "I wouldn't put anything past her. Look what she did to you."

The defeated resignation in her voice galvanized his hatred for a woman he'd never met. "Yeah, but I'm not her daughter."

Pilar ran her hands through her hair and re-anchored the blonde curls in the ponytail they were trying to escape. "I'm quite certain my mother would use whatever was at her disposal to get her way. With me, or you, or anyone else. Why do you ask?"

"If she taped you having sex..." He let the words drift.

Her eyes widened. "Is there a camera?"

"No, only audio."

She blinked and shook her head. "Ummm... yeah. That's really sick, but like I said, I wouldn't put it past her."

"When you are in your room, you'll need to be aware the device is active."

"As in transmitting or recording?"

"Recording only. The device is sound activated to save battery and space in the small device which collects the audio files. They won't get more than a couple hours on a device of this size."

Rationally she knew her mother monitored her actions. Actually seeing the extent Regina went to track her lanced her with an ice-cold spear to the heart. She took in the information, hating every corroborating shred of evidence. She closed her eyes and drew several deep breaths before she was ready to speak. "So, when do you want me to give you that data?"

"How about I take you back to your stateroom, and we'll both get a shower and change then we can meet in the lounge and work through what you have."

"What about the crew?" She glanced up at the bridge.

"They work with me."

"At Guardian."

"Yes."

"I take it Guardian has been briefed and has approved of your plan."

"We're here. We wouldn't be if they hadn't." Her eyes searched the upper floor of the yacht. He put his hand on her ankle and she jumped. "Pilar, do you trust me?"

She stared at him for several long seconds. "Like I've never trusted anyone in my life." She deflated in front of him. "I'm worried. I'm violating my oath by giving you this information. Regina will go to jail. I don't doubt it for a second as long as you can substantiate the information by an independent investigation, because anything I give you can't be used in a court of law."

He rubbed her shin with his hand. Her soft skin against his hardened hands held his attention as he spoke. "And what if she's involved with more than you know?"

"Then she pays for those sins, too. Look, the reason I'm giving you this information is because I know she's involved in more. She's opened the window, but I can only see pieces of information which are horrendous by themselves through the cracks of the blinds. My small glimpses of her acts will undoubtedly lead to other crimes." Pilar shook her head. "She's guilty of things I can't let myself say. I know what I'm doing, Luke. I'm condemning the woman who gave birth to me to jail. I don't want to do it. I want to pretend it isn't happening, but I can't. I... can't." Tears formed in her eyes, but she raised her chin and stared at him. "She deserves to be held accountable for her actions."

He squeezed her leg. "Then let's get cleaned up and get to work."

CHAPTER 11

Pilar leaned against Luke's strong arm as he guided her to her stateroom. "Remember, anything you say once the door is open will be recorded. I'm right next door. When you're finished you can either come through the door which connects the two rooms or go through this door." He pointed to the door immediately adjacent to hers. "And lose the flip flops. Barefoot is better. I'll re-tape your toe when you're done."

He leaned down and gave her a platonic kiss on the forehead before opening her door. The kiss halted anything she wanted to say. Things like *'You do realize I'm over thirty, not thirteen, right?'* or maybe *'Am I crazy for wanting you?'* She snorted as she hobbled into the room and shut the door behind herself.

Of course, she was crazy for wanting the man. Look at him! He was a fucking bronze god and she was... she lifted her arms and looked down at herself. A sticky, wine-stained, slightly overweight, sexually frustrated, thirty-year-old puppet about to cut the strings. She glanced down at her suit-case. What in the hell did she have to offer someone like Luke? Someone who worked for Guardian.

She stopped and shifted her attention to the adjoining door. What exactly did he do for Guardian? Man, she was seriously off her game. She sat down on the navy-blue comforter and stared at the door. What *did* he do for Guardian? Why exactly had he come back? It wasn't because he was interested in her. The peck on the lips and the brush-off kiss to the forehead just now sealed that door. She'd told him she wasn't holding him to his oath to come help her get away from her mother. He could have walked away, but he hadn't. Why? What did he want?

She straightened as the answer came to her. Her mother. Guardian was after her mother, and Luke worked for Guardian. His words played back through her mind in Dolby surround sound. *"And what if she's involved with more than you know?"*

He *knows* Regina is involved in more, and they are *looking* for a way to bring her down. Pilar drew a deep breath and chased away the thoughts and the scenarios it brought with it. She felt oddly... relieved. Guardian was building a case against others with which her mother was involved. It was a relief she wasn't the impetus of the entire investigation. She was the conduit, a channel marker giving Guardian directions to look. The small separation from the self-condemnation which had hung around her neck since she'd agreed to reveal her privileged attorney-client information was the breathing room she needed.

With a lighter and now flip flop free step, she gathered a bathing suit and cover from her suitcase, slung her bathroom case over her shoulder, and carefully step-heeled it into the bathroom.

The shower took a few moments to figure out, but she cleaned up and changed into a lemon colored, one piece swimming suit which dipped drastically low in the back and was cut to the waist in the front. Her gossamer wrap draped to mid-thigh, and was almost see-through, but it veiled the important parts of her. She wound her hair into a quick French twist and secured it with a wide barrette instead of the multitude of hairpins she usually pushed into her hair. That accomplished, she refreshed her lip balm and grabbed her planner.

So... Luke had no interest in her beyond the information she could provide against her mother. Guardian had been conducting an independent investigation on her mother, and her personal input was simply a boon. How... sad and liberating.

She rolled her eyes at her school-girl infatuation. She'd give Luke the information he wanted and spend fourteen glorious days lounging in the sun and mending her toe. Not a shoe in sight, no reasons to stress, and no more reasons to worry. She'd made the right decision in confiding in Luke. She chuckled as she exited her cabin and shut the door behind her.

Her imagination had played the worst-case scenarios for so long. Really? How bad could it be? Worst case, for her... disbarment and jail. But Guardian would never sully their pristine reputation of protecting their sources, so she wasn't in fear of that scenario playing out. The worst thing for her mother? Incarceration. Her knowledge was limited, on purpose, but if the right questions were asked and if Regina was involved in any way with the deaths of those wealthy donors? Well, if she was involved, then she would be sentenced as appropriate by a judge and jury.

She knocked on Luke's door and nearly choked on her tongue when he answered it. He wore a pair of black board shorts and nothing else. Granted it was just like what he'd been wearing earlier, but damn... "Ah, hey. Ready?"

"Yeah. Let me get a shirt. Come in. I'll re-tape your toe."

She looked down at the tape which flopped like a limp noodle against the top of her foot. "Ah..."

"Come on. You know I don't bite." He winked at her and tugged a black t-shirt over his head.

Oh, my heavens. Drool worthy shoulders, chest, abs, and the happy trail of dark hair leading down past the waistband of his shorts. She popped her eyes back up to his. He smiled and waggled his eyebrows a couple of times. *Shit.* Had he caught her checking him out? "Come in. Let's get you taped up so we can get down to business."

Business. "Right. Okay." She heel-toed it to a chair in the corner.

He returned from the bathroom with a small

red box and motioned to the king-sized bed. "Here. The light is better."

Of course it is. With a smile plastered onto her face, she squeezed her planner to her chest with a death grip as she limped to the bed and sat down. He kneeled in front of her and moved her foot to his thigh.

Oh, my god.

Her foot absorbed the warmth of his flesh like a dry sponge absorbed water. She started to shiver and not because she was cold. No, looking down at him holding her foot with such care sent a thrill through her. She closed her eyes and groaned.

"Did I hurt you?"

She popped her eyes open. *What?* "Ah... no. Not really. I'm fine."

"Let me know if I cause you any pain."

He stared at her, and she did the only thing she could. She nodded. If she opened her mouth her tongue would unroll and drag on the floor. Drool would flood the cabin. God, was it his soap or cologne? Whatever it was, the scent was intoxicating. His long fingers carefully removed the bandage the nurse had wrapped her little toe in this morning. Man, had it only been this morning? Since Luke had come back into her life, time had sped up. Moments which used to drag raced past her, leaving her playing catch up. He removed the non-stick pad and examined the bruising on her toe. Vibrant reds, purples and blacks filtered down the side of her foot from the bottom joint of her toe to the heel. "Pretty, huh?"

His eyes connected with her gaze. "Beautiful." He kept the connection for several seconds before he dropped his attention to her foot again.

Oh... wow... those gold-flecked green eyes could suck the air from her lungs.

She leaned forward and watched as he deftly taped her toe as efficiently as the nurse had this morning. "You're good at being a nurse."

He chuckled as he put the tape back in the case and snagged up the wrapping from the pad he used to cushion her toe. "I've had quite a lot of practice and several training courses on self-aid and care for others. Battlefield type operations." He carefully moved her foot off his thigh.

Wow. "Battlefield? You were in the military?"

He spoke as he moved around the cabin, throwing away the trash and stowing the kit. "Something like that, yes."

"How old are you? Or is that rude?" She chuckled. "I know it isn't polite to ask a woman her age."

He smiled and offered her his hand. "I'm forty-three."

She stood and stared up at him. "How tall are you?"

He chuckled. "Six-four. I wear a size thirteen shoe, and I don't have any allergies."

She snatched her hand away and spun toward the door on her good foot. "I'm sorry."

"Hey, no, really. I didn't mean to make you feel self-conscious." His hands landed lightly on her shoulders, and she froze. He stepped up behind her as his hands slid down her arms and gripped her biceps gently. "I want you to know me. I want to know everything about you, too."

She snapped her eyes closed and whispered, "Why?"

He gently turned her and waited until she looked up at him. "Because you saved my life. My very breath, my thoughts, my survival, are real because *you* cared. You are a God given blessing I don't deserve, but one I must acknowledge I want." He lifted a hand and cupped her cheek. "The connection we shared three years ago refuses to be dislodged from my thoughts. You have been with me every day. How can I not want to know you better?"

She stared up into those intense eyes. He towered over her. Men of his stature had always intimidated her, like the one who'd carried her down the pier today, but Luke had never intimidated her. This close to him, she felt shielded from the external forces of the world.

"You've always stayed with me. Here." She touched the skin above her planner which she still clutched to her chest. "I worried about you for so long."

"I couldn't risk contacting you until I was ready to come back for you." He folded her into a hug and dropped his chin on her head. She heard his heart beating under her ear. Strong, steady, warm. She sighed and leaned further into him. The planner dug into her chest, but she didn't give a damn.

"I'm so glad you came back. I'm glad you didn't leave after I gave you that note." She chuckled. "I wanted to do what was best for you."

"You're what's best for me." He moved away so she could look up at him.

"I think maybe you're what's best for me, too." Her eyes slipped from his gorgeous green gaze to his lips. She licked her own, wanting to taste his.

His thumb brushed across her cheek. "Before

this attraction goes any further, there's something you need to know. Because of information I've given them, Guardian believes your mother may be involved with a very well-organized criminal organization."

She leaned into his touch. "I know."

His finger stopped moving. "How?"

"I'm a pretty smart cookie. Top of my class, Harvard Law. You asked what I would do if my mother was connected to other crimes. Guardian is going after her, and I understand the rationale for their interest. The information I give you can be incorporated into your investigation, and Guardian will corroborate the information independently."

He stared at her for a long moment. "And if I were to tell you the justice you want may not be handed down by a US court of law?"

She moved away from his hand and drew a deep breath. "International crimes? I know she has a global reach." She shook her head. "She needs to pay for what she's done. Although I have only my suspicions, I know if you follow the open questions I'll give you, you'll no doubt discover evidence you can use. I didn't follow the trails. If I don't know for sure she has committed a crime or was going to commit a crime, then I'm not obligated to report it." She sighed and shook her head. "I reported you by the way. As soon as I made it back to my hotel in New York, I called 911. I told them you were being held against your will. I couldn't give them a location, and they didn't take it seriously. One call to Regina to confirm my statements and boom, zero interest."

"You shouldn't have tried to report it. What if your mother learned about it?"

"Oh, she found out. She mocked me for my ethics and lack of ability to see the big picture." And made sure everyone in her life reported what she was doing and when, gave her no freedom and limited her interaction with anyone she didn't approve of first. She sighed and stared at the space between them. "How bad is it? Guardian wouldn't be involved if the scope wasn't big. Right?"

His hand trailed down her arm and clasped her hand. "I don't know how deeply your mother is involved, but it's as bad as it gets."

She nodded and then stepped away from him. "Okay, well let's get this done so we can get the information to Guardian. What happens to her is of her own doing." She couldn't wear her mother's responsibility.

"Pilar." His husky voice secured her complete attention. "I'm sorry, in advance for what will transpire when Guardian confirms and acts on the information you give them. Your life will be disrupted and may never be the same."

She swallowed hard. "Change isn't a bad thing in this instance. Will you..."

"Will I what?" He stepped up next to her again.

"Will you still be in my life after this situation is cleared up?"

He lowered and pressed a kiss on her lips, but before he could lift away, she opened her mouth and swept his bottom lip with her tongue. The tortured groan which came from Luke emboldened her. She raised her good arm and wrapped her hand around his neck, keeping him where she could reach him.

His tongue met hers, and he slid his arms around the small of her back, riveting her to his hard, strong body. Oh, heavens, his board shorts did nothing to hide his interest. She leaned on her good foot and pushed against his hard cock. One hand traveled down her back and cupped her ass, pulling her closer to his erection. And dear heavens, the long hard ridge grinding against her lower stomach dispatched a flurry of electric sensations through her body. Her heart raced and her pulse pounded, sending curls of delicious want through her limbs and centered at her core. The need to breathe was the only reason she let him lift away from her.

He dropped his forehead to hers. "As much as I want to lock the door and forget everything outside this cabin, we need to get this information into the hands of the people who can use it."

She smiled up at him. "I was certain you didn't feel anything for me."

He blinked and cocked his head. A smile tugged at the edges of his lips. "So, subtlety doesn't work with you?"

A laugh bubbled from her. "I guess not. I thought maybe you were being kind because I helped you. Nothing more."

He cleared his throat and chuckled before he rubbed the back of his neck with one hand. "Ah, kind is not what I'm feeling."

She shifted and sent a hooded gaze at him. "What are you feeling?"

"Lust. Desire. Need. Want." He took a step toward her with each word. "And if we don't open the door now, we won't for days."

Oh. Yes. *Yes Please*. "Days?"

He leaned toward her. "Days." His arm snaked out... and he opened the door.

"Oh." She stepped away from him and hissed when she put too much pressure on her toe. "Damn." She shifted her weight, so her toes were in the air and she was walking on her heel again.

"Want me to carry you?" he offered as she exited the cabin.

"You? Anytime. That other guy? No thanks. I mean he's nice and all, but I don't know him, and he goes all He-Man, picks me up, and carries me down the pier. He looks really familiar, though. Like the actor––"

"Yeah, he gets those comments a lot. You'll be safer in the narrow passages if you walk. Once we have more room, I'll carry you to where we're going."

"No, really, you don't have to carry me. Seriously, it may take me a hot minute to get there, but I am capable of walking."

"Perhaps I want to hold you. You didn't consider that option, did you?"

His low rumbled words charged the plugged-in feeling again. The sensation was thrilling with an edge of excitement which bordered on anxious agitation in the most wonderful way. Stimulating, disquieting and a total composure wrecking ball. She swallowed hard and then cleared her throat as he gazed at her. "No. I didn't."

His smile spread across his face. "Perhaps it is time you did."

She watched him move forward to open the passage door at the end of the hall. Oh yeah, there was little room for thinking of anything else. *Ever.*

CHAPTER 12

Self-control had never been a problem for him. Yet, every time he was close to Pilar the only thing he wanted to do was plaster her body against his and revel in the soft, sensuous curves which teased him through the almost see-through coverup she wore. Her firm, toned legs were all the enticement needed at this point. Hell, a stiff breeze could give him a hard on right now and at forty-three, a horny, sex-crazed, teenaged boy was the last imitation train he needed to hop on, but *chugga-chugga*... there he went.

He waited for her, holding the door open. As soon as she passed him, he let the door shut and swept her into his arms.

"Oh! Seriously! I can walk."

"And I can walk faster." He strode through the back portion of the second level, a bank of chairs that centered in front of a theater sized projection screen.

"This is an amazing ship. Is it Guardian's?"

"No ma'am. It's mine." Smoke stuck his head out of the galley. "I'm rustling up some lunch. Sage has the helm."

"Pilar, may I introduce––"

"Dan Collins." He wiped off his hand and extended it to the woman he held.

She shifted the book she was gripping and took his hand. "Pilar Grantham."

"A pleasure to officially meet you." Smoke gave her a dazzling smile, the one he pulled out when he wanted people to fall under his spell. The same one his little brother gave to millions of adoring fans. The brothers were from the same mold. Magnetism surrounded them and siphoned people into their orbit. Which was probably why underwater demolitions was the guy's specialty. Not many rabid fans out on the ocean, even fewer under the water. Although the man had other skills. Specialized and deadly was a hallmark of all the Shadows.

"Has anyone ever told you that you bear a remarkable resemblance to--"

Smoke barked a laugh and spun on his heel going back to the galley. "All the time! Wouldn't it be awesome to be that guy? I'll bring lunch to the dining area in a couple of minutes."

Tempest chuckled, adjusted her slight weight in his arms and headed toward the aft of the spacious interior cabin. He sat her on a padded leather chair which swiveled but was bolted to the floor.

He noted the computer had inline encryption attached to the exterior USB device. Smoke and Sage were efficient. He lifted the lid and called up a blank document. Currently they weren't online, and they wouldn't be until he had a comprehensive briefing to give Guardian. When he did, he'd encrypt the document and have Guardian's cyber unit connect to the computer to ensure the link was shielded and unassailable. Physically, precautions were in place, and the yacht had state of the art sensors on the hull and stabilizers to ensure they weren't boarded without warning.

"So, as you know, I did not ask my mother specific questions, such as are you involved? Have you committed a crime? What is your role in this event? All of those questions would have involved me in a moral and ethical dilemma, but I've reached the point which I no longer care if I'm disbarred or serve time for complacency. My primary concern was who to get the information to so she couldn't... make it go away."

"How real is the possibility of her eradicating evidence?"

She carefully put the day planner down and flipped to a tabbed section in the back. "I don't know. Each page in this section represents a donation to one of her companies. Each one of these donations came after the death of the donor. Millions upon millions of dollars comes in on any given month."

Tempest looked at the writing. Shorthand. Nothing anyone snooping through her things would be able to decipher without effort. "So... none of it is illegal."

"True. However, with a few exceptions because of no next of kin, the donations were going to be contested by the families of the deceased. Those court cases never came to fruition."

Tempest leaned back in his chair. Damn it. If this was all she had, there was nothing but supposition on her part. "None of this is illegal."

She nodded her head and then pointed at a line

at the bottom of the page. "No court action ever resulted in any of the cases. None. Not one. Ever."

He leaned forward and gazed down at her shorthand as if he understood it, which he didn't. "How many cases?"

"*Twenty-seven* in the two years I've been tracking it. Twenty-seven donations totaling somewhere north of three hundred million dollars in less than two years."

"What happened to the complainants?"

"I didn't ask because I couldn't know. But the things I could ask, I did."

"Such as?"

"Such as how did the donors die?"

"And?"

"Without exception each donor died of accidental causes."

"Accidents?"

"Yes, none were from old age, cancer, heart conditions, anything remotely medical. The majority were vehicle and pedestrian accidents, some were reported as suicides, three breaking and enterings resulting in the deaths of the donors, and several accidental electrocutions."

"Interesting." Was Regina Grantham targeting liquid assets from families with skeletons in their past, families vulnerable to blackmail to remain silent? He leaned back and rubbed his jaw. Lycos' specialty was killing while making it look like an accident. Could her mother employ an assassin with similar skills? Guardian, Fury in particular, would know of any assassin currently freelancing with such a specialty. "What else do you have?"

Her shoulders fell. "You don't think this is enough?"

He placed his hand on her thigh. He nodded to the planner. "I think your suppositions have credibility, but I also see fifteen or twenty pages past the ones you've been talking about. What else do you have?"

"These are notes on things I've noticed while I've been executing my assigned responsibilities. I oversee The Continuum, the foundation where the donors' money is deposited. These pages show movements of money from the foundation to other businesses. Research into those businesses, done months after the fact so there was no link to the specific donation, led me into a labyrinth of shell companies. I believe the money is moved to foreign countries and exchanged into Euros, Pesos, Yen, Pounds and... legitimized."

"Laundered." Tempest gave her the correct wording.

"Yes. My ability to research the companies is limited, so while I was at the law library two years ago, I engaged the services of a law clerk to do the research. The research doesn't come back to me. I go to the law library once a month. She meets me there. I give her cash for her efforts, and she gives me a hard copy report which I read, transcribe in my notes, and shred."

"Are you sure the document couldn't be reconstituted?" He needed to ensure her mother wasn't any the wiser.

"I ordered a document shredder that was certified for destruction of classified material. The paper is powder by the time I'm done with it." She smiled at him. "I was afraid, but I had to know."

"What did your research find?"

"Twelve bank accounts totaling about three billion dollars. There are revenue streams I can't identify, but as Regina Grantham's lawyer, I can access her accounts. Her name and two others were on all twelve accounts."

"Do you have the names?"

"I don't. Access to that portion of the account

was shielded. I'm assuming she has business partners or perhaps other entities who are doing the same or similar things to acquire money."

Smoke came from the galley carrying a tray. Tempest shook his head, and the man pivoted on the ball of his foot and headed right back into the galley. It would have been comical if he hadn't been struggling with Pilar's revelations. They'd shaken him to the core. Regina Grantham could very well be one of the Fates. Instead of finding a way into Stratus, they may have located one of three women he'd been given the green light to eliminate.

"What? What did I say?" Her blue eyes swung back to him. "Why did you send him away?"

"I'll call him back shortly, but if you're okay to work for a while, I want to get this information to Guardian as quickly as possible."

"Why the change of attitude?"

He turned to her and shook his head. "I'm not sure, a gut feeling. Do you have anything else?"

She slumped back and stared at her planner before she startled, patted her wrap, and pulled her phone from a pocket. "Yes, she let me access her email to send her information on this charter. I'm sure she's changed the password, but I took photos of everything."

"Perfect. Let's start transcribing each page. I'll type, you read." He opened a document and they began.

"Oh, dear God in Heaven, we won't get out of here before the turn of the century if you're typing."

He stopped with his fingers poised over the keyboard. "What?"

"Two finger pecking is all right for typing an email, but good god, there are at least sixty or seventy pages here. Let me type." She made "give me" hands at the laptop. "Go get me food and something to drink. I'm so thirsty I could drink the ocean."

He slid the computer in front of her and watched as her fingers flew across the keyboard, five times faster than his tapping, even with an injured wrist. She turned and looked at him. "Food. Water, cold and lots of it."

He chuckled and swiveled in his chair so he could get up. "Anyone ever tell you that you are bossy?"

She shifted her attention from her work. "Are you *still* here?" She blinked her eyes at him.

"Food and ice water. On it." He stopped at the door to the galley and glanced back. Her blonde head bent over the book, and her hands flew across the keys.

"Sorry. I didn't expect you two to get to the serious stuff for a while." Smoke came to stand beside him. "What did you learn?"

He drew a breath and shook his head. "I think her mother may be one of the Fates."

Smoke dropped back against the wall and hissed, "Are you shitting me?"

"My gut tells me I'm right."

"And if she is?"

"I'll kill her."

"Fuck, man, don't. You can let someone else take the assignment." Smoke turned and looked at him with eyes which were serious and sincere. Those two things were rare in Dan Collins' world.

"The Fates held me and tortured me. They are mine."

"You can take down the other two. Don't put a canyon between the two of you."

Tempest stared at Pilar, busily giving him the information which would sign her mother's death warrant. "There isn't anything between us."

"You know I'd appreciate it if you'd do me the

courtesy of not lying to me. I've always played it straight with you. This woman is something to you, and by the look in her eyes, you're something to her, too." Smoke picked up the tray holding an array of sandwiches, chips and fruit. "Since there's nothing there, you won't mind if I make a play for her?"

Tempest slowly leveled his gaze on Smoke. Every possessive fiber in his body hummed with a confined surge of dominant fury.

"See, right there, your jealousy proves you're not only lying to me, but to yourself. Make sure you know what you're doing. Sure, you could do your job and never tell her it was you, but could you live with yourself? Would it drive a wedge between what you could have and what you end up with?" He headed out. "Drinks are in the refrigerator."

Tempest watched as Smoke set the tray down. Pilar smiled at him and laughed at something he said. A green monster the size of Kilimanjaro stirred and growled deep within him.

Could he forget the unfathomable connection between him and Pilar which kept him alive? No. Two things had fueled his survival and recovery. The first was Pilar's gentle strength when he'd had nothing left, and the second was the knowledge he would one day have his revenge on the people who'd imprisoned him. Killing her mother would cleave the connection he had with the woman whose memory had sustained him when nothing else could.

CHAPTER 13

Pilar rolled her shoulders. She was about three-quarters of the way through her notes. Luke had hooked up a second computer and split his screen so he could highlight pertinent information as she was typing, entering it onto another document which would be forwarded to his organization along with her transcribed notes. They'd been at it for hours.

"Would you like to take a break?" Luke didn't look at her but kept pecking away with his two fingers. In reality he was very fast but talk about inefficient.

"A short one. Didn't you learn how to type in school?" She chuckled when he stopped typing and turned to her.

"Ah, no." He leaned back in his chair and reached for a bottle of water.

"What? No typing 101 in high school?"

"No high school, actually. Well not much."

An iron weight landed somewhere in her stomach. "Oh... I'm sorry."

"No need to be sorry. You weren't responsible."

God, how did she so squarely put her foot in it when all she was trying to do was to tease him? "Well, no, but--"

He put a hand up. "Long story short. My mother died. My dad dealt with his grief by drinking. No abuse, no horror stories, but he didn't give a shit if I went to school or not. I spent my days at the beach learning to surf, smoking pot, doing drugs and getting into trouble up and down the coast of Florida." He chuckled and rubbed his face. "If I could only go back and have a talk with that kid."

"What would you say?" She moved in her chair, careful to look where her poor toe was in relation to the bolted table legs.

"Oh wow. Let's see... Don't believe everything your buds tell you. Don't let anger consume you. Don't make stupid mistakes or take the last hit of X at the beach party." He shook his head. "But if things hadn't played out the way they had, I'd probably be a drunk, a doper or dead at this point in my life. Getting into those scrapes got me attention from the person who threw me the lifeline which got me out of there. He probably wouldn't have known about me if I hadn't acted on my anger, so I guess I'd like the opportunity to tell the younger version of me everything will turn out all right."

She leaned forward and placed her chin in her hand as she stared at him. "You've been through so much. I wish the older version of you didn't have any connection to my mother."

He shook his head. "Then I wouldn't have met you."

"The cost you bore was too high." She put her hand on his arm.

He shrugged. "Acknowledging what we've experienced and putting it into perspective builds a strong foundation for forward progress."

"You *sound* like you have a very good education."

"Ah, well after a lifeline was thrown in my direction, I made strides. Still no typing classes, however." He winked at her and nodded to the notebook. "We can stop and continue tomorrow if you'd like."

She shot her notebook a glance and reached to ruffle through the pages left. "Let's get finished and maybe have a drink on the deck and watch the stars show themselves when we're done." She glanced at the clock. "Or look at the stars, I don't think I'll be done by sunset."

"Deal. Are you hungry? Thirsty?"

"No, I'm fine. I needed a mental break for a couple minutes. How about you? Are you finding anything you can use to build a case against my mother?"

He nodded and then glanced at her.

"What?" She angled her head, assessing him the way she would a client in her office. He didn't give away much, but just then he had. He wanted to ask her something, or perhaps tell her something.

"If all things were even and your mother had committed horrible crimes, crimes against people who had no defenses, would you want to know about it?"

A cold fist wrapped around her gut. "As her lawyer, no."

"As her daughter?"

"If I were only her daughter and not her lawyer? Then, yes. But I'm not just her daughter, so while I am giving you these open-ended questions and allowing you to draw your own conclusions, if you were to give me information on my mother it would place me in a moral obligation to report her." She drew a long slow breath into her lungs. "I have no doubt my mother is many things." She released a small humorless laugh and looked at Luke. "I know she hurt you. I tried to report it." God, he had to know she'd tried.

"You did what I asked. What I had no right to ask of you. When your mother found out, you could have been in grave peril."

She carefully moved her foot and turned in her seat to look straight at him. "Peril? Me? From the information you have, do you think she'd... hurt me?"

He twisted in his seat and faced her. Those gold-flecked green eyes were so damn serious. "It would be speculation on my part and as her lawyer, do you really want to know?"

Her eyes lowered to the tabletop. "Perhaps we should agree the information I am transcribing is sufficient and leave any discussion about my mother out of future conversations?"

His hand covered hers. "I'd enjoy that. Although our topics of conversation may be limited."

Her brows furrowed. "Why?"

"My past with Guardian is... classified."

"And? Does classified mean I can't ask you if you like pepperoni on your pizza or if you like your steak rare?"

"I'm a carnivore. I love all the meats on my pizza, but I haven't had one in... damn, years and as far as the steak, the rarer the better. Still mooing would work. What about you?"

Laughter bubbled past the guilt and self-doubt which had threaded through the earlier conversation. "I'd prefer my steak without the sound effects and give me a cheese and veggie pizza. You can keep all the other stuff."

"Wine or beer?" His eyebrows rose in challenge.

"Beer with pizza, red wine with steak."

His grin spread into a brilliant smile. Lord, he took her breath away. He was absolutely gorgeous. "I like you, Pilar Grantham."

"And I like you, Luke Wagner. Should we get to work so we can continue our discussion?"

He slid his hand off the top of hers. The warmth which had infused her skin evaporated, but still flooded the recesses of her being. The tingle of radiant hope skittered through her body.

She readjusted in her chair and stared at the computer screen. The feelings she'd been nursing for the man had taken root. Every time he smiled or touched her, those small seeds of hope had flourished, grown, and shaded the dry, forsaken parts of her life. *Careful does it, girl. Don't pin your future on someone you barely know.*

"Is something wrong?" His question snapped her back to the present.

"Oh, no. I was thinking." She flipped the page in her notebook and started another set of circumstances, times, places and events which could only lead to one conclusion. Her mother was a criminal.

It was completely dark by the time she'd typed the last words. A heavenly smell from the galley produced a wicked roar from her stomach. She clutched her cover up and felt her face flame. "Sorry."

"Don't be. I'm going to save these documents, then I'll go grab us a cocktail and something to nibble on to hold you until dinner." He moved the mouse and clicked to save the documents. "What would you like to drink?"

"Ah... A glass of the white wine I had when I boarded?"

"Perfect. Let me help you to the deck. You deserve some fresh air." He stood and offered her his arm.

"Such a gentleman." She leaned carefully as she put weight on her foot. The toe had swollen from not being elevated all afternoon, and she could definitely feel her heartbeat in the darn thing again.

"I have been accused of many things; being a gentleman isn't one of them." He smiled and walked slowly as she hobbled across the open deck to the chaise lounge. Once she sat down, he moved to grab a large pillow from another lounge and placed her foot on top of it. "I'll bring some ice for your foot, too."

She watched him go back into the interior cabin before she glanced heavenward. The multitude of stars unfettered by the lights of a city wrapped around the heavens. She sighed and relaxed against the warm canvas of the deck chair. With her work complete, she had thirteen days of sun, and hopefully, thirteen nights of adult fun with Luke. Presumptuous? Perhaps, but there was an attraction and even if it went no further than the confines of this ship, she wanted to know him, as a man, not as a prisoner, not as a person working a case against her mother, but as Luke Wagner, the young man who'd gotten into trouble and the man who'd worked his way out of a bad situation. She smiled at the sky imagining a tall, lanky boy with too long hair and a wickedly beautiful smile.

"Here you go." Luke carried a tray and set it on the deck between the two loungers. "Ice, for the foot." He picked up a small bag and wrapped it in a hand towel before he carefully laid it against the side of her foot. "We should have elevated your foot while we were working."

"It will be fine." She took the wine he offered her and a small plate holding cheese, crackers, grapes, and apple slices. "Thank you, I'll nibble, but I don't want to ruin my appetite. Dinner smells wonderful."

"No worries. Dan and Sage take turns cooking. They are pretty fantastic in the galley. I believe we are having fish Sage caught this morning off the pier."

"Perfect." She motioned to the stars. "The marvel of the heavens. It makes you realize what you can't see when you're consumed inside the city with daily worries and strife. Even from the beach house, the stars are diminished."

She sipped her wine to shut her mouth. She'd never been chatty, but around Luke she wanted to talk, to interact, to get to know him. The wine was oaky, buttery smooth and a delicious accompaniment to the soft brie cheese which adorned the sesame crackers.

"For the last three years I lived in a place where I could see the stars like this. There was no light pollution."

She placed her small plate down on the tray and turned to her side without dislodging the icepack on her foot. "How bad did it get? After I left?"

He turned toward her. In the darkness the conversation seemed more intimate, even though she could see movement inside the cabin. "After? Not as bad as it was before."

She pushed up on her elbow. "Why? Did they leave you alone?" A spring of hope bounced forward. Maybe her mother had...

He gave a humorless chuff. "No."

She stared at him. His eyes focused behind her, distant, lost in memories, or in his case, nightmares. "What happened then? Why was it better?"

His eyes tracked to her and a soft smile tilted his lips. "You happened."

Her mouth dried and she couldn't breathe. "Me?"

"Yes." He set his wine glass down and sat up, leaning toward her chair. He took her hand in his. "You."

He threaded his fingers through hers. Resolve settled around her as she looked at their joined hands, and she whispered, "I want you to make love to me."

His eyes moved from their hands to meet her gaze. "Why?"

"What?"

"Why do you want me to make love to you? Sympathy for what happened?" He stared at her, those gold-flecked eyes so serious.

"No. God no. This has nothing to do with what happened. No, wait that's not right." She shook her head and carefully sat up, being cautious of her damn toe. "What happened three years ago, it impacted the way I think of you, but not the way you may think. I'm in awe of your internal strength, of the way you've overcome what happened. I really didn't think you'd live." She blinked back the tears forming in her eyes. "I wanted you to. I prayed so hard for you, but I didn't know. I even had these fantasies of you coming back and sweeping me off my feet." She laughed and swiped at tears which fell from her lashes. "And not because I broke my toe, either."

"There are things you don't know about me. Things you can never know about my past." His thumb caressed a circle on the back of her hand. Soothing and gentle.

"Does my mother change the way you think about me?"

He drew back a bit, his eyebrows high and a shocked expression on his face. "No. Absolutely not."

"Then why would you assume whatever is in your past would change the way *I* feel about *you*?"

Those serious eyes softened a bit. "Who your parents are and what they do isn't your responsibility. My past is an amalgamation of my decisions, and I wouldn't change a single choice I made."

"Then there is no need to dredge up either of our pasts and examine them, is there?"

"Perhaps it is an oversimplification of where we find ourselves, but I'll let you win this argument." He leaned forward until their knees touched, and their faces were inches apart.

"That means you'll make love to me tonight." She leaned forward and felt the warmth of his lips land on hers.

"D-Dinner!"

She groaned into the kiss. "I'm really starting to dislike those guys."

Luke chuckled and stood. She was eye level with the evidence of his desire for her pressing against the thin nylon of his board shorts. Oh, dear merciful heavens, he was impressive. His hand appeared in front of her face, breaking her rapt attention. "Dinner then I think an early night." His deep rumble filled her as he helped her to stand.

She swayed against him and closed her eyes as his arms wrapped around her. Warmth and a sense of rightness permeated the moment. "I'm suddenly not very hungry."

He tucked a finger under her chin and tilted her head up. "You should eat. I haven't been with a woman in a long, long, time, and I think you'll need the energy for what I have planned for you tonight."

At his words, a flux of liquified desire flowed through her veins. Oh yes, she wanted whatever he had planned. Now. This instant. Food be damned. "Don't make me wait. Three years is long enough."

He bent down and swept her up into his arms and devoured her mouth in a kiss which spun her world and stole her breath.

Sage headed to the bridge with Dan's dinner. He'd made a tray for the two love birds, put it in the refrigerator, and tidied the galley, securing everything in case they hit rough water.

"Hey, you're early."

"The l-love b-b-irds are nesting." He'd talk around Dan. The man had never judged him and had helped him sort through a fuck-ton of baggage. He had a job with Guardian based on Dan's recommendation.

"Tempest doesn't know how far he's fallen for the woman."

"He's d-doing b-better." When Sage had first seen Tempest at the Rose, he'd been a shell of the man he was now.

"Yeah." Dan stared through the bridge window.

"What?"

"I see storm clouds on the horizon."

Sage glanced to the horizon. Crystal clear sailing as far as he could see, so his partner was talking about Tempest. "H-he'll b-be okay. He's s-strong."

Dan gave him a quick glance and a sad smile. "He'll need to be if he plans to move on his vendetta."

"Sanctioned?"

"Oh yeah, but it's the worst idea of the century."

"And i-it's n-ot yours?" Sage ducked the quick swipe Dan sent his way.

"Get out of here. Relieve me about two?"

"Yep." He headed back to his room with a smile on his face. What would he ever do without his partner? *Lord, please don't make me find out.*

CHAPTER 14

Mysteries like how he managed to get Pilar to his quarters without stopping to ravage her perfect body were best left unanswered. He didn't care, but the knowledge he managed to do so was an emboldening observation.

He laid her gently on the bed and grabbed a pillow from the vacant side to prop up her foot. She moved onto her elbows and watched him. Those vivid blue eyes darkened with a hunger which he knew only too well. The last time he'd lain with a woman was before his capture. Years. He pulled his t-shirt over his head and watched her eyes dance across his chest. There were scars darkened by the Arizona sun, but there was nothing he could do to cover them. She sat up and wiggled out of her gauzy yellow wrap. The one-piece bathing suit hugged her curves and accentuated her legs.

He lowered and carefully crawled on top of her, moving her to her back and into the pillows as he stalked his way to her succulent mouth. Ravenous. God, he couldn't get enough of her smell, her taste. He was an instant glutton for the soft little sounds she made against him. The sensations of her skin and the shiny fabric of her suit as it slid across his skin fed his voracious cravings. His hands traveled the length of her waist as he tenderly bit her bottom lip only to kiss the swollen flesh before consuming her again.

Her soft fingertips explored his skin as boldly as his fingers feasted on her flesh. She found his waistband and tugged at the material. In frustration she moved away from their kiss. "Off. Now."

He was only too glad to oblige. He hopped off her and the bed in point zero seconds to strip his board shorts, ready to... Oh, fuck. The little yellow slips of material which constituted the swimsuit peeled from her shoulders. Slowly the fabric fell from one perfectly taut rose-colored nipple and then the other.

He gripped the base of his cock and squeezed, trying to stave off the rapidly approaching end to his sexual abstinence. Half-starved and eviscerated with need he dropped a knee on the bed, waiting like a deprived animal famished for its next meal.

The material peeled down and down. The expanse of ivory skin she revealed left him panting. She lay down and arched her hips. "Help me."

Fuck yes. He was on the bed and straddling her calves in a heartbeat. A gentle tug extricated the material from under her hips. Oh, damn. She was beautiful. Her soft mound was covered in dark blonde hair, natural and beautiful. He eased the material off her legs careful to replace her foot on the pillow.

Now centered between her legs, he lost the battle and dropped down, easing her injured foot onto his back. She shifted onto her elbows and licked her lips. Fuck, she was hungry, too. He licked a trail from her inner thigh to her sex. Her body shuddered at the slightest caress of his tongue. He kissed her inner thigh and repeated the trail to her core again. This time, he spread her and lapped at her swollen flesh, indulging in her taste.

Her grip in his hair tightened and her soft sounds became louder as he targeted the tight pearl at the top of her flesh. The muscles of her legs flexed and bore down against his shoulders, the pressure increased with each pass of his tongue. Her thighs trembled and her body arched against his mouth. Her orgasm inflamed his almost compulsive yearning. He braced above her and reached toward the nightstand. Her hand on his arm stilled him instantly. "I'm on birth control."

He moved back above her. "Are you sure? I know I can't give you anything."

"Nor I you. Take me. Now." Her arms wrapped around his neck, and she tugged him down for another breath-stealing kiss. He centered himself and slowly rocked into her heat. He moved away from her mouth when he slipped in, seating himself deep inside her. "Oh, God." He dropped his head to her shoulder and, as if she knew what he needed, her legs rose to cradle him as her arms slipped to his back, grounding him in this moment. Their connection, one he'd imagined for years, blew his fantasies out of the water. She was exquisite in her sensuality. He kissed her collar-bone and slid away only to move back inside her again. He groaned; the sensations too vibrant to endure in silence. Her breath hitched, sighed, and hitched again. Fingernails dug into his back, and her soft frame arched under him as her legs constricted around him. Her body grabbed his cock. Fluttering contractions immobilized his hips and shattered him. Red and white blotches formed behind his eyes as he struggled to keep his weight off her and breathe at the same time.

He had to think for a moment before he rolled, ensuring he wouldn't touch her injured foot. When his cock, sated, slipped from her, he rolled her with him and tucked her into his side.

Her fingers threaded through the hair on his chest. Petting, touching, just being, they lay there for long minutes without speaking. He kissed the top of her head. The crown of her head tipped back, and those blue eyes sparkled up at him. She pushed her body closer and whispered, "I'd like to do that again."

"I think it can be arranged." He dropped a kiss on her upturned lips and rolled her onto her back again. He didn't need any more encouragement.

Her body quaked under the onslaught of his touch. She'd had lovers before but none who mattered. None were important; none had a connection. The sex had been functional, utilitarian, and completely forgettable. Not with him. Not with

Luke. He worshiped her body as if she were something special. His reverence and restraint were
tinged with a hunger which made them both shake
with anticipation. He carefully moved her, always
making sure her foot was out of the way of his
long, long limbs. On her hands and knees now, she
felt him place a pillow under her foot before his
hands found her hips. He leaned down and kissed
his way up her back, vertebra by vertebra. As he
folded over her, the arm which wasn't supporting
him snaked around her, and his fingers found her
clit. He entered her slowly and the pressure of his
fingers echoed the languid strokes and soft kisses
to her neck and shoulders. She arched her back as
he slid forward, and they both sighed.

She looked back at him. "Don't be afraid to go
deeper or faster. I won't break."

He pushed her hair away from her face and
they kissed. A sloppy, wet, sideways kiss that rock-
eted her craving for the elusive summit he'd driven
her to the last time. He backed away from her and
rested on his knees, his large hands wrapping
around her waist. He tugged her to him as he
moved forward. The slow and sensual motion
increased in pace. She closed her eyes and floated
on the electricity which skittered under her skin.

Never had sex been this way. Never had she ignited so quickly or exploded with such intensity. There was something special here, between them. He thrust into her, harder now, and she reveled in the pleasure his excitement and strength created.

His fingers once again swept lower and moved to her clit. Instantaneous combustion and incendiary orgasmic bliss flooded her. Her shout echoed around the room right before his. He held her up, against him, hands on her hips, rooting her to the spot where they were still joined. She panted with her head down and her hair sweeping the sheets. "Well, the first time wasn't a fluke."

He chuckled behind her and moved away from her before he carefully moved her injured foot and flopped onto the bed. He tugged her down beside him and wrapped her in his arms. "I think there may be some chemistry at play."

He couldn't stop the outright laugh when she popped up onto an elbow and gaped at him. "Maybe? I think you need to reconsider your statement, sir."

"Definitely. There is definitely chemistry." He held up a hand in surrender. "I didn't want to force you to agree to salvage my ego."

She reached across and pushed his long brown

hair from his eyes. "Ego? No. Skill. Superior skill and definite finesse."

He brought her into his arms again. "You have no idea the monster you've let loose."

"Oh, if your monster wants to consume me, I'll let him. Over and over and over again."

"You'll be sorry you agreed."

She loved it when his eyes twinkled with joy. She'd seen it a couple of times but only in the last twenty-four hours. She wanted to see more of it, and drawing his attention, she teased, "Nope, don't think I will be, but you could try to get me to that point. I won't object."

Luke rolled her onto her back and stared at her. "Neither will I."

Luke stiffened and looked at the clock. Just after 2:00 a.m. He listened intently for what had awakened him. Silence. No motor. The yacht bobbed at rest on the water. He slipped his arm from under Pilar's neck and settled her before he pulled on his board shorts and left the cabin. Padding carefully down the hallway, he stopped at the galley where the light was still on. Smoke was pulling a couple of trays from the fridge.

"Why did we stop?"

"We're anchored off the Keys. I was going to keep cruising, but we can dance around in the Keys for a week or so, restock, and then head to Freeport and spend some time fishing off the Bahamas."

"We may have to go in earlier, depending on what action Guardian wants to take after digesting the information Pilar's providing."

"Not a problem. Plenty of ports to head into should we need to get you and her off the ship in a hurry. Hungry?"

He glanced down at the food and shook his head. "Not really. Thanks." He was pleasantly tired thanks to three great orgasms. "Do you need me to take a shift?"

"Nope. We have all the sensors deployed. Sage will monitor them for about an hour to make sure they are all functioning and then we are grabbing some sleep. Breakfast is on your own tomorrow. The galley is yours, feel free. Coffee is there." He pointed with a knife which had a glob of stone ground mustard on the end. "If you empty the pot, make a new one. Filters and grounds are above it."

"Got it. I'll need a secure link to Guardian tomorrow, probably mid-morning." He grabbed a bottle of water from the fridge.

"Not a problem." Smoke flopped a piece of bread down and slathered it in mustard. "I really hope you're wrong."

He knew exactly what Smoke was talking about. "I do too."

"Is the evidence in the information she's giving you?"

"It's between the lines. The truth is there, and it isn't a reach."

"But you'll let Guardian make the call, right?" Smoke took a bite of his sandwich and munched while looking at him.

"Of course. I'm not going to start a vendetta without solid corroboration and approval from our handlers."

The sandwich which was once again on the way to Smoke's mouth stopped mid-way. "Who the fuck are you, and what have you done with Tempest?"

"What do you mean?"

"They released you. Gave you a Go and I'm speculating told you to go find who was holding you. There should be blood and gore in at least ten different locations by now."

He chuckled. "Three years of intensive therapy, compliments of Guardian, have changed my mental processes. I've learned patience."

Smoke snorted. "Right. I'm not buying it."

"The truth doesn't need to be purchased, asshole." He rolled his eyes.

"Whatever, but do yourself a favor and call Fury. He can get someone here to take care of the woman's mother."

Tempest turned toward his friend. "Fuck. You."

Smoke huffed and dropped his sandwich. "I wasn't slighting your skills, my man."

"Really? I'd imagine the entire organization doubts my skills because I was compromised." His anger at himself for that mistake hadn't diminished.

"Stop the pity party. I've seen you dismember men with your bare hands. There isn't anyone I'd rather have on my six. You are one of the best, if not *the* best, currently in the field, but you aren't seeing the entire board here. I know you're a fan of chess. Back up and look at the pieces currently on your board. You're willing to sacrifice your queen when the game isn't going to be won unless three separate kings are checkmated. There is no back-wash if you take down two of those pieces and let someone else handle the third. You aren't alone in this. We aren't lone wolves, isolated with no backup. Not anymore. The organization has changed." Smoke damn near hissed the last words.

"I might have changed but I haven't weakened. These three targets are *mine* alone."

Smoke picked up his sandwich. "I make things go boom. I'm good with my hands, but not as good as the rest of you. I know my limitations and I *apply* them."

He laughed at Smoke. *Damn, really?* "You're suggesting I have limitations?"

"I know very well you don't. I'm saying maybe you *should* have one. One, for her." Smoke took a huge bite of his sandwich and a glob of mustard hung from the side of his face. Tempest didn't react to the man-child temper tantrum. His friend was trying to help... in his own way.

"I'll go where Guardian sends me, do what they tell me to do and yes, I'll make sure all three Fates are dead. That is my fate, and Pilar's. I'll see you in the morning." He lifted the water bottle and saluted Smoke with it. Grumbled words like "idiot" and "asshole" followed him down the long hallway to the bedroom.

He slid back into bed beside Pilar and smiled as she purred and drew closer to him. Wrapping himself around her, Smoke's words echoed in his ears. Unfortunately, those words were trumped by the years of torture he'd endured at the hands of Stratus and the Fates. He was going to kill all three of the Fates and dismantle Stratus from the top down. If his vengeance damned him to a life without Pilar, he'd deal. Somehow.

Smoked watched Tempest walk down the hallway and continued to send one liners after him. The asshole needed to listen to him. Sage came into the galley from the other door. "P-problems?"

"Yeah, big problems brewing."

"How so?" Sage started to slap together a sandwich. "Sensors d-deployed are working."

Dan pointed down the empty hall. "My gut tells me that man is going to explode. I've worked with him for a long, long time. He's not a finesse operator. He annihilates his targets. Obliterates them like direct hit from a Cat 5 hurricane. Nothing is left. Waiting for the explosion is fucking freaking me out."

Sage handed him a napkin and pointed to his cheek. He swabbed at the area he indicated. "Maybe he's changed." The fact his partner didn't stutter as much around him was not lost on him. It gave him a sense of pride that Sage could be comfortable around him. His partner had had a shit life and he was damn glad he could provide some stability.

"He hasn't. Not inside. This guy is going to go nuclear. When he goes after his targets, the reverberations will be heard around the world." He really hoped Guardian had control of the blast area. Tempest's statements were legendary when he *wasn't* pissed. When he was emotionally involved... Well hopefully Guardian had a strong hand on Tempest's bridle.

"Can't be t-that bad. You're probably w-wrong."

Smoke stared down the empty hallway. "Yeah, I really hope so." The world wasn't ready for what was coming for Stratus or the Fates.

CHAPTER 15

"Where is she?" Smoke looked behind him as he entered the bridge.

"Sunbathing. Rear sun deck." Tempest carried both computers and set them on the long counter on the port side of the bridge. He'd spent ten minutes rubbing lotion on her body and five minutes cooling down enough to be presentable for this meeting. The feast of desires he'd consumed last night and again this morning hadn't satiated his appetite for the woman. She was ambrosia, and he was a compulsive addict.

"P-pink today." Sage winked at Smoke as he stepped onto the bridge and shut the door. Tempest glanced up; his possessiveness lifted an acid-laced claw.

Smoke snorted. "Damn it. I owe you five bucks, man. I thought for sure it would be orange."

"What the fuck are you two talking about?" Not Pilar's swimsuit. It was red.

"Sunrise colors. You know the amazing thing people come to the Keys to see? Sunrise and sunset? What did you think we were talking about?" Smoke talked while he hooked the computers together with a USB cord and then hard wired the computers to the ship's internet.

"I had no clue, which was why I asked." The "you stupid shit" was left unsaid, but Sage got it loud and clear. His shoulders bounced in silent laughter.

"Are we ready?"

"Wait, plug the phone into the computer." He handed Smoke the phone and the cord which Pilar had given him this morning. Smoke complied and then signaled Sage to connect them to Guardian.

"Operator Two-Seven-Four. Standby Sunset Operative Six."

"How the hell do they do that?" Smoke looked at him. "Have you ever asked yourself how old that woman is? And she never mis-identifies the caller."

"Artificial Intelligence?"

Smoke shook his head, his brows laced

together. "No, if you talk to her, she answers, and I even made her laugh once. What AI does that?"

Sage shrugged, "F-freaky."

"No shit." Smoke agreed.

"Alpha online." Jacob King sounded off.

"Dom Ops online." Jared King's voice was now recognizable to him.

"CCS online. The line is secure." The woman. Bengal's wife.

"The annex online." Anubis' voice whipped across the connection.

"The Rose online." Fury's growled, "Why the fuck are we here?" tipped the corners of his lips. The grumpy asshole.

"Archangel online. What do you have for us?"

Smoke nodded to him. He leaned forward and braced himself on the countertop where the comms equipment was installed. "The computers are hardwired into the ship's interface. From what I can see, Pilar is onto something. She's been diligent in documenting every question she had without asking her mother for clarification. She's got good instincts but didn't have the resources to follow the money past her mother's accounts."

He could hear someone going after a keyboard

with a vengeance. "You should all have access to the reports now in the shared folder."

"Is there anything in particular we need to address?" Archangel's voice cut through several keyboards and clicks.

"Yes sir. The financials. She said her mother had two partners, and she believed the partners were making money in the same fashion her mother was."

"Illegally," Smoke interjected.

Tempest rolled his eyes and continued, "Two partners."

The silence which hovered on the connection lasted three seconds. "Jewell?"

"On it." The woman's voice sliced above the tapping of a keyboard.

"Also, there are some photos on the phone which is attached to the computer. Her mother allowed Pilar one-time access to her email. She took screenshots of what she could see."

"Okay. Just a minute. The phone has a four-digit lock," Bengal's woman muttered under her breath.

Tempest started to speak. "The code ––"

"Don't need it. Got them."

Tempest watched the phone's screen light up.

"*Oh shit.*" The woman's expelled gasp came across the connection.

"Use your words, Jewell," Archangel's tired voice prompted the woman.

"Did I tell you her phone had a tracker in it? I killed it yesterday before they left the pier, but I didn't go any farther because it would have been an invasion of her privacy, and someone said this lady was a good person. Didn't they? I think they did but—"

"Jewell!" At least four male voices shouted at the same time.

"What! Holy crap y'all are on edge, aren't you? You should lighten up on the caffeine, maybe work out or something."

"Jewell, maybe you could tell them what you found?" Bengal mused softly in the background. "*Oh*, right. Sure. Guys, I know the financials are important, but you've got to see this." A flurry of clicks sounded before a momentary silence.

"What the hell am I looking at?" Fury growled.

"Screenshots off the Darknet. Her mother's email server is *on* the Darknet. Tempest's woman captured the address with these pictures. Holy shit. I can totally hack this. It will take time, but if I can get into her email system without her organization knowing about it..."

"Do we need a warrant?" The comment came from Dom Ops.

"For the Darknet?" the woman asked and scoffed, "What is she going to do? Complain I hacked her illegal email account?"

"I meant for evidence reasons. Bringing these people to justice."

Archangel responded, "We will need a warrant if the server contains data we want to use to prosecute them in the future. I'm authorizing CCS to work on the information for now, pending a federal warrant. Jewell, we need to know what country the server is in, and do not hack the email server until we get the warrant. Tempest, the summary you provided appears concise and to the point. Regina may well be one of the three we are looking for, but until we can verify suspicions, everyone will stand by for instructions. Archangel out."

"Guys, you made my freaking year. Honey, you get Alonzo to take the day-to-day ops and order us a pizza for dinner. No way I'm leaving until I get this puzzle solved. What? Oh, right. CCS. Out."

"If you need assistance let me know. Sierra team is in south Florida on standby. Alpha Out."

"Dom Ops will start working on this information. We'll keep you apprised as we can. I'm out."

"Well my friend, I miss one day, and you launch a multi-department operation." Anubis laughed. Tempest could imagine the man shaking his head as he was doing it.

"The world was a much quieter place when you were sitting your ass on your porch every night," Fury agreed.

He snorted his reply, "I have years of inactivity to make up for."

"I think you're doing a hell of a job." Fury's evil chuckle came across the connection. "Tell that knucklehead and his partner, they're with you until this op closes."

"I'm the partner." Smoke presented a hand for a high five from Tempest. He rolled his eyes and left the man hanging.

"No, you're not. I'm out."

"You know, a guy could get a complex." Smoke crossed his arms over his chest.

"Don't blow up any more substations," Anubis scolded.

Smoke pointed to Tempest as if Anubis could

see his actions. "*What*? It was *his* idea! Why am I taking the shit for this?"

"I'm sorry, Tempest. I don't know how you're going to remain sane after two weeks on a boat with him."

Sage chuckled. "Amen."

"Hey? *Et tu Brute*?" Smoke gaped at his partner. Sage shrugged and smiled. "Fine, see if I offer to help again."

"You owed me for the free rent," Tempest reminded him.

"Oh. Yeah. Okay. Whatever it takes, man."

"For as long as it takes." Tempest and Anubis finished the statement, but Anubis continued, "Two weeks. Damn. Good luck, my friend. Annex out."

Warmed from the sun and rocked by the soft waves which lapped the side of the boat, Pilar drifted in contentment. They'd eaten a huge lunch and were being lazy in the setting sun. Luke lay beside her. His tan, shades darker than hers, took on a reddish hue today. "I think you've gotten a little too much sun."

He shifted at her mumbled words. "You're not pink."

She tipped up her head and glanced down at her exposed skin. "I have on protection."

He sat up and scanned her from head to toe. "Not that I can see."

"Does it bother you?"

His eyes held hers as he slowly shook his head from side to side.

The bleating, sharp, ringtone she'd assigned to her mother wailed from the phone she'd tucked away under the chair to shield it from the heat of the sun. "Crap."

"Who is it?"

"My mother."

"Answer it. Keep up the story."

She rolled her eyes and patted around on the deck to find the phone. She put it on speaker. "Hello."

"Where are you?" The uncaring, modulated tone bordered on disinterested.

"Umm... I don't know? And to be honest, I don't care. I've been lying in the sun, drinking yummy frozen drinks with copious amounts of alcohol and eating way too much food. Oh, I slept in this morning. The first time in *years*."

"You mean you have no idea where you are?" The snip in her mother's voice got a little tighter.

She glanced at him and he mouthed, "Florida."

"I don't know. I think the captain said something about cruising around Florida. Why? Is something wrong?"

"No. Have you been online?"

"Me? How in the world would I go online? On my phone? Sorry, not interested in the news, or what this idiot is saying about that idiot. Besides, I dropped my phone in the hot tub earlier today. The internet works for like one second and then blanks out. I can't dial out, though apparently I can get incoming calls."

"You dropped it in water?"

"It happens."

"The next time you're in port get a new one."

"Why? You can call me if you need me. I'll get it fixed when I get back home. Two weeks, Regina. I'm unplugged, and for the next two weeks, I don't care what happens anywhere in the world. When I get back, I'll fall into line and march to the beat of your drum. I am going to be the first female President after all."

She rolled her eyes at the sanctimonious Regina-kowtowing-minion she'd channeled.

"Be prepared to work. It won't be easy."

"Nothing worthwhile is," Pilar answered, but she was sure her mother had disconnected the call before she'd finished her comment. She turned off her phone and tossed it on the cushion beside her.

"What a lovely lady." Tempest stood and extended his hand to her. "Shade and one of those frozen drinks you told your mother about."

"Sounds wonderful." She let him assist her from the chair and then hobbled to the large round rattan daybed currently sitting in the shade. A gentle breeze moved the light drapes at the head of the futon. "I guess I should ask. Where are we?" She glanced off the port side of the ship. A series of islands dotted the vista.

"The Florida Keys." He helped her sit down and put her foot on top of a pillow before he walked to the daiquiri mixer on the bar. The thing had been tumbling the icy concoction all day. She accepted her third, fabulous, mango and rum drink since noon.

"This is so good." She took a strong pull on the straw and hummed in appreciation. Sending him a sideways glance, she asked the question she'd been wondering all day. "Tell me what happens next."

"I sent the information you gathered to my

organization. They are taking the questions you asked and working them. Until they find something, we do this."

"This? As in float, lie in the sun, and drink?"

He chuckled, "Food and sex need to be in the mix somewhere."

"Sex before any of the rest." She waggled her eyebrows several times.

"Hungry?"

"For food? Nope." She wound her tongue around her straw and watched as his eyes followed. She sucked the thick drink through the straw. "Very good, but I think I want something else." Her eyes traveled down his rippling abs to the waistband of his trunks. "I definitely want something else." Luke shifted and yanked at the leg of his swimming trunks. The bulge was impossible to miss. "A nap."

His eyes snapped up to hers. "A nap?"

"Absolutely. I'm suddenly very tired. Would you help me back to your cabin?"

A wolfish smile flashed across his face. "A nap sounds wonderful." He stood and extended his hand to her. When she stood, he swept her into his arms.

She laughed and leaned into him, wrapping an arm around his neck. "I can walk you know."

"I know, but I don't want to wait for you to hobble the length of the ship." He dropped a long, hungry kiss on her lips.

Pilar sighed, happiness drowning everything but Luke. "Dear heavens, neither do I. To the cabin, sir."

CHAPTER 16

She trailed her hands down Luke's chest as he held himself above her. They'd made love, napped, eaten dinner and were back in bed again recovering from another yacht-shattering orgasm. Her lungs drew deep in an effort to regulate her breathing. "Wow, as a legal professional, I would be remiss not to mention death by orgasm is punishable by law." Her arms hung limply around his neck, and she sighed happily when he chuckled and rolled to her side.

"And what is the sentence for death by orgasm?"

"Ah, you are forced to reenact the crime every night for the duration of my vacation."

"Such a harsh sentence?" He narrowed his eyes at her.

"Absolutely." She traced one of the scars which littered his body. Needing to be sure, she asked, "Are all of these..."

His hand covered hers, and he brought her fingertips to his mouth, kissing them one by one. "My scars are healed."

She propped herself up on her elbow. "Are they, really?"

He angled his head and studied her. "Why?"

"Because I don't understand how they could be. I don't understand how you're not screaming for justice. My mother knows things about your captivity. Why haven't you had her questioned or arrested?" She blinked back her emotion. "The information I gave you has nothing to do with what she's done *to you*. How can you be so calm?" She pushed her curls away from her face. "I'd be so hateful if I were you."

He brought her down and kissed her gently before tucking her into his side. He ran his fingers up and down her arm for a moment. "For the last three years I have undergone both a physical and mental reconstruction. I've worked with a psychiatrist and examined almost every aspect of my captivity. Is there still rage and hatred? Yes. Do I want revenge for what happened to me? Oh, yes. Will it be unleashed when the time is right? Absolutely. But in my line of work, you learn to compartmentalize. My time with you has nothing to do with your mother."

She looked up at him. "But you are going to confront her, right?"

"I will."

"When?"

"When my superiors allow me to do so."

"How can you be so damn calm?"

"Who said I'm calm? I've thought of only two things for the last three years."

"And they are?"

He gave a quick, sad smile. "You and revenge."

"Me? Why?"

"The day you were thrust into the cell... I'd given up. I wasn't going to survive. My... will to live had dissolved. You gave me a reason to keep fighting. Hope is a dangerous thing to nurture when you *know* there isn't any chance of rescue, but your promises made me believe there was a reason to keep going."

"I'm so glad I was able to help get you out of there." She ran her hand across his chest. "You gave me purpose, too. I probably wouldn't have started digging or had the law clerk do research for me if I hadn't met you. I hate my mother for her role in what happened to you."

His fingertips stopped their caress. "Do you know what her role was?"

"I think she was the one who directed you be questioned. She wanted information from you. She said it was nothing personal. No emotion involved. You had information, and she wanted it."

"Explain that." He sat up; his bulk loomed over her.

"I mentioned you in conversation, and she said there was no emotion involved in the process of breaking you down. You were... business as usual for her."

"You know your mother could be involved in things which are dangerous."

"For her? No. She'd never sully her hands. For others? Yes, and as much as I wish it weren't true, I do suspect she's dangerous."

His gold-flecked green eyes stared at her as if he was trying to see into her soul. "When the investigation is done and I finish my duties for Guardian, come away with me."

"Where?"

"Anywhere in the world, you name it."

"What? Like for a vacation?"

He shook his head slowly. "No. Forever."

She startled and blinked up at him. "We hardly know each other."

He shook his head. "I know what I need to know about you. I know your character. You despise unfairness. You want justice for everyone. You don't know how beautiful you are, and you're terrified of becoming like your mother. You're brave and even if life scares you, you push forward. I know who you are here." He laid his hand over her heart.

She stared back at him. "Do you want to know what I've learned about you?" He cocked his head and nodded. "You work for Guardian. You have been through hell and survived. You believe there is a sharp line between good and bad, and in your job, you keep the line distinct. You're a man of your word, no matter the cost. You honor your debts and..."

He prompted, "And?"

"And I believe you care about me as much as I care about you, which is illogical. We've spent a total of what, four days together?"

"Four days in each other's presence. Three

years in each other's lives. Illogical, perhaps. There is more between us than couples who have known each other for years."

"I feel like I've known you a lifetime." She traced his lips with her fingertip.

"You have. My life started again the day you found me."

He lowered his lips to hers in a tender kiss before he pulled away. "In full disclosure, I am not an angel. Some would consider me a nightmare. I have a dark past where I worked top secret missions. Those were the secrets your mother wanted me to disclose. My past and my association with Guardian, which I've never acknowledged to anyone but you, is why I was tortured. I have one final mission with Guardian. If you so desire, I will walk away from all of this when I'm done with it. Come with me."

The breath in her chest caught at the emotion he'd laced through his words. To leave everything she knew for this man was insane. Yet, all she had to do was look at her life, truly look at it, to realize she'd never be anything but her mother's game piece. "You'll regret asking me."

"Never."

"We'll see." She pushed his hair from his brow.

A slow smile spread across his face. "Is that a yes?"

"How could it be anything else?" He wrapped her in a tight embrace, and she closed her eyes tight. *God, please never let him regret it.*

The single knock on the door jacked him to his feet. The gun which had been resting in his nightstand was in his hand and pointing at the door. He extended his other hand when Pilar sat up and grasped the sheet to her breasts, covering her nakedness.

He moved silently to the door and opened it with a quick jerk, his weapon centered on the man outside the door.

Smoke lifted his hands. "Don't shoot. Me friend. Comms, for you."

He nodded, releasing the grip he had on his weapon. "Be right there." He shut the door and placed the weapon on the bed as he searched for and found his shorts and a t-shirt.

"You have a gun?"

He glanced at her and chuckled. "Guardian is a

federally recognized law enforcement entity. Guns are in our wheelhouse."

Pilar pushed her mass of blonde hair from her face. "Oh. Yeah, I guess. It surprised me." She blinked at him and then blinked again. "Where are you going?"

"I'll be right back. I have a call from Guardian. Go back to sleep." He leaned forward and kissed those full pink lips.

"Bring back some water, please?" She snuggled down and grabbed his pillow, pulling it toward her.

"Roger that." He slipped out and headed to the bridge.

Smoke nodded to the headset. He put it on and adjusted the mic.

"Go ahead."

"Who else can hear this conversation?" Anubis asked.

"No one. Headset with mic."

"Authenticate Teacup."

"Teapot."

"We have confirmed your theory."

Adrenaline flooded his body. "Targets?" God please let it be the Fates

"All three are coded but will be taken down as

directed by Archangel. This is a delicate balancing game, Archangel was adamant. You'll take down all three, but in the order that is best for the entire operation. "

He glanced sharply at Smoke who was actively listening to his side of the conversation. His friend's gaze drifted his direction. A slight shake of his head was the only indication Smoke knew what was going on.

"They will all be brought down––by me."

"Affirmative."

"Send me the information."

"Negative. Sierra team will meet you in Tampa at the dock with the packet tomorrow night. They will accompany you. Whether or not you use them, they will be in the area. This is nonnegotiable."

"You don't trust me?"

"It has nothing to do with trust. Every Shadow has a team in the vicinity when they are working. Everyone. Lone wolves no longer exist at Guardian. We protect our own."

"All other Shadows are assigned a team?" He glanced at Smoke. The man nodded.

"Assigned a team for backup if they are identified as a single asset or, if they can mesh with another, they're given a partner. You saw the process at the Rose. We aren't singling you out. As I said, it has nothing to do with trust and everything to do with supporting our people to the fullest extent possible. Sierra team is your asset on this operation. You'll be in charge of their placement and utilization. The end game is still your show. Instruct Smoke to proceed to his usual berth in Tampa. Miss Grantham will stay with the yacht. You will disembark at 0230hours and rendezvous with Sierra team at the end of the pier."

"I'll need a few things delivered to the ship when we arrive." He rattled off what he wanted.

Anubis sucked a breath through his teeth. "I'll get it to the boat, if not this stop, the next one."

He glanced out the window into the darkness. "The next one?"

Anubis made a sound of agreement. "Information you don't need right now."

"I'd prefer if you could get the items here this stop. If her mother goes underground, she could take Pilar with her. It may be a way to track her."

Anubis grunted. "I'll see what we can do. I may be out of my quotient of miracles this quarter."

"I'm sure you have at least one more in your bag. Whatever it takes, remember?"

"For as long as it takes, my friend, but some

things require *time.* I'll try to get your items to the boat before Smoke and Sage leave Tampa. Tell Smoke to stay in port if possible. If he sees something he doesn't like, have him head to the open water, cruise north, and we'll meet him and Miss Grantham in Panama City Beach."

"I'll do that."

Anubis cleared his throat. "Take these women down, for all of us. I wish I could join you for this one. These women are the worst kind of evil."

"You don't have to tell me. I'll use my tech to check in."

"Good hunting." Anubis cleared comms.

He closed his side of the connection and set the headset on the counter. "Go ahead." He knew his friend was going to spout off some advice he didn't plan on taking.

"I got nothing man. Are you disembarking soon?"

"I am. She's not. Anubis instructed you to make your way to Tampa and stay in port until we return if possible. If not, make your way to Panama City Beach." He relayed the rest of the instructions he'd been given.

"Will do." Smoke kept his eyes directed toward the panoramic view from the bridge.

Tempest nodded and started toward the door. He stopped and turned slightly. "Do me a favor? Take care of her while I'm gone."

"You didn't need to ask; I know what she means to you even if you won't acknowledge it." Smoke turned, giving him a smart-ass smirk before he picked up the onboard phone. "Yo, Sage, my man. We've got orders to head to Tampa. We need to lift anchor." He laughed at whatever Sage said before he hung up. "We'll be moving in ten minutes. Tampa area by mid-morning. I'll pull in at last light, and we'll deploy motion sensors at the dock so we can all get some rest before you head out."

He inclined his head and padded down the stairs, through the massive living area, to the galley. With a cold bottle of water in hand, he headed back to his cabin. He slipped into the space and quietly took off his clothes, placing the water bottle on his nightstand.

She hummed contentedly and moved toward him as he slipped into bed beside her. "Everything okay?"

"Everything's fine. Go back to sleep." He settled her against his chest and stared at the ceiling. He'd find a way to keep his employers happy. One target at a time, just as Archangel decreed. He'd wait if it meant he'd be the one to take out the Fates and make them pay for what they'd done to so many.

Pilar sighed and snuggled into him again. He reveled in the feel of the woman in his arms. When hope had disappeared, she'd saved him. When death had him in its grasp, her strength freed him.

His fingers caressed her soft skin. Soon. He could feel the anticipation building beneath the peace he'd constructed over the last three years. The careful composition acted as a drape which prevented people from seeing the abyss of anger and hatred which moved in a molten river through his veins. He drew a deep, cleansing breath. Never again. Never again would he allow anyone to fall into the hands of Stratus or the Fates. He'd paid an unspeakable price, but he'd recovered. He'd repaired his damaged body and shot an azimuth to his destiny. Tempest, the personification of death, was coming for the Fates. This time he would not fail.

CHAPTER 17

"Is this work connected to the information I gave you about my mother?" Pilar watched him as he put on his clothes. Black cargo pants, black boots, a black t-shirt and jacket.

"Yes and no. This operation is connected to activities Guardian believes your mother is involved with."

"What exactly are you going to do?" She stood and limped to him.

"Follow my employer's orders."

"Is this where you tell me its classified, and if you tell me you'd have to kill me?"

She pushed his hair away from his face. He smiled. The gesture had become second nature to her in the small time they'd been together. "I promise I won't tell you, so I don't have to kill you."

"Whew. Deal." She rolled her eyes. "When will you be back?"

"I'm really not sure. It depends on how this assignment goes and what my superiors want me to do next."

He frowned at a knock at the door. When he opened it, Sage handed him a small box. "Just d-delivered."

"Thanks, man."

Sage nodded and headed back down the hall as he shut the cabin door.

"What's that?"

He opened it and smiled. "A miracle."

"What?" She leaned over the box. "Oh, that's nice."

He produced a mother of pearl and gold cell phone case which would fit her phone. He pointed to the side. "See this?" He slid a small tab up.

"Yeah, what does it do?"

"When it is down, I can't track you. Nobody can. Completely private, on your own, and self-sufficient. But, if you ever get into a jam, slide it this way. I'll get an alert and I'll find you."

"Well that's cool, but what happens if I don't

have my phone with me and I need you?" Pilar slipped the case on her phone.

"Well, then you just need to think of me, and I'll come running. Look, the case is a precaution. That's why it has an on and off switch."

"Right. I understand." She stood on the toes of her good foot and leaned on him to peek into the box again. What else is in there?"

He removed a ring from the box. It was a band, inlaid mother of pearl with gold borders on both sides. "It is a keepsake of this vacation I'd like you to have. I hope it fits."

"It's beautiful." Pilar took the ring and slipped it onto her right hand. "I've never worn much in the way of jewelry. It seemed to me if you wear something, it should have a sentimental value and not be a pretty bauble.

"Hopefully this will be something you'd wear."

"Absolutely, I'll never take it off. How did you know I liked mother of pearl?"

"The clip in your hair the day we met at the deli was gold and mother of pearl. I took a chance."

"You couldn't have chosen better." She held her hand up and smiled at the ring before she turned her attention to him. "Please be careful."

"That, I can promise. I'll be back as soon as I

can. Sage and Dan will take good care of you." He wrapped his arms around her. "Don't fall for the pretty boy image Dan has going on."

"Nah, I have a different type."

"You do?"

"I do."

"What type is that?"

"You." She slid her arms up his biceps, across his shoulders, and around his neck. "Come back to me, Luke."

"Wait for me, Pilar."

"Always."

He lowered and kissed her, trying to infuse all the emotion he was feeling but couldn't explain. Their connection, so strong and yet so new and fragile, held him next to her for a few extra seconds. He drew away and nodded to the bed. "I like the idea of you sleeping in my bed."

"I'd like it better if you were there."

"So would I. I'll be back as soon as I can." He stared at her for a moment. Tears brimmed her eyes. He smiled and opened the door. Closing it hurt more than he wanted to admit, but he had a mission, one which required his focused attention, and focus was exactly what he'd give it.

With each step down the pier, he shed the

layers he'd carefully pulled around him. His instincts were rusty after years of non-use, but his skills weren't. He was ready, and the team who met him at the end of the pier looked world-weary, pissed, and lethal. A perfect combination for this mission.

The man in front extended his hand. "Travis. I'm the skipper of Sierra team. This is Ricco, he's our comms specialist and marksman. That's Scuba. Entry and weapons specialist. Harley is our demolitions specialist. That's Coach. He's our medic and jack of all trades. We are here to cover your six on the trip overseas."

Each man tipped his chin at the quiet introduction. Tempest assessed them as a unit and individually. There was no backdown in any of the team's gazes. Solid and dependable, but not needed, at least in his opinion. "You have information for me?"

"We do and transportation to a private airport with an aircraft waiting to take us to our destination." The skipper handed him a large packet, sealed with tamper resistant tape. "The van is this way."

The trip to the airfield and the waiting C-17 took a half hour, even with almost no traffic on the roads. The tarmac was deserted except for the two flight crew members who were performing a pre-flight check. The skipper of Sierra team headed to the flight crew, no doubt to authenticate their identity and assure himself the aircraft hadn't been compromised. Tempest headed directly for the open rear loading ramp and walked inside the aircraft. He found a pallet of equipment resting underneath adequate lighting. Using the crates as a seat, he opened the packet given to him earlier.

Two photos of the same woman fell out imme-diately. The woman was breathtakingly beautiful, but plump to the degree he'd call her moderately overweight. The weight didn't detract from the woman's attractive features. Dark brown hair, a charismatic smile and in both pictures, diamonds dripped off her ears, throat and wrists. She did not wear a wedding band.

Folded papers slid from the envelope when he tipped it. He carefully unfolded them. The first page was a dossier. Francesca Clarke. Fifty-one years old. Tempest examined the photo again and stared at the image. He would have estimated early forties. He placed the picture back on top of the equipment pallet and continued his review of the documentation. The woman was a prominent supporter of several humanitarian efforts. A socialite who'd traveled extensively in support of her causes. Nothing new. Evil hid in plain sight. She was connected to the fringes of royalty through marriage several generations ago. An eyebrow arched as he read the notes attached to her packet. The woman had been in Colombia during the time Guardian had first learned of Stratus. She had also been active in Russia and the United States during the year-long operation where Guardian took down a human trafficking ring.

He leaned forward and tilted the paper toward the light as the rest of the team entered the plane. Two pages of financial ties to terrorist organizations, and... damn... the woman's money led to an account which had been identified as one used by Lobo, a freelance assassin who he'd crossed paths with once. The payment coincided with the death of the woman's father. She was the sole inheritor of a very wealthy estate. Circumstances suggested the Fates and Stratus utilized assassins to take out the people they were stealing from. If so, what level of killer were they utilizing? He needed to determine if Lobo had been active while he'd been out of commission.

There was an itinerary for Francesca for the next three days. He reviewed it and the map of London included. He smiled. Yes. Yes, it would work. After reviewing the evidence, schedule, and map again, he tipped the envelope. Six passports and a stack of British pounds, six credit cards and a set of keys fell onto the pallet. He studied the last piece of paper and the words written there.

Code Authenticated, Sunset Clearance. Confirmed via Counsel. Locality a non-issue. TOD to be inde-terminable. Report when mission is accomplished.

TOD to be indeterminable. They didn't want the death to be a known assassination. The reins on the mission sucked, but he could understand why. They still had two other targets they didn't want to drive underground.

Tempest refolded the documentation and examined the passports until he found his. He took some of the money and the card issued to the same name as his passport. He tossed the ID packet to Travis and nodded to the back of the plane. Travis gave him a thumbs up, distributed the identification, cards, and cash, and headed back toward him.

Travis stopped next to him, still examining his passport. "How the hell do they get these things? They always look authentic."

Tempest glanced at the passport. The Rose was producing them. He'd seen the machines which were installed in the underground facility, but it was not his information to give.

"It's best not to ask. I have a plan. I may need some logistical support, but until I get eyes on the target, I won't know for sure what assistance I'll need."

"Really? There's a bet going on at HQ. They said you wouldn't ask for support."

"Ah. Normally, no, I wouldn't. However, I'm going to make a statement—a statement which can be heard around the world."

"That's pretty damn loud."

Tempest smiled. "Not really. Haven't you heard about the butterfly effect?"

Travis chuckled. "I have. When a butterfly flaps its wings, halfway around the world a tornado is the direct consequence. In plain English, a small change can make much bigger changes happen; one small incident can have a big impact on the future... Not a technique we generally employ. We are more of a shock and awe, get-in-and-get-out type of force of nature."

Tempest chuckled and watched as the rear cargo door was raised in preparation for departure. "As was I, but this is a multi-faceted mission. The first strike will be a single flap of the butterfly's wing."

"The last facet will be a tornado."

"No. The last facet will be a *tempest*." He eyed the man.

Travis held his gaze for a moment before he nodded his head. "I'm getting the distinct impression what you have planned will be worse than a tornado."

"You have no idea."

"Probably not, but no joking, I kinda want to see it. From a safe distance."

Tempest shook his head. "There is no distance safe enough for the ones I'm hunting."

"I'm getting that vibe." The plane's turbine engines cranked. "We need to get strapped in. How long are we going to be in the air?"

Tempest cocked his head. "You didn't ask the pilots?"

"Nope. Once I validated their identity, I

checked in and brought my team on board. This is your show. We are here to make sure you get your job done and get your ass back to Tampa, and those words are a direct quote from Alpha."

"Settle in. We'll be landing outside London."

"Sweet, figured so from the money. My guys can use some sack time." Travis gave a whistle and made a few hand signals. His men found seats and strapped in. "Let me know what you need us to do. I suck at reading minds."

"Noted." He found a seat and strapped in. The butterfly effect. This kill would look like an unfortunate accident. Not his forte, but he knew what he was going to do. The second would be an epic statement and the third, the third would be a soliloquy. A personal monologue on the end of life for those who abused innocents and thought they were above reaping the consequences of their evil.

London:

"Sierra Five, the back of the residence is secure."

"Sierra Four, West Side secure.

"Sierra Three, East Side secure.

"Sierra Two, Front of residence is quiet. No movement."

"Sierra One to Sunset Operative Six, in position. The residence is yours."

Tempest aimed the laser pen at the motion detection activated lighting. He hit the sensor and temporarily blinded it. He pocketed the pen and moved from the darkness along the stone wall. He worked his way across the side yard, past the neatly trimmed bushes, to the back of the house. At the communications box at the rear of the house, he looped the telephone line which thankfully wasn't fiber optic. The punch-down block was almost too easy to access. He shut the box and made it to the back door in less than two minutes. The lock, a deadbolt, was one of the latest pieces of shit electronic locks which were controllable via an app on the homeowner's cell phone. He used his screwdriver and popped the cover with the cute little combination buttons on the face. Three wires, two twists and a penny activated the looped circuit. The door unlocked and he was in.

Just inside the door were two tiny bowls

inscribed with the word "Meow". Cat bowls. Perfect. The woman had a cat.

He visually inspected the kitchen for an alarm panel. *There*. There was a flashing light. Motion detector.

As he examined the room, he heard the heavy steps of dress shoes heading down the hall. When he'd done his surveillance today, he'd determined there were at least two interior guards. He could see the man's shadow in the hall light as the guard approached the kitchen. In absolute silence he crept across the room and pushed his back against the wall. He channeled every fucking cat he'd ever heard and meowed quietly.

"Bloody hell, you berk, it's the cat. Probably jumped up on the counter. I thought you put the damn thing in her rooms," a deep voice called down the hall.

He heard steps as the man in the hall reached around the corner and turned on the kitchen light. Tempest flattened against the wall and readied.

A man with a heavier accent answered, "I did. The little arsehole escaped. Leave the bugger alone. The show's about to come back on."

"Fine, but you're catching the bloody beast."

"A little mackerel and it's snagged. Come on already, it's starting."

The light went out.

Tempest tracked the sounds of the man's footsteps. Glancing up at the motion detector, he slid down the wall and slithered on his belly to the doorway. The hall light was on. No cameras and no motion detectors which he could see. He shimmied from the kitchen and then stood up.

He made his way down the hall and past the off-shoot where the men were watching television. Quickly assessing each room, he either jogged or low crawled through the house to the back. The grandeur of the upstairs quarters was opulent to the point of being obscene. Finding Francesca's bedroom took ten minutes. He knew it was exactly ten minutes because Sierra One gave him a time hack as he opened the bedroom door slightly. The cat swiped at the door and purred loudly. He let the animal out of the room, which would satisfy the guards. After the cat trotted out, he slipped in. The woman had a mask across her eyes and lay in a repose of utter luxury.

He opened a pocket on the inside of his shirt and produced a small box of extremely expensive chocolates. The type, according to Guardian's background information, Francesca preferred.

He opened the box quietly and set it on the bedside table next to the woman's cell phone. Withdrawing his gun, he screwed on his silencer. He wouldn't use it unless necessary. He needed a butterfly wing to flutter tonight, not a statement, only a small ripple of air.

He placed the barrel of the gun on the woman's forehead. She startled and jumped, but the pressure of his weapon against her head kept her down on the pillow. She clawed at the mask and pulled it down to her chin.

An evil glint overtook the shocked look he'd first seen. "You fool. Do you have any idea who I am?" she spat. Her hand moved toward the bed side table.

A duress button or a weapon. He didn't care. He leaned into the barrel of the weapon. "Move again and you die, Francesca. I know exactly who you are. You are one of the Fates."

Her eyes widened in a surprise she couldn't hide although she tried to blunder through her obvious shock. "I have no idea what you're talking about. Who sent you?"

He smiled. "I came of my own volition, but this is a sanctioned removal."

"Sanctioned? By who?"

"My employers."

"I'll scream."

"Your personal rooms are heavily sound-proofed." He shrugged. "Scream away."

"I'll quadruple whatever they are paying you." She sent a furtive glance toward the side table. He saw the moment she recognized the chocolates.

"Poison? How droll and ineffective, not to mention traceable. My sisters will take cover, and you'll never find them."

"That's where you're wrong. We've already found them." He reached down with his free hand and took one of the filled Swiss chocolates. "Eat this."

"And if I refuse?"

He grinned widely. "Oh, yes, please refuse. I'd enjoy killing you slowly and watching you bleed out. A cut for each person you've sold into slavery, a chunk of flesh carved away for each assassination you paid for and benefited from, a finger removed for each political maneuver that deprived citizens of needed governmental help, a toe gone for each armed conflict you supported or prompted. We could be here all night." But he had that death planned for another.

"Who sent you?"

"I am an angel of death. Who do you think?"

"Guardian," she hissed. "I told her... Wait, I can be of use to you. I can give you information, show you things." Her eyes darted around the room. "I can help you."

He rolled his eyes. Bargaining. His targets rarely made it to this point. It was a waste of time. He knew it and she knew it. He saw the resignation in her eyes.

"You can kill us, but there will be others."

"There are always others." Humanity had a way of spawning monsters like Francesca and her ilk. He handed her the chocolate. "Unwrap it and eat it."

Her red claw-like nails extended and grasped the beautiful foil wrapped treat. "Let me sit up?"

"No."

He watched as she unwrapped and examined the confection. "My death will be investigated. They will know."

"Yes. Eventually." But not until he was ready for them to know.

She popped the chocolate into her mouth. The

poison would be almost instantaneous and unde-tectable. Her eyes swung to him. "He'll come after you."

Tempest gave her a bored look. "He? Your assassin? Bring it on."

She coughed and her breathing became labored. "Insurance policy. Fifty million. Paid only when my murderer is killed." Her laugh ended in a cough and a wheeze.

He moved the gun away from her forehead and smirked. "First, he'd have to identify who'd been here." He watched the woman take her last breath and then unwrapped another piece of candy, this one not laced with the drug. He put it in her mouth, forced her jaw to manipulate it slightly and then pushed it into her throat, lodging it firmly. It took a few seconds to unscrew his silencer, tuck it away, and holster his weapon. He wiped the chocolate off his glove using the inside of his coat as a towel.

Sierra One sent another time hack. Fifteen minutes. He retraced his steps and alternated between low crawling and rapid movements to make his way back down to the kitchen. The cat was sitting in the middle of the floor. It meowed at him. He darted into the kitchen, picked up the cat, set it on the counter, and slipped out through the back door. He worked the electronic lock, reengineering the components and snapping the cover back on. The phone lines were disconnected, reattached to the proper block, and the box closed.

He heard the muscle talking in the kitchen. One laughed and the other cussed. He shot a beam from his pen to the automatic eye of the motion detector which would deactivate the outdoor sensor. A quick thirty count and he was sprinting through the side yard. He vaulted the fence and contacted his overwatch. They rendezvoused with the rest of the team and were in the air and flying from the country an hour later.

Tempest closed his eyes. Her death was not... satisfying. His specialty was death on a grand stage. Tonight, his stage was small, but the death monumental. The butterfly effect. The wing had flapped. Now he'd wait for the chaos to start.

CHAPTER 18

J ason King walked into Jewel's section and headed up the stairs to his sister's office. The electronic lock buzzed as he reached the top, and he stepped into a full room. Zane, Jewell, Jacob, and Jared stood in an arc around the monitors Jewell controlled. Every eye swung to him.

"We've got the warrant. Go for it."

"Awesome!" Jewell removed a pencil from her hair and put it in her mouth, biting down on the wood as she typed. Her fingers flew across the keyboard, and the monitors switched screens rapidly.

"Date and time mark." Jewell's screen flashed. "I've captured the data for the legal beagles to prove I waited to go in until after it was approved."

The printer activated and started whirring out the screenshots. "I'm in the backend. She isn't online right now. I'll know if she logs in. What do you want first?"

"How far do her emails go back?"

"Ummm... ten, no... twelve years. What are the parameters of the warrant?" She stopped typing, her hand hovering above the mouse.

"I went back to the beginning in the request for a search warrant, stipulating the documentation we found in Colombia, the sex trade operation, and several earlier incidents we now believe may have been tied to the Fates. I also tied in the Russian hacker, Vista. So, anything you can find on the server should be covered. At least it will be up to a defense attorney to prove it isn't."

"Perfect. I'm going to copy her files and not touch or open anything. Unless you want her to know we've been here?" Jewell double clicked on the mouse and files started transferring at an incredible rate.

"Not yet." Jason watched his sister work.

"What about the other two?" Jared leaned in and spoke to him as everyone watched Jewell perform her magic.

He nodded. "Jewell, the other two accounts, the

ones tied to the financials Jared's team have followed, can you get in?"

"I am in. It is a matter of getting your blessing." She lifted a hand and snapped her fingers. "Easy Peasy."

"Copies only and make sure they don't know you were there." He smiled at the middle finger he got in return and the, 'as if' his sister tossed at him while typing faster than a human should be able to type.

A chime cascaded through the room. Jewell jerked her head up and scanned the upper right monitor. "Francesca Clarke. The London team reports an ambulance has been called to the residence."

Jason sent a glance to the world clocks arranged at the front of the theater. Five hours ahead of them. Which made it noon in London.

"Why so late? Were they covering their tracks?" Jacob glanced at him.

"I don't know. Jewell?"

"Hold on. Hold on. Damn it." A flurry of keystrokes later. "Regina is back online. The other account went active, too. Crap on a cracker. I have all of the information I need for Regina and

Francesca, but I haven't gotten all of the third account."

"Get out. We don't want them to know we're on to them," Jason ordered and Jewell's fingers flew.

"Okay. I'm out. I'll keep an eye on the accounts and try again later. But for now, we can process the... seventeen thousand emails." Jewell scrunched up her nose. "Zane, honey, I'm going to need an energy drink."

"Here." He handed her an orange juice from the mini fridge under her desk.

"Not what I wanted."

"And yet you knew what you would get." Zane put his hand on her shoulder.

Jason watched his sister beam up at the former assassin, the man he didn't think would be good enough for his sister. Proved what an idiot he could be at times.

"Jared, I need your team to go through anything Jewell sends your way. I'm sure you'll end up with all the emails eventually, but right now we are focusing on the Fates. We'll get to Stratus." Jason popped off the orders, organizing their searches.

"Ummm... yeah, here, here it is... no, wait that's not it, but I saw. Yeah, here is the unknown Fate's schedule for this week." Jewell slid a schedule onto the monitor."

"Decipher it and see if we can extract a location for the woman without going back into her computer. We have the appointment schedule. We need to put eyes on who is at these appointments and determine the identity of the unknown Fate.

"Jacob, have Fury put two of his best teams in the field and track where Regina Grantham is this week. I want eyes on the woman. She will not slither away before we can complete this op. Am I clear?"

"Crystal." Jacob picked up the secure handset in Jewell's office.

"Hold on for a second, Jacob, before you make the call, remember this, when we take these women down we are protecting our own. We are doing this by the numbers. Every T crossed and every I dotted. No exceptions." He glanced from his brothers, to his sister, to his brother-in-law. "We can't afford to let anyone walk due to an overzealous employee or someone who is complacent."

Jewell cleared her throat. "We won't let you down, Jace."

He smiled at his sister. "You could never let me down, Button. Let's get to work. Zane, a word?"

Zane followed him outside the office and let the door shut behind him. Jason glanced around to make sure they were alone at the top of the stairs and whispered, "Anubis and Fury called."

Zane nodded his head. "Yes, they called me, too. I'm in."

"Did you clear it with your wife?" Jason glanced at the darkened glass where Jewell worked.

"We talked. I'm going to be there to support them, but I won't go in with them. That isn't what I do anymore. I can't go back to that life, and she agrees."

"Then let's get it done." Jason spun and headed down the stairs. All the threads were coming together. Now if he could keep the whole damn thing from unraveling.

"Operator Two-Seven-Four. Standby Sunset Operative Six while I transfer you to Thorn One."

Tempest moved the phone away from his ear in surprise. "Wait, I don't need to speak with Thorn One."

"No sir, but he needs to speak with you. Standby."

"Authenticate Teacup."

"Teapot."

"Where are you?" Fury growled.

"Just landed outside of Tampa. I'm heading back to the ship unless you have intel on my next stage?"

"No. We received confirmation of your success. Choking to death on a chocolate while in bed. Original, I must admit. I give you props for it."

He glanced at the van where Sierra team waited for him. "I'd rather have made a statement. Do you have my next assignment?"

"Not yet. It will be a couple of days. The information we've been able to access needs to be worked. Have Smoke make his way back to the east coast of Florida and then stay within four hours of a port at all times."

"Roger that."

"So you know, the information your woman gave us... it's priceless."

He closed his eyes tightly. The statement was... good and profoundly bad. Pilar had provided the means for Guardian to take down the Fates and signed her mother's death warrant with the same information. As Regina Grantham's executioner, he'd find the closure he needed, but in doing so, he could quite possibly sever the connection he had with Pilar. No matter how strained the mother-daughter relationship was, there was a bond. Destiny had to be laughing down at him right now. The vicious bitch.

"Sierra team is to set sail with you."

"Excuse me?" The idea of five other men on the damn yacht was not hitting his happy place.

"Boss' orders. When you get the word to go after the next objective, it is going to be fast. They are your support team."

"I don't fucking need a support team."

"You do if you want the name of the next Fate." Fury chuckled. "Get over it. It is the way we are working now."

"So much for independence."

"You're in charge. They follow your command. You're as independent as you ever were, but if your ass gets forced into a crack, you won't end up in some Stratus cell for years, asshole."

"Fuck you."

"Nah, my wife would object."

Tempest chuckled and rubbed the back of his neck. "All right. They're onboard." He could keep

Pilar on the upper deck and ask Sierra team to stay on the lower deck. They'd have a sun deck and could fish with Sage if so inclined, plus it would keep Pilar's interaction with others from his world to a minimum. In the meantime, he meant to spend every minute he could with Pilar. Alone.

CHAPTER 19

Pilar stood at the back rail of the yacht and watched six men saunter down the pier toward the yacht, but she only had eyes for the one leading the procession. When he looked up, she waved. His wave in return and the bright smile on his face flooded her with lighthearted happiness. Was it foolish to feel so deeply for a man she'd spent so little time with? Perhaps, but the connection was there, nonetheless.

She watched as Luke made the introductions between Dan, Sage and the five other people with him. A small smile spread across her face. Yes, her assumptions had been right. His work for Guardian wasn't that of a run of the mill employee. She tracked him as he dropped his duffle by the rail and headed to the stairs which would bring him up to the level she was on.

Her hand flew to her hair, checking to make sure it was still held securely in a ponytail before she smoothed her sundress. He jogged up the stairs and strode to her. She met him halfway. "Hi. Are you all done with your assignment?"

"Partially. I'll have to go out again, but not for a couple of days." He wrapped her in his arms and lowered his lips to hers. His taste, the way he kissed her, and the possessive way he held her as he claimed her lips, sent incandescent warmth across her skin.

A rousing round of applause rose from the lower deck. Pilar laughed against his mouth when he groaned. "Who is our audience?"

Luke guided her back into the interior of the ship.

"The men who have been assigned as my overwatch."

"Overwatch? Are you doing something dangerous?" She stopped. A quick scan confirmed he wasn't injured.

"I'm doing the same job I've always done. The overwatch is a new addition. I don't like it, but policy has changed since I last was given an assignment. When the boss says jump, you jump." Luke shrugged.

Pilar narrowed her gaze. "I'm not an infant, and believe it or not I'm fairly intelligent."

Luke stopped, turned, and frowned at her. "I haven't treated you in any other way."

"No, but you're assuming I can't put two and two together. What you do for Guardian isn't the usual investigative thing is it?"

His stare went blank. The happiness in his eyes faded. He didn't move, didn't even seem to breathe. So, it was likely she was correct in her assumptions. "Luke, I'm not going to judge you. I am aware of the rumors about Guardian's reach and their use of teams overseas." She closed the gap between them. "In fact, if you are part of those teams, it would explain a lot."

"How so?" His expression gave absolutely nothing away. If she didn't know the man behind those cold, emotionless eyes, she'd be very cautious. He was scary.

"Well, I've been asking myself why my mother would want information from you if you were a run of the mill Guardian investigator? I mean sure, it could have been a single case you worked, but if it was a routine case, why did you resist giving her the information? Why the... torture?" She swallowed hard as the memories of the way she found him flashed through her mind. "Then there was the other side of the equation. Why wouldn't you give me your name or tell me to call Guardian directly? You never said you were part of the organization. Was it to protect me? Or maybe them, or even yourself? Then the message I replied to was weird. It interested me, so I did research on that type of communication. It is old school in methodology, rather like a dead drop during the Cold War era."

She'd had plenty of time to think during the last two days, and she'd started to string all the tidbits of information together. She didn't get off the boat while he was gone and besides sunbathing and sleeping, all she'd done was think, ponder, and weave possibilities with the information she had, making leaps in logic to fill in the spaces. Nothing had been as neat and tidy as what had occurred to her when the men walked down the pier with Luke. The whys and hows of everything which flew around her brain *ad nauseum* fell into place when she saw the men come aboard with him.

He looked down at the floor and rubbed his neck. Her words made him uncomfortable, but it was better than the emotionless stare he'd been giving her. "I wasn't part of a team, but my operations were classified. I can't and won't talk about that part of my life."

"If it is classified, that's understandable. I'm not going to ask you any questions about what you did. I don't care."

He flicked a questioning glance in her direction.

She chuckled. "Seriously. I could never talk to you about cases I've handled. Well, except for..." She drew a deep breath. "I've also come to the conclusion that I'll likely be disbarred for releasing this information to you. I could also face criminal charges, but I'll deal with that if it should come to pass."

He stepped closer to her and slid his hand behind her neck. She tipped her head up to stare up at him. Way up. He searched her face and then smiled softly. "You won't be implicated. Guardian is working around your involvement. What you did was the morally correct thing to do. As far as anyone knows, you aren't involved."

"If it does get out, though, I'm prepared to face the consequences." She elevated on her toes, and he bent down and dropped a tender kiss on her lips. "I'll never ask again about your work," she whispered against his lips. "What you do for Guardian is between you and Guardian."

"And if my job was in the vein of Black Ops?" He kissed down her jaw to her ear.

"Then I trust you'll stay safe and come back to me." She shivered as he took her earlobe between his teeth and tugged lightly.

"I've done things. Things nightmares are made of." He stood tall and stared into her eyes.

"When those bad dreams come, I'll hold you until they pass." She reached up and pushed his hair from his eyes. "Your work is between you and Guardian, but I'd like to ask a favor."

"What?" Those eyes with the gold flecks bored into her soul, searching in a way which sent a thrill through her.

"Be careful." *With your life, and with my heart.*

He smiled almost as if he'd read her mind. He dipped down to kiss her, stopping before his lips met hers and promised, "Always."

"Luke, we're getting underway and you need to check in. The bosses want a word," Dan interrupted a kiss which promised to lead to much, much more.

He groaned and snapped his head toward the captain of the ship. She heard Dan laugh. "Hey, don't shoot daggers at me. You know the protocol."

"I'll be there." He glanced down at her. "Give me twenty minutes?"

She smiled up at him. She'd give him forever if he asked. "Absolutely. I'll be waiting for you. In your cabin." She hitched her eyebrows several times and laughed when he groaned again. "Go. The faster you finish work, the faster you can come to me."

Before he headed down the hall toward the stairs which would lead him to the bridge, he dipped down for one more kiss.

"Here. Look." Jared swiped his tablet and the page went to the screen in front of them.

"Okay, and?" Jewell stared at the calendar.

"Show me the calendar you have. Didn't it have this?" He drew a circle around several letters. "VC23"

"Um..." Jewell swiped through the electronic calendar she had. "No, close. VC12."

Jared leaned forward. "Zane, on Francesca's, what does it say?"

Zane glanced at his tablet. "VC13"

"So, follow me on this. Video Conference or whatever else you want to place there for the alphabetic sequence, but then consider this. Regina is One, Unknown is Two and Francesca is Three."

"You don't actually think they went by numbers, do you?" Zane started swiping through the emails he had.

"Oh shit. That works. Look!" Jewell swiped her finger across her tablet and a series of emails popped up.

"What am I looking at?" Jared scanned the documents.

"Here." A white circle formed around several of the messages. "*1>2. Confirm* and then look, here. This, the sequence of numbers after it, could be a date and time." She circled the message. "Zane, you have Two?"

"I do." Zane's brow furrowed as he dug through the emails. "Here." He swiped the document up onto the monitors.

Jewell grabbed the mouse and zipped through the document. "Here! I found it." She sat forward as the document opened. "Shit."

Jared looked at the email. "It's gibberish."

"Code." Zane leaned forward and stared at the screen.

"Cassie." Jewell said. "Time is of the essence. We need Cassie." She swung around to look at him. "You'll need to tell Jason and get transportation for her and her family, ASAP."

"Cassie, the code breaker?" He'd never met the woman, but Jewell sang her praises, with just cause. From all reports, she was a miracle worker. Jared stared at the screen. Yeah, there was no way in hell he'd be able to decipher the mess.

"Yep. She's the best in the world. I'd futz around with this if we had the time, but now is not when I should be refining my code breaking abilities." Jewell nodded as if agreeing with herself. "We need to find all the emails in code and segregate them so we can decipher them as soon as we get Cassie to tell us what kind of code this is."

Zane nodded. "You do it, and I'll take the schedules and try to marry them up with the time and date stamps of the coded emails. It will assist in determining if we can glean any usable information."

"I'll be back after I get transport set up. Don't have all the fun without me," Jared quipped.

Zane snorted and gave a middle finger salute. Jared chuckled and left Jewell's office.

Luke put on the headset and dialed the number after Smoke gave him the thumbs up, indicating a secure connection. "Operator-Two-Seven-Four. Standby Sunset Operative Six."

"Authenticate Teacup."

"Teapot." Tempest responded to Anubis' prompt.

"Any problems?"

"No. What's the media saying?"

"No indication of any foul play. Smoke has been given directions to the next port of call."

"Where?"

"Back to where you started."

"I was told it could be a couple days."

"Something has been found. By the time you get to port, we'll have a plan of action and a way forward."

"All right."

"Now on to the primary reason for the call. How are you?"

"Fine."

"Quit the bullshit. It has been years since you went on an assignment. Mentally, where is your head? Talk to me or I'll pull your ass for a Go/No go."

"The mission went smoothly. The woman begged and bargained. There was never a second of question as to my purpose or the rationale for her demise. I'm solid, but tired. I forgot what a bitch jet lag could be." He'd examined his feelings on the flight back to the States.

"And you aren't getting younger, old man." Anubis chuckled on the other end of the line.

"Fuck you and the horse you rode in on."

"Ah, now hell, man, how rude. My horse has done nothing to you." Anubis' voice sobered, "Also, the computer people found some information you need to know. We believe we found out how they suspected you in Tahiti. One of the techs found an un-coded email with your picture as you walked out of the hotel. There were four or five other pictures attached. We believe the others were taken as well."

"So, it was a chance happening?" He closed his eyes and internalized the information. A photo had changed his life forever.

"Yes. Do you need to talk with Doc Wheeler?"

"No. In actuality the information shuts many doors. Permanently." The questions of how he was identified had always plagued him. Now that he knew he could move on.

"Take care of yourself and go to bed. When you dock, call for instructions."

"Roger that." He heard the connection click off and took off the headset.

"I'll leave a couple of plates in the fridge for you and Pilar. Sage is rustling a meal up now, and he'll feed your entourage." Smoke snickered when he threw him a finger. "Hey, she didn't make a call out, nor did she leave the ship. In case you were wondering."

Tempest glanced at his friend. "I wasn't, but thanks for the confirmation."

Smoke shrugged. "I figured knowing she's really on your side of this equation might make the decision to let someone else go after her mother a bit easier."

"All three, Smoke. I'm taking down all three. I've waited for years. They are mine."

"You'll ruin what you have."

"Maybe. Maybe not. It's a risk I have to take."

"You don't have to take it, you know."

He stared at his friend for a moment. "I do. For

this to be over. All of it, the years of pain and rebuilding, I have to do this, or it will never be *over* for me."

Smoke nodded. "Got it."

A wave of exhaustion swamped him. He turned and headed for his cabin. What he needed was a shower, some private time with Pilar, and six to eight hours of uninterrupted sleep.

CHAPTER 20

Cassie stared at the papers for thirty seconds before she raised her head and spoke to Jewell. "This is either a Caesar shift or an Alberti's disk code. I see a consistent pattern, so I don't believe it is a Vigenère square which would use multiple Caesar shifts in the document." They both leaned over the stacks of paper again.

Zane glanced at the women as they studied the papers. Cassie's husband lurked behind her, a silent sentinel. He got it; he really did. The woman had been through hell, and as an ex-Guardian, her husband was all about protecting Cassie.

"How's life on the ranch?" He leaned across to Van and asked.

"We are doing well." Van smiled at him and

shrugged. "I never saw myself as a rancher, but when part of my grandfather's old ranch was put up for sale, it was a foregone conclusion."

They watched as Cassie grabbed a pencil and a pad of paper. Van chuckled and glanced at the clock. "Won't be long now."

"Why do you say that?" Zane glanced back at the women. Cassie's hand hovered over the pad.

"When she grabs a piece of paper and a pencil, she's found the common core of the code and she's extrapolating the rest of the sequence in her mind. It's like chess. She won't move the first piece until she's run the entire game in her head. When she starts to write, she'll have the cypher for you to use."

"Man, I wish we could have done this via video chat." Zane chuckled. "It would have saved you a trip."

"You don't want shit like this on a video chat, no matter the encryption." Van nodded to the stack of papers his wife was staring at.

"Ever think of coming back to work for us?"

"Never. We have no problem doing special projects for Guardian, and we make exceptions for this organization, but the rest of the Alphabet soup has been asking for access. We've declined with emphasis. I've taken a shotgun to the porch a time or two. They've gotten the idea. She's still fragile, and I'll be damned if I'll let anyone take advantage of her gift. Those two women have a connection. Jewell was the reason I was on the mountain to help her. Honestly, it's because Guardian cared and sent us to check on her that she's alive. That is the only reason we make the exception for Guardian."

"Got it. Okay, it is a Caesar shift, see here?" Cassie wrote the alphabet on the tablet of paper. "Use this six-letter coded word here."

Jewell nodded her head. "Got it."

"Okay, there are two letters in the sample word which are the same letter, right? The letter L?"

"Yes." Jewell nodded.

"Here we use simple knowledge. The most common consonant in the English language is the letter R. So, we start with the assumption these two letters are the letter R."

"Okay, I'm following."

"Now we look at the alphabet I've written. If we assume the letter depicted here twice is the letter R, we count how many letters the letter L is from the letter R. Six letters behind. So, using this premise we can decode this word assuming the letter L in this code is in fact the letter R."

Jewell nodded and grabbed a pencil from the messy bun her hair had been scraped up into. So... this would make the G in the code word an M."

"Right. Do the rest of the word." Cassie smiled like a proud parent as Jewell finished the cypher.

"Murder."

Cassie nodded. "After I was able to see the pattern, I gave you an easy one to decode. Thankfully, this code is in English, or it would have taken much, much longer." She glanced up at the screens full of coded messages. "These people are talking about heinous things." Cassie shivered and crossed the office to stand beside her husband. "Thank goodness we live in the middle of Montana. I don't want to imagine what they are doing."

"I can make an algorithm to decipher these emails." Jewell smiled up at Zane. "She's freaking amazing!"

Cassie laughed and shook her head. "No, I recognize patterns like other people recognize the makes and models of cars."

"Can you stay for dinner? I'll be free in about... three hours?" Jewell bounced on her toes. She didn't have many friends so Cassie being here was a big deal for her, and no doubt the idea of creating an algorithm to defeat the coded messages had her wound up, too.

Cassie glanced up at her husband. "Can we?"

"Sure, I told Jason we'd spend the night and fly back tomorrow." Van chuckled when both women squealed.

"Okay, to work I go then!" Jewell stopped and spun around, a stricken look on her face. "Where is Samuel?"

"He's with our ranch foreman and his wife. He's happier running after Mack than he would be sitting here trying not to squirm." Van smiled down at his wife.

Jewell smiled. "Oh, okay. Honey, would you help them leave the section and find out where to pick them up..." Her words trailed off as she sat in front of the computer.

"Yep, we are alike, aren't we?" Cassie quipped and smiled up at Van.

"Same pea, different pod." Van agreed. "You both zone out when there is a challenge in front of you."

Zane glanced at his wife as they left the office. He knew for a fact she had no idea they were leaving. Damn, he loved her intensity.

~

Luke closed the door behind him. The sound of the shower in his bedroom drew him toward the small bathroom. He took the time to remove his pistol and secure it in the bedside drawer. Pilar's shock when she'd seen him arm up was fresh in his memory. He didn't want to jolt her with his reality again. At least not tonight.

The door pushed open and a wave of warm fragrant mist wrapped around him. The shower stall's frosted glass obscured a perfect view, but the undulating texture of the fogged panel framed her beautiful body, hinting at the curves and softness beyond the panel. He'd seen artwork crafted by the Old World masters, and he hadn't appreciated any of their talent. Now, gazing at the sight in front of him, he wished *he* knew how to craft the long lines and sensuous sways standing before him. He'd give his life savings to be able to create with brush-strokes a rendering which would capture the beauty of her form forever.

He shed his clothes quickly, stacking them in the corner, away from the door. She turned when he opened the door and backed into the wall making room for him. "It's a little crowded in here, but I thought you might let me take care of you for once."

His hands found her hips as he stared down at her. Those big blue eyes exposed her soul to him. "You've been taking care of me since the moment I saw you. You just didn't know it." He lowered and drew her into a kiss, slowly advancing and retreating until she wrapped her arms around his neck and held him against her mouth.

She finally allowed him to pull back. "That's not the kind of care I want to give you." She kissed his chest and slowly lowered to her knees. Her mouth brushed his stomach and then his cock. She nuzzled his balls and licked around one and then the other. He ran his hands through her hair, not to hold her to him, but rather to steady himself. His earlier exhaustion got pushed to the side, and he braced his stance and closed his eyes. Her mouth brushed against his skin. Kisses slanted across the head of his shaft. His thighs shook against her tender onslaught. Gentle hands cupped his balls at the exact time her hot mouth sucked the cap of his dick into her mouth. An explosion of whites and reds fired off behind his eyelids as he tightly screwed his eyes shut. The soft suction, pulling and releasing, was going to kill him.

He pried his eyelids open and gazed down at her on her knees before him. Sex had always been mechanical. A means to an end. Only with Pilar was sex a conveyance to something more. He stroked her cheek with his thumb, and she glanced up at him. He could read every emotion in those beautiful blues. He felt the same way, and he hoped she could see it in his eyes. The intense connection shredded him. He gently tugged on her hair. "I'm close."

She moaned around the tip of his cock and rolled his balls in her hand. Oh, God... His orgasm kicked through his body, and the fireworks behind his eyelids exploded again. The sharp bark of his exhale echoed in the small bathroom. The sound of water falling and his deep breathing replaced the echoed sound of his release.

He helped her stand and wrapped her in his arms, lowering to kiss the woman he'd fallen in love with all those years ago. Label him a sap, a romantic, what the fuck ever society wanted to tattoo on his ass for wanting this woman more than anything in the world.

He froze for a second at the realization. She sighed and leaned into his chest as he held her tightly. Did he want her more than he wanted his revenge? Yes... no... fuck... maybe? She'd distorted his reality, and although they hadn't shared the words, he felt her emotions and saw the same feelings in her eyes.

The water blasted cold, jolting him. Her shriek and laughter bounced through the small bathroom. He hit the faucet, turning off the water, laughing as she shivered and grabbed for a towel.

"Well that's why they tell you to take a cold shower. Oh, my God! It was freezing!" She shoved a towel toward him and wrapped herself in cotton.

He laughed at her. "We'll have to try it again when hot water is guaranteed." She nodded and shivered. "Bed, under the sheets and covers. I'll be there in a moment."

"Okay." She bolted from the bathroom with a slight limp and squealed. "Air Conditioning! OMG, I'm turning into a popsicle!" Her words were muffled by a flurry of flapping sounds. He leaned to his right and chuckled at the lump huddled in the middle of the bed *underneath* the bedding.

He finished drying off, picked up her towel, and replaced it on the rack along with his. He checked the lock on the door and lifted the blankets, slipping into the bed. She snuggled up against him, and he held her until she stopped shivering.

The blankets rustled, and her head popped up from under the covers. "Was the call about work?"

"Always. We are heading back to the Palm Beach Yacht Club."

She deflated before his eyes. "Time to face reality?"

"Afraid so. You'll need to concoct something your mother will believe when you get home." He traced a circle on the soft skin of her back.

"No, I won't. I'll tell her I got bored."

He tipped his head so he could see her. "Is getting bored a thing with you?"

"It used to be, but about three years ago I met this guy who changed my way of thinking." She reared up on an elbow and tipped a tentative smile his way. "I grew up entitled and rich. I thought nothing of having a butler, a cook, a nanny, or a chauffeur. It was the way I grew up." She reached forward and traced a scar near his collarbone. It was from an old battle, a lifetime ago. "After I tried and failed to report you being held in New York, I did some serious soul searching. Things I'd never paid attention to started to matter. I didn't want my life to be a shell, and that's what it felt like. I'd always done what my mother wanted, when she wanted it done because as I said, it was the way I was raised. I'd started to question her, argue, and deviate from her plans. It got ugly. I was a freshly minted lawyer with the law on my side. She needed to stomp the independence out of me. So to quell my rebellion, she sent me into your cell, and then discredited me with the NYPD. She needs to have complete control, or in my case for the last three years, she needs to *think* she is in control."

"Be careful, if she thinks she's losing you, she could react badly." He had no doubt the woman would teach Pilar a lesson, but would she eliminate her own flesh and blood?

"Regina Grantham lash out?" Pilar cocked her head and then shrugged. "Maybe. I've seen it once or twice, but she needs me. I'm a pawn on her board." She snuggled down next to him. "Can we talk on the email account?"

"If you need to get information to me, it would be the best bet. You'll need to keep your head down, at least for the next week or two. Guardian is working on tying up all the loose ends. If you need help, activate your phone case. I'll have someone monitoring it. I'll come for you when all of this is done."

She leaned down and kissed him. "I'll hold you

to it." Pilar sighed and shook her head. "You know, there is a part of me which hopes she'll be exonerated and everything I've questioned is wrong."

"She's your mother. Of course, you'd want her to be innocent." He went back to drawing circles on her back.

Pilar's voice drifted up to him sometime later, soft and sleepy. "Luke?"

"Yeah, babe?"

"She's not innocent."

"I know." He dropped a kiss on her hair and stared at the ceiling.

CHAPTER 21

"Where are we headed, boss?" Travis asked as the ship moored at the pier.

"We don't go anywhere until the lady is off the boat, and we have night to cover our exit."

"Of course. Do you think she's being watched?"

"I do." He gazed through the darkly tinted windows of the main cabin. The languid pace of the strolling people along the pier didn't give him any peace of mind. He hated the fact she'd been forced to go back to that damn house and under her mother's observation once again.

"Do you have a team or someone who can keep an eye on her while we're working?" Travis leaned back in one of the white leather chairs and glanced down the hall when his men's laughter echoed from the galley.

"Putting a tail on her would cause problems if they were discovered." Her mother could be guaranteed to watch her closely for the next week or so. Her spur of the moment trip and the death of one of the Fates couldn't be connected, yet the coincidence would be there. How tight the surveillance of Pilar would be depended on how much of a paranoid bitch her mother had become with the death of one of her... hell what was she, a coworker? *Fellow world dominatrix, evil bitch of the East? Whatever.* He had a way to track her.

He assumed her mother would too, once Pilar left the boat. He glanced at the team skipper. "How long have you been doing this?"

Travis glanced up at him and shrugged. "I joined up and served. Did two tours, most of it in the Middle East." The man's eyes clouded. "I was approached when I got out by a recruiter for Guardian. I signed on and haven't looked back."

"That good?" The itch to know what the other side of the business looked and felt like was new for him.

Travis drew a breath and nodded his head.

"Yeah. I have a permanent team here. No one is rotating on or off every six months. We know each other and are closer than family. The training and equipment are top-notch, and you can't beat the pay. "

"Do you miss family time?"

"Ha! Well if I had a family, then yeah, it might be an issue. We are deployable assets, you know? Ricco has a steady girlfriend, and they're serious, but they work at it. He calls when he can, and they email when he can find a secure server. The rest of us aren't locked in on any single lady. This line of employment can be hard on a relationship, but I know guys who are married and still work in the business. Usually their partners have busy careers too. The ones who sit at home waiting are the ones who are distressed when a mission goes long, or we get pulled to deploy. Those who have a life outside the couple seem to do better."

"Sounds like you've been taking note. What's stopping you?" Tempest watched a white limo pull up at the end of the pier. Pilar's transportation home.

"I *have* been observing. Human nature is a curiosity to me, and as far as what's stopping me, well it's the right woman. So far I haven't found anyone who can put up with me." A laugh followed. "Looks like you got yourself one hell of a catch, though."

Travis nodded to Pilar as she walked slowly across the lower deck. A slight limp was still discernible, but greatly improved. Dan trailed behind her down the wide boardwalk with her two suitcases. The limo driver trotted from the driver's side to the rear of the vehicle and popped the trunk before he opened the rear door for Pilar. He watched Dan approach her after he'd placed the luggage in the trunk and then she slid into the interior of the vehicle.

He wanted nothing more than to pull her back into the confines of the ship and shield her from the vileness of her mother. They'd said their good-byes earlier, yet watching her walk across the deck toward the ramp which Sage placed to allow her access to the pier was excruciatingly painful. An ominous feeling swamped him. Pilar was balanced on a narrow precipice between two atrocities—her mother's predation on one side and his violent past on the other.

He'd fought Satan's hellhounds with his bare

hands and won. Vengeance was his to redeem, and he would cash in the ticket with emphasis. When he was done, perhaps he'd try to walk in the light, or rather the black ops side of the house. How hard could it be to become legitimate?

"C-comms for you." Sage's voice snapped both him and Travis from their silent contemplation of the pier.

"On my way." He spun on his heel and followed Sage up to the bridge. He signed in and authenticated.

"We've got it all. The evidence was in the emails on the Darknet server." Anubis' voice held a tinge of excitement. "Bengal's wife and her team are putting together the superstructure of the organization from the top down."

"What is my next step?" He glanced at Sage who was leaning against the far counter beside Smoke. Both men looked at him.

Anubis cleared his throat and began, "The top of the organizational structure goes by numbers. Francesca, the woman you eliminated was called Three. One is Pilar's mother, but as she is domestic, we need the Council to reconvene for unanimous approval due to One's location. Archangel is mustering the players as we speak. In the meantime, we've located Two. Two will be your next assignment. A van will be waiting for you at the end of the pier at 0300hrs. You are to utilize your usual technique for this mission."

Make a statement. He'd most certainly do it, with pleasure. "And One?"

"The best way to eat an elephant is one bite at a time, my friend. Don't worry, the assignment is still yours. Guardian has identified a host of 'middle management' personnel who will keep our teams and specialists busy for a very long time."

"Making a statement will drive her underground."

"We have eyes on her. If she goes under, we'll know where she is."

"She's mine."

"Acknowledged for the second time. Rest up. You've got a hell of a long flight ahead of you. Jet lag is a bitch."

"Don't I know it."

"Check in fifteen minutes before departure for any updates."

"Copy all." He signed off and leaned against the counter on his side of the ship.

"Well? What's next?" Smoke's eagerness nearly dripped off him.

"What happened at the end of the dock?" He wanted to know what words they'd exchanged.

"Caught that did you?" Smoke rubbed the back of his neck. "The chauffeur wasn't the same one who dropped her off. He said the regular guy called in sick. I think your lady was suspicious, but she said everything was fine."

"Did you get any bad vibes off the guy?"

"No, but I sensed her tighten up. Want me to call her? Tell her she's forgotten something? Make sure she's okay?"

Hell yes, he wanted Smoke to contact her, but would further contact be suspicious? Probably, especially if her mother still had her under a microscope, and it was what they'd have to assume. "No. If she said it was fine, I'll trust her judgment. We can't risk contact at this point unless we're sure something is wrong." He shrugged. "I'm leaving with the team at 0300hrs. Beyond that, I wasn't given specifics on what management wants you two to do."

"Okay. If we weren't given any specific instructions, I'll check in with Fury after you disembark." Smoke pushed off the counter where he'd been leaning. "I guess this is a 'see you later moment'." He extended his hand.

Tempest grabbed it and pulled the man in for a half clench, half hug. "You're feeding me before I go, and you know I'll be around. So, get your shit out of my bedroom at the house."

"Damn, well if you insist. Whatever it takes, my man."

"As long as it takes, and you better not take too long clearing your shit out of my room."

Sage barked a laugh at their interchange and waved a hand at him. He returned the salute and headed down to pull his gear together for the mission.

He had every intention of home basing in Florida. Pilar had passed the bar here, and she could practice here while he worked. Travis' words had burrowed quick and deep. However, those dreams were going to be nothing but figments of his imagination if he didn't handle the next two portions of his assignment correctly. He'd get the brief on the next target and watch as the ripples from the butterfly's flight intensified. When his current job was complete, a cyclone would bear down on the lone remaining Fate. But first he had work to do.

Pilar breathed a sigh of relief as the limo turned into the beachfront mansion. Security, a guard she recognized, waved them through the gate, and the driver drove up to the front door. He opened the door for her. "Would you like me to bring the suitcases to your room, Miss?"

The man looked at her with a carefully manicured expression. She got the feeling whether she liked it or not, he was going to carry them in. "Thank you."

She made her way to the front door opened by her mother's butler.

"Welcome home, ma'am. Your mother will be arriving in six hours. Please be prepared to meet with her as soon as she arrives."

The chauffeur walked past her with both suitcases and headed up the stairs.

She leveled a stare and arched an eyebrow at the butler but didn't acknowledge the man's words. *He* was the reason there was a tracking *and* recording device in her luggage. What other devices had he planted at her mother's behest? Well, she had six hours to discover if there were any monitoring devices in her rooms. By the time she was at the top of the stairs, the driver was heading back down.

She turned and watched him walk away. Her head swiveled to her rooms and then back down the stairs. How had the driver, a person she'd never seen before, known which set of rooms was hers?

A chill raced up her spine, and gooseflesh prickled down her arms. Forcing a lungful of air into her chest, she counted to three and exhaled. She had to be imagining things. She was paranoid because she'd actually made the leap and had given her carefully gathered information to an agency which could investigate and do something. The door to her rooms stood ajar, and her cases were inside her quarters, the case with the monitor in it closest to the door. She walked past the dirty laundry, carrying her cell phone and day planner. When she reached her chaise lounge, she dropped into it and called her mother.

"Why did you return early?"

"I got bored. The boat had mechanical issues and had to dock for a couple of days." It was a shade of the truth, and Luke said to stick as close to the truth as she could without revealing what really happened.

"We have several meetings. Did you review the material provided at the last meeting?"

"I've looked at it. How did you know I'd be home?"

"Go through it again and be dressed professionally."

She rolled her eyes. "I won't disappoint you."

"Time will tell." Her mother disconnected the call.

Pilar set her phone down and stared through the window. The ocean rolled onto the beach and a runner passed by. She drew a deep breath and scanned her living room. Her home inside the mansion. She'd had these quarters since she was old enough to be left alone at night, so for as long as she could remember. Her first memories were of waking up afraid in the middle of the night. She glanced at the shelves which held her most cherished mementoes. The little purple stuffed elephant... *What in the hell?*

She rose off the couch and went directly to the shelves. The elephant was on the wrong shelf. She picked him up and moved the little notebook her second grade teacher had given her for perfect attendance and switched their location. She sent a critical gaze around the room. The plants were arranged differently. She'd always made sure they were closer to the window. She moved behind the bar and pushed the pots back. A small wire dropped from one of the plants, black where the plant was a vibrant green. She turned her back on the plants and ran a cup of water from the bar sink. Pretending a nonchalance she wasn't sure she could sustain, she poured a small amount into every plant and examined the leaves. Whatever had been hidden in the plant was connected to the stalk. She couldn't get a good look at it, but it didn't matter. She was being monitored. *Better to know. Right?*

Her toe throbbed, but the wedge heel she was wearing was bearable. She chose a pantsuit, well aware Regina didn't like the idea of ladies in slacks, but it was the best way to cover the shoes she wouldn't approve of either. She'd found two more devices in her rooms. God only knew what they were, but they were there, and she wasn't paranoid. She was being monitored. Those things hadn't been in her room prior to her leaving on the yacht. She would have noticed them.

Her campaign manager looked up as she entered the office area. Not even a smile in her direction. Yes, the woman knew exactly who she worked for––Regina.

The door closed moments after she arrived, and the meetings began. Her schedule was drawn up, events were finalized, and a platform was agreed upon. No one consulted her. For the last two years of her pro bono work, she'd won judgments against the city for negligence and corruption, so she knew how Regina would attack the sitting mayor. She watched from her perch as the minions bobbed their heads and deferred to Regina's decrees.

Regina dismissed the minions and held a hand up as Pilar stood. "A moment."

She stretched briefly and then took her seat again. Regina's attention focused on her computer until the door shut behind the election staff. "I'm very concerned about your recent indiscretions, Pilar. You must know I am aware of your actions at all times."

She blinked repeatedly. "Ma'am?" Fear gripped her muscles, freezing her to the spot.

Regina turned the monitor, and Pilar leaned forward to view an aerial picture of a ship.

"Are you topless?" Her mother clicked the mouse, zooming in on a picture of a blonde woman wearing a multi-colored swimsuit bottom and no top. Pilar shook her head vehemently. "No! That's not me! I don't even have a tie-dyed swimsuit."

Her mother's eyes narrowed. "Not you?" Regina's eyes swung back to the picture. It was grainy and there was no way anyone could tell who the woman actually was. "Were there other people on the ship?"

"No. Just me and the crew." Still shaking her head in disbelief, she pointed to the picture. "I don't know where you got *that* picture, but I would never sunbathe topless. You've raised me to understand what a professional in the public eye can and can't do." She crossed her arms across her stomach. "Besides, look at her foot. She doesn't have her foot wrapped." Pilar lifted her foot displaying the padding and white medical tape which still cushioned her swollen black and blue toe.

Regina's mouth puckered slightly as she moved her eyes from Pilar's foot to the screen. "Not. You." She turned her computer monitor and stared at the picture. Without breaking her concentrated stare at her monitor, Regina waved to the door. "You are dismissed."

Pilar sent a final glance at her mother and

exited with as much dignity as her limp would allow. She had no idea why her mother would think the woman in the picture was her. She shut the door behind her and tried to breathe. Seriously, an aerial photo? What in the world had happened to her life?

CHAPTER 22

They were driven to a private airfield about an hour inland. The aircraft's pilot met them with the briefing packet and showed him a crate of supplies that had been delivered and marked for him. Tempest took the offered envelope and once again entered the aircraft first. Travis held the team outside while he dissected the packet's contents. Several pictures of a middle-aged woman with light brown hair dropped from the envelope. There were no full-frontal pictures of the woman's face. He examined each of the photographs. It was as if she always knew where the cameras were and concealed most of her face on purpose.

He reviewed two pages of financial transactions that tied her to several international terrorist organizations. Highlighted was the same financial tango which linked this woman to an assassin referred to as the Raven. To his knowledge, the operative wasn't a freelancer. Last he'd heard the man... or woman, was attached to the Mossad. Guardian had tracked the payments through whatever cyber magic they did, and the transfer of money coincided with the death of the woman's husband. *Well, well, murder for inheritance was becoming a trend, wasn't it?* Francesca offed her father to inherit her fortune, and Nadia Volkov, a Russian born entrepreneur, inherited her wealth from her late husband. *Coincidence? Hardly.* Which led back to the question, were the Fates and Stratus utilizing assassins?

He tipped the envelope and Nadia's calendar for the next three days slipped into his hand. A map of St. Petersburg was next. He spread the map and studied it and the itinerary. This one was going to be a bit more difficult. Not impossible, not by a long shot. He slid his eyes to Sierra team as they loitered by the door giving him time and privacy. A smile tugged at the corner of his lips. He had the assets; he'd use them. With methodical precision, he once again studied the evidence

Guardian had provided, committed the schedule to memory, and pocketed the map. He tipped the folder. Six passports, a stack of Russian rubles in various denominations, six credit cards, and two sets of keys fell onto his lap. The last piece of paper was stuck inside the envelope. He reached in and extracted his instructions.

Code Authenticated, Sunset Clearance. Confirmed via Counsel. TOD to be a statement. C, E and I requested. Delay discovery if possible. Report when mission is accomplished.

He found his passport and took a thick stack of money before shoving his credit card into the pages of his Russian passport. He tossed the envelope with the rest of the money, keys, passports and credit cards to Travis when the man entered the aircraft.

Travis glanced in the pouch. "Fuck. I hope you speak Russian, my friend. None of us do."

Tempest spoke perfect Russian, but he shook his head. "If we do this correctly none of you will have to speak Russian."

"Well then, by all means, let's do this correctly. Are we the perimeter again?" Travis looked at a passport and tossed it to Ricco, then glanced at another and sent it airmail to Scuba. Both passports sailed past their targets.

"Stop throwing stuff, Skipper, you can't hit shit," Coach mumbled as he picked up one of the passports which had hit him in the back.

"Stop bitching. It isn't a hand grenade." Travis laughed and handed the envelope to Harley who continued to disburse the contents.

Tempest laughed and turned his attention back to the conversation. "No. You'll be a little more involved this time."

"Well all right. Do you have a plan?"

"I do." He spread the map and began a detailed explanation. When he finished, Travis wasn't smiling. The guy wasn't even looking at him. "Are you good with this?" He pointed to the map and the places he'd pointed out.

"No. I can't say as I am. We haven't done the stealth mode breaking and entering gig before. Enter quietly, take down the bad guys, rescue a hostage, and get the hell out without losing a team member, yes. Enter quietly and steal all the electronics without setting off alarms? Not so much, but we'll do our best." Travis rolled his shoulders and cracked his neck. "This target is for sure keeping information we need to remove?"

"Affirmative. My handlers are requesting all computers and electronics on this one."

"So, I gotta ask, why?"

"An assumption only, but I'd bet it is because this target is responsible for kidnapping and selling children, and young men and women, into the slavery. She's made money off drugs, guns and believe it or not, starting wars. She has politicians in her pocket and several very unsavory characters who would kill you for the thrill of it alone. No payment required. *These* are the people who went after the Kings."

Travis' head snapped up. "*These* are the mother-fuckers?"

"They are."

"Dude, you should have led with that bit of information. You make whatever statement you need to make. We'll take care of our end. Not saying it will be completely silent, but we'll do our best." The man extended his hand and Tempest grasped it. Only time would tell if Sierra team would fulfill their end of the mission, but it was theirs to conquer. His fate lay in another direction.

The line of cars snaked along the Mokhovaya Ulitsa. Commoners' vehicles sped by the slowly crawling line of luxury vehicles. She scanned the oncoming cars from where she stood on the street outside the ballet house. The gold Aurus Senat coming to pick her up crept further along the avenue toward the entrance of the ballet. Chauffeurs were prohibited from exiting their vehicles, thus stalling the slow creep of vehicles. Instead, a uniformed assistant opened the side door of the vehicle, allowing the occupant into the climate controlled comfort.

Nadia Volkov tapped her foot in irritation. Her driver was supposed to be at the front of the line. Instead, her gold Senat was midway in the line. Unacceptable. She'd have the driver fired and then find a way to make him pay. Perhaps he had a son or a daughter she could dangle from a string. Yes, she'd see how the man liked waiting.

The attendant opened her door and she slid in. The curtains had been closed. Another strike against the man. She *wanted* to be seen. Was he a fucking imbecile? She drew a breath and reached for the chilled champagne which waited for her. At least the halfwit had remembered to chill her wine. She removed a crystal wine glass from the holder she'd had the manufacturer make specifically for her. She had two vices in this world. Wine and caviar. Indulgences for the most refined tastes, unlike that pig, Three, who'd choked to death on common chocolate *while eating in bed*. Obscene. The conference call with One tomorrow would no doubt stretch into an uncomfortable duration. One was so... banal. In truth, *she* should hold the position of First. The woman's plodding in the United States was becoming irritating.

She took a sip of her wine and wrinkled her nose. *What vintage was this?* Definitely not her Louis Roederer Gold Label Cristal Chardonnay Pinot Noir, 2002. She placed her glass back in its holder and removed the bottle from the bucket. *Strange.* She blinked at the label. The swirling R blurred. She braced herself against the soft leather of the back seat. *No! This...* Nadia fell to her knees and crawled to the front of the car. She ripped the curtains back. "No!"

The driver wasn't the man she'd hired. Dead eyes turned to her and a sneer curled his lip. She clutched her stomach as waves smeared across her vision. *No. This couldn't be hap...*

The old warehouse at the edge of St. Petersburg was a shell neglected to the point it had partially collapsed. The barb wire fencing around the structure was as old. Nothing and no one had been in the building for months if not longer. The dust, cobwebs, and decomposing garbage covered in dirt told a story of abandonment to anyone willing to look. Tempest had been willing. He'd turned off the headlights of the expensive luxury car about a mile ago and hadn't passed a soul, either on the road or walking. This corner of the city was desolate and perfect for his plans.

He dragged the woman from the vehicle and placed her on the quickly constructed frame he'd built after landing in the country. His watch vibrated and he glanced down. Sierra team would be engaging with security at the woman's home soon. He hit the mechanism on his watch, checking in. So far, so good.

A razor-sharp knife made quick work of the woman's designer gown. The fabric fell to the ground in a pool at her feet. With practiced ease he slid the IV needle into the woman's arm. Guardian wanted a statement. They were going to get one.

Tempest opened the port to the IV and let the chemicals mix. The tip of his knife made multiple, fine cuts, opening her veins. She moaned as he finished the last cut.

He moved away from her and watched as she regained cognizance. "What? Release me!" she bellowed in Russian.

He cocked his head at her. "Why would I do so when I've gone to such trouble to kill you?" His Russian was practiced and precise.

Her eyes widened, and she swung her gaze to the IV and then down her body. "What is this? What are you doing?"

"I'm making a statement. Humanity has had enough of your manipulation." This time he spoke in English.

"I don't know what you are talking about." The woman's chest heaved, and her arms tightened as she struggled to loosen the zip ties which held her to the frame he'd thrown together.

Tempest crossed his arms over his chest after he put his knife away.

"These cuts are not enough to kill me," She sneered. "I will be missed. I will be found."

"By who? Your guards are dead. Your computer and all your electronics—" he extracted her phone from his pocket and waved it at her "—have been secured." At least he hoped Sierra team was in possession of the woman's computers.

"You will find nothing!"

"We already have access to your email server on the Darknet."

"Which will be useless." Nadia spit at him. A red tinge to the spittle colored the cement floor.

Tempest meandered a few steps forward and examined the puddle of saliva. "It's pink. You are already bleeding inside. Your cuts will continue to ooze a slow push of blood from your body. The IV contains Coumadin and Heparin. Your blood will not clot. You are going to die of exsanguination. I wonder if your tears will turn to blood before you're gone."

A nasty smile split the woman's face. "Killing a *woman*? How heroic of you."

"You are not a woman. You'd have to be human first. You have been found guilty of crimes against humanity and sentenced to death."

"By who?" She struggled against the bindings. The blood pulsed from her cuts. Red rivulets streaked down her legs and started to pool at her feet.

"Does it matter?" He walked back to his kit and grabbed a paintbrush.

"What do you want?"

He smiled. "I want you to die." He made his way to the blood on the floor and dabbed the brush in it. He moved in front of her and started lettering a message.

"You! Are you the one she held and toyed with for years?"

He stopped what he was doing and looked up at her. "I am." He resumed his work as if her words were inconsequential.

"The other... she said you died."

"She lied."

"Did she send you?"

He couldn't avoid the temptation to fuck with her. Tempest chuckled. "Yes."

"That bitch! I can pay you more. I have resources she doesn't know about."

"There is nothing I can do for you now. The damage the chemicals are doing is fatal and irreversible." He continued his macabre lettering on the floor before her.

"Kill her for me."

"No." He'd kill the woman for *himself*.

"I can give you wealth beyond your comprehension."

"No." He only needed one thing to be rich beyond this woman's understanding and the one thing was Pilar.

There was silence for several minutes as he walked back and forth reloading his paintbrush and forming the message that would sign this as his work. His assassinations usually bore messages. His statements let the target's organization know who and what was coming for them.

"There is a hard drive. She has it. It has information about Guardian. I can get it for you."

"If she has it, she has it." He continued his work without looking up at her. A hard drive? Did Guardian lose a hard drive? He didn't think Bengal's wife would be sloppy. No, it had to be from an outside source.

"They've almost cracked the encryption, only the last layers remain. I can get it. I have people inside her inner circle."

Interesting. The Fates didn't trust each other. He didn't look up as he spoke, "She knows."

More time passed. He finished his work and dropped the paintbrush. It had no identifying marks or fingerprints. It was trash.

"You can kill me, but I have insurance."

"You will die; and I'm sure you do."

"He will remove whoever kills me."

"Ah, Francesca alluded to an assassin." Was it Lobo or Raven who had the contract?

"You killed her." A statement not a question.

"She begged and bargained, too."

"I have not begged." The vitriol of her original anger settled into resignation. "He will not get paid unless you are killed. There are controls. This, what you paint in my blood, it is your calling card, is it not?"

"It is."

"He will track you down."

"Lobo or Raven? I'm not worried."

"No, another."

"One who exists only in your imagination doesn't bother me." He crossed his arms and assessed his mark. She wasn't going to be conscious for much longer.

"He exists."

"If you believe so. You have no leverage anymore. No power. She will protect me."

The woman reared her head and glared at him. "She cannot protect you from Akuma. He will find you. He will collect his reward. She won't be able to stop him."

His smile spread, and he knew the moment she realized her mistake. She'd named her asset. One he'd never heard of, but it wasn't exactly a billboard moment. Assassins worked in the shadows. Most he knew by the way they killed, not by name. Raven and Lobo had been around for as long as he'd been working for Guardian. They were second rate, not the caliber of professional Guardian insisted on. If memory served, Lobo was keen on keeping trophies from his kills. Raven? The assassin had a body count in the hundreds, not of paid kills, but of bystanders, innocents. Messy and dishonorable.

The woman struggled to breathe now. "I'm cold."

"I know. Death won't be long now. Why did you do it?"

She tilted her head with effort, a grey tinge around her mouth and eyes accented the pallor of her face. A trickle of blood ran from her nose and the inner corner of one eye. "Because *men* have ruined the world."

"And sex trafficking, drugs, guns and wars repair what has been ruined." He shook his head. "What a screwed-up way of righting a listing ship."

"To propagate power, one needs money. The easiest means are often illegal. The people who we used were sacrificed for the greater good."

"I think they'd disagree." He watched her lower her head.

She mumbled something. He moved closer. "I didn't hear you."

"She will not let you live."

"I don't work for her. She's my next target. *She* will not live."

A huff of air pushed from the woman. "She will not die alone. If she gets to... bunker. She will..."

He assessed his mark. There would be no further words. Intelligence gathered, he waited for the end. It wouldn't be long. He removed the IV from her arm and made a small cut, dipped the paintbrush in the blood and dropped a trail of blood from the mark the IV left. No sense in making the medical examiner's job easy. Nadia had died a tragic death. Small cuts. None deep enough to kill her and yet with the help of the IV blood thinners, the woman who'd ordered the ruthless murders of innocent people, sold children into ungodly horrors, and created wars to further her goals, had bled for those she'd hurt. An eye for an eye.

He looked at the message illuminated by the moon through a gaping hole in the roof.

One Fate for All

Written in English, it was a message sent to an entire organization, but directed at the one who remained. Mission complete, he moved through the dark warehouse and made his way to where he'd left his vehicle. He'd meet up with Sierra team and head back to the States. There was one more step to take on his road to vengeance. One. More. Step.

CHAPTER 23

Pilar made her way to the insistent knocking on her living quarter's door. Pulling a robe around her, she yanked the door open and glared at the security guard. "What?"

"You will get dressed and pack a small overnight bag. Your mother requires your presence at a meeting she will be hosting in the morning."

"What? Where is she? Where is the meeting?" Leaning through the doorway, she blinked down the dark hallway.

"I did not ask, and she is not here. In order to comply with her directions, we will need to leave within the next twenty minutes. Please do hurry, I value my job." The man gave her a resigned and slightly put-out look.

"Fine." She shut the door and headed back to the shower. It wasn't the first time her mother had demanded she drop everything and go to a meeting, but she'd never been summoned in the middle of the night. Regina had lost her mind. She showered quickly, drew her hair into a tight French twist, and slipped into a business suit and a pair of flats. She threw her heels into her overnight bag, added two changes of clothes, and her toiletries. She threw her phone into her purse and dragged her almost awake form to the front door. The security guard opened the door for her.

She stepped out and the guard behind her grabbed her in a tight hold. A cloth covered her nose and mouth. She screamed and tried to get away. Panic bolted through her as her vision started to tunnel.

"Did she make any calls?" Regina emerged and crossed her arms as the security guard manhandled Pilar into the back of a black panel van.

"No," said a man who'd been hidden in the shadows.

"You know where to take her."

"I do."

"She isn't to be eliminated, yet. But do ensure she knows her place." She turned and walked back into her Florida residence and flicked a disdainful glance around the entryway. The home was a mildewed stone around her neck. She'd put it on the market immediately. The humidity and heat were ever present, save a handful of days in the middle of winter where one could breathe without feeling as if they were drowning in water. Pilar's things would be removed tomorrow. Her assistant had seen to it.

She mounted the stairway en route to her office. Two was due to call in a few hours. They needed to nominate candidates and start the scrub to appoint another to the council. A shame, the former Three was just becoming tolerable. Regina shook her head in disdain. The fat bitch had choked to death on a chocolate, of all things. A horribly apropos reckoning.

She moved into her office and glanced at the report on her screen. The ship the tracking device was found on wasn't the ship Pilar had chartered. The surveillance and photos taken of the blonde woman on the boat had been of a sixty-year-old banker's new trophy wife, which meant they had no intelligence as to where Pilar had been during her absence. The only conclusion which could be drawn was her daughter had help in removing and transplanting the tracking device. The oaf of a butler had been relieved of his duties––permanently, as had the previous chauffeur. One for being an imbecile, the other for getting too close to the person he was required to monitor. Two would need to order those two eliminations. The chauffeur first, and then the butler. Pilar should never have been able to detect the tracker, yet it was removed from her luggage and placed on another ship. What was she hiding?

Her eyebrows pinched together as she stared at the report. Whatever she was concealing, her deceit was intolerable. She would no longer invest time or effort into the ungrateful foundling she'd agreed to raise. Yet another strike against her predecessor's edicts and way of doing things. Pilar's upbringing and education had been directed by the Fates before her and they had been superseded. She'd been interested to see if the elder Fates' incompetence in administering the rest of their programs would carry through into this effort. Of course, she'd been proven correct. Pilar was unacceptable.

The woman's recent change of mind had been too sudden, and in hindsight, she could see Pilar had used her malleable stance as a ploy to get her way. Very inventive and probably directed, although who was directing Pilar's recent actions had yet to be seen. Speculation at this point would be useless, however, she would find out. Eventually. Two would not give her any problems as far as disposal of the now useless asset. The law office would close; the house would be sold; and all records of Pilar Grantham would disappear. Before she did, however, the woman would tell her exactly what she wanted to know. There were drugs which would hurry the disclosure of information, but why deprive her interrogators of a reward? They did deserve a fresh candidate, and it had been a long time since they'd been given a woman on which to practice.

Regina minimized the report and logged into the Darknet email account. Two had not provided her updates, but that was not uncommon when they had scheduled telephone calls. She handled the minutia of her legitimate business and had her assistant bring her a fresh cup of coffee as she waited for the call from Two.

Her ire hit its limit when Two was thirty minutes late calling. The woman really needed to be replaced. This show of disrespect was appalling. One clicked on the icon and hit send. She was going to tear the skin off the woman, verbally of course. She'd never get her hands dirty. The call rang through. And rang again. And again.

One disconnected the call and switched screens.

A chat box popped up. One typed in her query to the person she had on the inside of Two's inner circle, the trusted security team's leader.

>**Is she doing this on purpose?**

The guard would answer when he could, usually within minutes, sometimes as long as ten. When twenty minutes elapsed, she leaned back in her chair. Three was dead and Two? Where was Two? Where were Two's guards? What would cause both Two and her guards failure to answer? She tapped on another screen and previewed world events. Nothing which would preclude Two from initiating contact.

One spun in her chair and gazed through the window to the rolling tide. Precautions had to be taken. If Two was dead, it would mean somehow the Fates had been identified and two of them eliminated.

"Get in here!"

Her assistant flew into the office. "Ma'am?"

"Execute Ground Zero, immediately."

"Of course, ma'am. I'll contact New York and divert the plane back here to retrieve you."

"No. Not yet. I have time. Let them deliver her before they come back for me." She would go to her safe place in New York City and leave the US from there, but Pilar was unfinished business.

"Of course, ma'am." The little man hurried from the room.

She watched his door shut and sighed. Too bad the last step of Ground Zero was his death. He was a loyal little curmudgeon. But there could be no one and nothing to implicate her. Her office building in New York would be cleared out, the offices vacated, and all personnel would be eliminated. The corporations would receive her resignations, but the legitimate business would continue and, as a stockholder under another name, she would continue to amass her fortune.

Watching the water, she sighed. She would disappear and reemerge in another country, as another person. She'd purchased a rather large private island in the Maldives which was untraceable to her. Unfortunately, the humidity and heat of the tropical location, her primary fall back location, wasn't any better than Florida. A few years of relaxation before she began to rebuild the Fates would be in order. There would be changes this time.

It was unacceptable that Two and Three would have the same influence and power as One. One should reign without the continued irritation of the lesser women. Yes, there was much work to do. Unfortunately, there was little to be salvaged as far as political connections. There was work to be done behind the scenes to ensure the people she had in place remained loyal and committed. Money made the world go around, and as Three had been removed from the picture, and presumably, Two also, she'd have access to their accounts as well.

One narrowed her eyes as she focused on a

runner on the beach. She depressed the intercom. "I need to speak with the insurance broker."

"At once, ma'am."

Two and Three had implemented insurance policies, as had she, still she needed to verify with the... adjuster that Two and Three's policies were going to be fulfilled. After all, if she didn't have to track down who killed them, all the better.

CHAPTER 24

"**O**perator Two-Seven-Four. Stand by, Sunset Operative Six. I'm transferring you to Alpha."

Alpha? What in the hell..."The line is secure." The operator spoke in the same damn voice. She had to be AI. Cutting edge intelligence.

"Alpha online."

"Operator Two-Seven-Four is clear."

Alpha growled, "Authenticate Lipton."

"Iced tea." Tempest rolled his eyes when Travis shot him a weird look and snorted a laugh. Sometimes he wished he could go back and re-write his authentication codes. Whoever made them up was obviously stuck on a tea theme.

"Status?"

"Target confirmed and mission complete. Sierra team acquired the products required. In addition, I have some intel."

"Go on."

"There is a computer hard drive. The owner believed it had information about our organization. Apparently, there are a few levels of encryption still remaining, but they are close to accessing the drive."

There was complete silence before Alpha muttered, "Fantastic. I thought this shit was done."

"Obviously not." He had no idea what shit his old boss was talking about, but the implication was the ordeal wasn't finished. "Additionally, both targets indicated the existence of an insurance policy. Fifty million US dollars for the successful termination of their murderer."

"Indeed?"

"Inquire about the name, Akuma."

"I will."

"Anything else?"

"The one who remains is suspected to have a bunker. The target's words were, 'She won't die alone.'"

"Wonderful, we still have eyes on her. Any collateral damage?"

"Sierra team encountered two."

"And from you?"

"No." He didn't do collateral damage. He wasn't Raven. When he killed more than one, it was on direct orders. Like Tahiti.

Alpha was silent for a moment. "Do you still have tabs on your... ah, on your woman?" Alpha chuckled at his own lack of words.

"I can locate her." He glanced at the men across from him. The aircraft was on final approach. He'd ping her location as soon as he could power up his computer and get a secure link. Unlike the satellite phone he was currently using, his computer did not have built-in encryption. There was a secure network at his safe house, and he could access one on Smoke's ship if it was still in port.

"Find her and make sure she's okay."

"That was my intent all along."

"Yeah, well sometimes men are stupid when it comes to women. Take it from an old married man, you've got no idea how many ways you can screw up in a relationship."

"And yet you're still married."

"Yep. My woman is a saint. Stay available. Things are moving fast."

"May I ask why you're the one taking this call?"

"You may ask, but I'm not answering."

Tempest chuckled. "Message received." Alpha wasn't going to tell him shit. It didn't matter. He didn't give a flying fuck who he reported in to as long as the next step of the mission went according to plan. "Has the last mission hit the media yet?"

"No." Alpha's response was immediate. "When you are debriefed by Anubis, provide the location so we can drop hints if need be."

Tempest closed his eyes. He'd left the body in a very remote location. "Not unanticipated. I was told to keep it remote."

"Fortuitous actually, for a number of reasons. Keep Sierra team. I want them immediately available when you need to move. When we're ready, I don't want to wait for personnel."

"Roger that."

"You will receive further instructions."

"Affirmative."

"Alpha out."

Tempest turned off the satellite phone and

rolled his shoulders. "Have your team standby in the local area."

When he spoke, Travis' eyes popped open. "Copy. I could use a bed. These jump seats suck."

Hell, he'd agree with the statement even though he was in the best shape of his life. The seats were guaranteed to stiffen muscles. "I'll be in the Boynton Beach area. Stay local to me."

"Can do." The plane banked and the interior bay light dimmed. "Someone coming to get the computer equipment?"

Tempest blinked. Alpha hadn't given any instructions on the equipment. "I didn't get any intel on what to do with the computers. I'll take them with me." He could secure them at his house until Guardian could meet him and take custody.

The plane touched down and the roar of the engines reversing stopped all attempts at conversation. He glanced at the backpack holding the computer equipment Sierra team had obtained. Why hadn't Alpha mentioned the disposition of the electronics? Why hadn't he? Damn it, he'd briefed the man they'd seized it. It seemed strangely unlike Alpha not to have all the I's dotted and T's crossed.

The aircraft slowed and taxied while the team

stood and gathered their personal equipment. The kit Guardian had prepared for him and the computer equipment salvaged by Sierra team took up residence on his shoulder.

The plane parked, and they waited for the cargo bay door to open. The load master for the aircraft made quick work of engaging the hydraulics, and the ramp lowered to the ground. Tempest stepped off the plane with Sierra team right behind him. A whistle drew all their attention.

Holy Shit.

Fury, Anubis, Bengal, Asp, Thanatos, and Moriah stood beside a large, blacked out, SUV. The only member missing was... Lycos exited the vehicle with a phone plastered to his ear. *Son of a bitch.*

He strode across the space and extended his hand only to have it batted away. He got man clenches and back slaps from the men and a nod from Moriah. She wasn't the touchy-feely kind, unless she was killing you, so thank you, but no thank you.

"What the fuck are y'all doing here?"

All eyes moved to Fury. "Big mission. When

you take off the serpent's head, we are taking down the body."

"I know I haven't slept in a couple days, but how in the flying fuck do you think you're going to do that?"

Bengal answered, "We cracked the code they were using. Do you have the computer equipment from the last mission?"

Tempest nodded. "Yes."

"Good, we've set up a temporary headquarters in Del Ray Beach. Your sleep will have to wait for a few more hours." Lycos motioned to his phone. "There are rooms at the hotel we've set up in for you and your team."

"Thank God," Travis said behind him.

Asp tossed Travis a set of keys and pointed to another blacked out SUV. "Follow us."

"You got it." Travis and his men piled into the second SUV as the most elite force of assassins in the world piled into the one they were standing beside.

"Whoever said this thing seats seven comfortably was a fucking liar," Moriah bitched from the jump seats in the back row.

"Count again. We have eight packed in here. You're fucking tiny. What about me?" Anubis groaned and shifted, moving the second-row seat with his knee.

"Just hold still for a couple minutes, and would you please stop bitching. Worse than a car full of toddlers," Bengal growled as he put the vehicle into gear.

"You drive around toddlers on the regular?" Asp twisted in his seat, sitting almost on his hip giving Tempest and Lycos a bit more room. Asp had gained at least fifty pounds of muscle since the last time he'd seen the man.

"No, he doesn't, but I do, and he's right." Anubis unbuckled Moriah and pulled her onto his lap. "Sorry, but I need leg room." He stretched his legs toward the center and Thanatos flipped sideways on the third row seat and moaned in relief as his knees came up where Moriah had been.

"Her husband may kill you for your boldness." Lycos looked back and laughed at the tangle of arms and legs behind the second-row seat.

"Don't fucking worry about my husband 'cause if you don't move your hand, I'll kill you myself." Moriah shifted and Anubis hissed.

"Damn it, that wasn't my hand, those were my keys, and you may have punctured an artery."

Moriah huffed, "Then I'm losing my touch

because that's exactly what I fucking wanted to do."

"How much longer?" Fury asked.

Bengal merged onto I-95 Southbound. "Ten fucking minutes."

Fury glanced at his watch. "Make it five or we'll be cleaning blood from the carpet."

"Hold on." Bengal hit the accelerator.

Tempest shook his head. Guardian had rented the entire fifteenth floor of the hotel, which was also the top floor. A tactical advantage unless someone blew up the building. Then it would suck, but as of yet, Stratus hadn't been that bold.

Travis and his team were given keys, and they said goodnight, even though it was four in the afternoon. Tempest dropped his kit inside his room, washed his face and hands quickly to wake up, and then headed to the room Bengal had told him they'd set up in. Only it wasn't a room. It was a communications center. The windows, walls, floors and ceiling had been draped with a mesh which appeared to have metal coils tightly woven through the material. There was a man who searched him and the backpack he carried with a wand as he entered, and only then was he allowed to proceed to the interior room.

"Wow." The word escaped him as his eyes traveled from one screen to another.

"Thanks!" said a woman as she sped by. She had long black hair pulled up into a bun with several pencils sticking from it. "It's a work in progress, but we've got most of the equipment I require. Where is the computer? Oh, and the phone and anything else the team picked up." She spun and held her hand open in anticipation.

"And you are?" Tempest held the backpack without surrendering it.

"Huh?" The woman looked at him like he had three heads.

"Tempest, this is my wife, Jewell. Jewell, honey, this is one of the Shadow operatives, code name Tempest."

"Yeah. I know. Luke Wagner. Recruited and trained under the original Shadow program. Held by Stratus for one thousand twenty-one days before he was recovered in Atlanta by an operation––"

"Jewell, how about you say hello?" Bengal interrupted his wife.

"Oh. Oh! Hi! It's nice to finally meet you face to face." The woman grabbed his hand and pumped it. "I forget to people sometimes. Do you have the equipment? Wait until you see the information we're getting from the emails on the server alone. I'm hoping she has something on the hard drive. At a minimum, I can recreate her history, extract the sites she visited, and retrieve deleted docs, unless she used a military grade hard drive eraser." The woman spun and headed toward a computer with no less than eight monitors. "I didn't think about a military grade wipe. We can recreate the documents, but we'd have to sift through each line of entry and filter the scrubbed data, like mining for bits of information. It could take an enormous amount of work, but we could recreate those documents. I think if we..." The woman bent her head and started typing.

Bengal chuckled and extended his hand. "I'll take the equipment."

"Is she always like this?"

"Yeah, her mind operates like no one else's. She's brilliant but forgets most people don't understand what she's talking about because she starts in the middle of a conversation she's having with herself." He took the backpack and set it next to the woman who didn't even glance up at him.

"Anubis and Fury are in the next room. Alpha has briefed them on your conversation. Head there, and they'll fill you in on the scope of the operation."

"Where is everyone else?" He glanced around the comms room.

"Asp went to get food for everyone. Go figure. Moriah and Lycos are heading down to the docks to get Smoke."

"Is his specialty needed?"

Bengal shrugged. "Don't know. I'm in charge of this area. I don't go into the field unless absolutely necessary." The man pinned him with a stare. "If you need me, I'm there. Make no mistake, however, I prefer to do this these days." He held his hand up and circled it, indicating the comms room.

"Understood completely." He extended his hand and Bengal shook it.

"Get next door. If your last mission is discovered before we are set up, all hell is going to bust loose."

He nodded and headed to the next room but heard Bengal's woman squeal and spin around.

The woman clapped her hands and literally bounced in her chair as Bengal removed the laptop and three hard drives which Sierra team had found at the residence. Damn, the woman was definitely a computer geek.

He found Fury and Anubis staring at tablets. "Bengal has the equipment."

Anubis looked up and nodded to a seat across from him. "Perfect. Now let's get down to brass tacks. Have a seat."

He took the proffered seat and extended his legs in front of him. "How are you planning on removing the body of this serpent?"

"With the information we've deciphered from the coded emails and the information found from following the information provided by Pilar, we've been able to positively identify sixteen in the organization."

"Are these people with Stratus or are there more in the organization that spawned the Fates?" He retracted his legs and leaned forward, placing his elbows on his knees.

"To our knowledge there are only three Fates. The organizational structure of Stratus appears to be a compartmentalized mess until you understand the reporting structure." Fury flipped his tablet and pointed to a graph.

Anubis added, "It appears each Fate had direct lines of responsibility. Francesca was the one who oversaw expansion. Her duties included moving and planting new layers of Stratus in different countries. She sent intelligence back to Regina and Nadia and directed which local leadership would be eliminated and designated the families to be kidnapped and tortured to ensure the foundations of their organization received no pushback. The woman is responsible for a vast cartel expansion in Colombia and Venezuela. Her role was to seed and monitor the newer organizations, but it appears she's also provided funding through the illegal drug trade her new organizations took over.

"Nadia was in charge of eliminations. She directed what appears to be a sizable squad of personnel who terminated anyone she, or the other Fates, needed eliminated. Normally these people were killed by incidents which were miraculously classified as accidents. Of course, most of these 'accidents' befell the individuals in jurisdictions which were controlled or manipulated by the last Fate, Regina. Those accidents which didn't happen inside friendly jurisdictions were covered up with bribes and eventually other murders.

"Then we can focus on Regina. From what we can tell, her role was oversight of the other two. She was called One, and according to the emails we've deciphered so far, she is neck deep in political blackmail, bribery, and individual replacement as necessary. We have the email which was sent to Nadia instructing her to set the murder of a New York Senator, two sitting judges, and a Representative from Virginia. Each of those women agreed on each operation. There are votes which are recorded in code and show each agreed in turn to every crime committed."

There was no doubt about the depravity of each of those women. His mind flitted to Pilar. "The sixteen you've identified?"

Anubis put his tablet down. "Seven have been coded. Six if you don't count your next mission."

"What about Nadia's army of... hell, are they assassins?" He glanced from Anubis to Fury. "I'm thinking she has access to several that are fairly skilled, Lobo, Raven, Akuma."

"Which is strange. Lobo has been out of the game for a long time." Fury rubbed his chin as he gazed across the table.

"Maybe someone else is using that name?"

"They're a fucking fool. That old wolf will hunt them down and make sure they don't do it again." Fury shook his head. "That is a discussion for another time. We have coded personnel to go after."

"Almost one for each of us," Anubis agreed.

Fury leveled a stare at him. "Pilar isn't one of them by the way, although she was mentioned recently in the emails."

Say what? He was wide awake now. He leaned forward and clarified, "Pilar?"

"Yes. Regina had sent an email inquiring what Two and Three's opinion was to her suggestion they eliminate her."

Rage coursed through his body. He ground his teeth together. "Killing her own daughter? Mother of the fucking year."

"Here's the thing, we aren't positive Pilar is Regina's daughter."

"Clarify." He wasn't in the mood to play guessing games.

"There is no record of birth for a Pilar Grantham."

"She's attended school and college." He frowned at his handlers.

"True and she has a birth certificate, but it isn't real. It wasn't created in Florida, although it is an excellent copy of a Florida birth certificate."

"So..."

"So we believe Pilar was probably given to Regina to raise."

"She was supposed to be the first female President of the United States," he said almost to himself.

"A project. Not a child."

"Good God." He breathed the words. "I need to access a secure connection."

"Here." Fury handed him the tablet he'd been holding.

He tapped in the website and waited for it to populate. He typed in the sixteen-digit number he'd assigned her. A map of the world populated, and he waited as the red dot which was supposed to pinpoint her location blinked, and the globe behind it spun. Finally, it greyed out. *'No information available.'*

"Shit." He erased the numbers and repeated the sequence, gaining the same result. "The trackers aren't working."

Fury stood. "Let's take this to Jewell. If there is a way to track her, she'll know it."

The men barged into the comms room. Fury plopped down the tablet in front of Jewell. "Can you find where a tracker in this program was before it stopped working?"

The woman's fingers froze, and she glanced at the tablet. The pencil held crossways between her teeth dropped, and she caught it without looking. "What do you mean? Like a history?"

"Yes." Tempest confirmed.

She leaned forward again and started typing. The tracking program appeared on one of her monitors.

"The code?"

Tempest rattled off the sixteen digits, and she pounded them into the keyboard. "Okay, yeah. This isn't a constant monitor situation, but each tracker has a ping process. It allows the program to find the tracker in a nominal amount of time." The screen turned into a fast moving scroll of numbers as the woman typed. A printer spit a list of numbers.

She highlighted the code on the screen and opened another program, entering the coordinates into the database. "Longitude and latitude of the phone's tracker movements since its activation. It looks like about three days ago. Here is a virtual track of her movement."

"Fuck." He watched the red dots move from the port of Palm Beach to Del Ray Beach. From Del Ray it moved north and west. There were no stops between Del Ray and its location in the Florida Panhandle.

"Are they taking her to the same place we found you? The phone is moving north." Anubis leaned in and stared at the red dot.

"No, the place they took me was a place to die. For most of my tenure, they kept me in a different facility. I only knew the address they were going to transfer me to because the guards thought I was unconscious, and they were giving directions to the man they were bringing in to make me talk. They discussed the plans they had for me, how it would take months for me to die. My death in Atlanta was their fun for having to put up with me for years." That conversation had marked the end of his resilience. That's when he'd given up. He was going to die, and he'd longed for it. Then Pilar was pushed into his cell and... "I was moved the day Pilar was taken from my cell. I was weak, but the trip took hours."

Jewell gasped softly. "You heard them plan your death."

He nodded. "I didn't have much longer."

"How did you answer the dead drop and let Thanatos know where you were?"

"Pilar." Fury answered for him. "She was the one who wrote the message."

He held the assassin's eyes. "Yes."

"Now her mother has her in the same place."

He nodded.

"Wait, what is this? She has another tracker?" The woman started typing, her fingers a blur across the keyboard.

"Yes. A ring."

Jewell nodded and continued typing.

Bengal put a hand on her shoulder startling her. "Babe, what are you doing?"

"Pinging Pilar's second tracker, the ring, and verifying it against Regina's cell phone number. We have the information. I have a Federal warrant. I'm completely legal. Unique for me, but hey, when you got it, flaunt it, right?" Jewell worked her computer system and stopped, looking up at the screen. "Yeah, okay. I think Pilar's cell phone is a red herring. Regina was in Florida until this morning. Here she is and next she's acquired here, less than five hours later. She flew into New York City."

"That's what our teams have told us. She's been in her office building in Manhattan ever since," Fury agreed.

"Yeah, ten bucks says she's not." She typed again. "I asked the office in D.C. to determine what her mode of transportation was, private or commercial, and to get flight plans. I'm assuming we'll need to be able to prove she moved north and when..."

Tempest watched the woman work. She was remarkable. "Here. We have Regina's phone and the last ping from this cell tower. I'm overlaying Pilar's ring. Here. Yes. The same tower, twelve hours earlier. Pilar's in New York."

"What buildings in the area are owned by Regina?" Tempest shot the question to the room.

"Oh, snap! Excellent idea!" Jewell started typing. "It is going to take a hot minute, and I'm going to need help from D.C. There are so many damn shell companies at play in this."

"Then we head to New York." Fury cuffed him on the shoulder. "Anubis, gather the clan. Bengal, get us air transportation and *two* vehicles on the ground in NYC."

"I'll brief Archangel," Jewell said as her hands flew across the keys.

Tempest sprinted from the comms room and into the room where he'd dropped his kit. That bitch had taken Pilar. Was she at risk? Was the woman running? Hiding? Did Regina know about the assassination of the Russian? There were too many questions and only one way to get answers. He needed to get to his woman. Now.

CHAPTER 25

The aircraft had landed fifteen minutes ago, and they had been whisked away by drivers sent for them from the New York Office. The small brick building they were in now was a remote comms station the detachment used when they were on this side of Manhattan. Tempest stared at the assembled assassins as Bengal came through on the phone's speaker. "We haven't found any structures owned by Grantham or any of her known shell companies."

"What do you have?"

"A hunch," Jewel said. "The tower we triangulated is between SoHo and the Lower East Side."

Fury pinched his nose with his thumb and forefinger. "Jewell, what does it mean?"

"Well, follow me on this. There is nothing above ground in the area or any area adjacent to this location which belongs to Grantham, right?"

"Right," Tempest answered quickly and headed to a map of New York mounted on the wall of the small building.

"Well, what *is* in this area is the Basilica of St. Patrick's old cathedral which got me to thinking maybe what we are looking for *isn't* above ground."

"Wait."

"Why?"

"What?"

Tempest wasn't sure who said what because every one of the assassins in the room spoke at once, except for Moriah. She dropped a massive F-bomb after everyone else popped off.

"Let her finish," Bengal growled across the connection.

"Thanks... ah, well, the cathedral has extensive underground features. As a matter of fact, New York is riddled with these underground chambers built in the mid to late 1800's as the city was expanding with traffic and people. The tunnels, caves and structures were built so animals could get to slaughterhouses without causing traffic jams, people could store ice, you know, a multitude of reasons. Some were used during prohibition as breweries. There is all kinds of folklore and little to no real documentation on where these structures are located. So maybe, instead of looking above ground, maybe we look below."

"Nadia spoke of a bunker." Tempest stared at the map. "I was kept in a location that did not have windows. When I was moved, it was probably to ensure any remains which were found weren't located in the same city or state. Is there any way to see under New York City?"

"Yes, but it is in the trial stages. The intel might not be perfect," Bengal answered.

"What method?"

"We have a modified P-band X-ray cartography unit which is capable of examining, or scanning if you will, underground. It could tell us if there are tunnels existing where we don't have confirmed knowledge. It isn't perfect, but it is a start."

"I thought P-band only worked in desert locations due to the moisture in the soil." Lycos' question drew every eye to him. His brow furrowed, and he shrugged. "Ethan was doing a school project on the uses of different radars. We went down a rabbit hole. Sue me."

Bengal answered, "There has been some work

on the system in Israel which is cutting edge. The Mossad has been generous to Guardian because of the information they've received from their interrogation of Kowalski."

"How long until we know where to start?" Fury snapped and glanced at the clock on the wall.

"Permission has already been granted to fly over this location. The plane is en route. We can download as it scans real time, so to answer you, as soon as the aircraft makes the passes it needs."

Jewell interrupted her husband, "This would also explain why both Pilar and Regina's phones disappeared in this location. Last time I checked, there wasn't cell service underground."

"But she would have to have electricity and a means to communicate, right?" Tempest stared at the speaker on the table.

"I've checked. There are no unknown power draws, so I'm assuming they've tapped into the power source of a building above them, which eliminates individually metered businesses." A map appeared on the screen depicting the section of the city where the phones had gone silent. Several squares were blacked out. "When we receive the scans, I will overlay the newly indicated underground structures like this." The map tipped to a

3D image. A red block rectangle and several smaller blocks appeared under the cathedral. "What about phones?" He was grasping at straws, but damn it, there had to be something to indicate where they were.

"That's harder to determine. All they would need was a person who knew what they were doing and access to a punch down block. They could piggyback on any company's service without anyone being the wiser. Sorry, but we are in a holding pattern now. All we can do is wait for the aircraft to perform its magic."

"Good job, Button. We're standing by." Fury disconnected the call and crossed his arms over his chest. "What can you tell us about where you were held?"

Tempest turned to face his boss and leaned on the counter where he'd been standing. "I assumed it was underground. Steel doors, steel ceilings, floors, walls. Cold as fuck." An unbidden shiver dusted lightly across his skin raising gooseflesh. "There were at least twenty guards during my tenure. Some left and returned, some left and never returned. I believe there were others like me being held."

"Believe?" Anubis prompted.

"Screams, smells of flesh burning." He shrugged and closed his eyes. He was not going to let his mind slip back to the past. Not now.

"So, it is well manned. Were they armed?"

"Yes. Heavily. Several had converted M-4 type rifles, automatic."

"Alarms? Cameras?"

"I didn't see any. I don't believe the cell was monitored, but I don't know about the rest of the facility."

"Facility? You think it was more than a holding area?"

"Yes. The corridors were about twenty feet long, well-lit and had offshoots with closed doors." He shut his eyes and thought of the times he'd been dragged down the hall, leaving a smear of blood along the floor. "Three doors to the right, two doors to the left. My cell at the end of the corridor. There was a kitchen or a break room. I could smell food being prepared." An effective torment when they didn't feed or check on him for weeks on end.

"Anything else?" Moriah said from beside him. He opened his eyes and blinked back to the here and now.

"No." Nothing he cared to share.

Moriah stared at him before asking, "You think this bitch has your woman down there?"

"I do."

She grunted before she followed up, "You think she knows? About you?"

Tempest sighed and shook his head. "That I don't know, but my gut tells me she's put two and two together. The woman is smart but making that kind of leap, connecting Pilar to me would take a confession from Pilar, and I don't see it happening, at least not this quickly. If she couldn't reach the other Fate, would she go underground?" He shrugged. "Yeah, she could."

The phone rang again, and Fury punched the button activating the connection. Bengal's low voice came through the speaker. "Heads up. We got notification Nadia has been found."

"Details?"

"None. Only that a respected businesswoman had been found dead. The Russians aren't going to let the details out. If the other Fate didn't know, she does now."

"The plane completed its first pass; the graphic should start receiving the overlay soon," Jewell interjected.

All eyes swung to the monitor. It was painfully

slow to watch the program populate the radar image below the maps. Jewell followed behind, changing the color from red to blue if the indications were not on the map.

Tempest leaned forward. "That's it. The perpendicular hallway and the off shoots. See, here." He tapped against the monitor. It was basically a pod off a larger area. "Is it a cave or something else?"

"I can't tell from this information. Sending the longitude and latitude."

"How can we access the site?" Fury headed to the map. "What buildings are on top of or around this structure?"

Tempest joined him as Jewell rattled off buildings, "A bank, security surrounding it would be impossible to deal with. There is a retail and office building which would have metered units, so the power thing would be an issue. Next to it is... an event management facility. It also rents small areas accessible twenty-four-seven."

"That's where we start. Find us a way in."

"Wait, across the street is a twenty-four-hour gym. She could tap into the gym too, and the pod underground looks to be halfway between the two."

"All right, we'll split into two teams. Everyone has comms, weapons of choice and spare ammo?" Fury's eyes snapped up and measured the affirmative responses. "Let's go then."

"Wait." Tempest's word stopped them all. "Regina Grantham is *mine* to kill."

"What the actual fuck?" Moriah snorted. "It's like you don't know us. We won't kill her. Maim, yeah, maybe, but she's yours. Now can we fucking go? You guys talk more than the women I know." The tiny assassin spun on her heel and exited the squat brick building.

"What she said." Smoke cuffed him on the back. "Who is going where?"

"You, you, me, and him--" Fury pointed at Thanatos, Smoke and him, "--are going to the event management facility. The other four are going to the gym. Lycos, corral that woman and make sure she doesn't kill anyone because she's bored."

"Dude, she is *so* fucking not my job anymore," Lycos muttered, but headed toward the door.

Asp sniggered and cuffed Anubis on the back. "Come on, Pops, time to dip your toes back into the operational world. Then I want to go to this little cafe I found on East Houston near Broadway. Excellent food."

"Food. Oh, yay, just what I want." Anubis groaned and left the building.

Tempest turned to Thanatos. "Are you sure about coming along?"

"Yep. Discussed this with Eve. She knows and understands. We're solid, but you damn sure better call her when this is done. She wants to set up an online chess game with you."

"Let's leave the chit-chat for later." Fury threw him the keys. "Get us to this building. It is time to go to work."

The event center reminded him of a tidal pool. Entities which should not be together stuck in a small location swimming around each other while trying to keep a safe distance. There was a man, probably the event director, in the middle of the mayhem holding a clipboard.

"No, those are for the Wesley wedding. They go in the holding area until tonight. We aren't cleared into the facility until ten." He ran after a couple of men wheeling carts of tables. "Wrong, wrong, *wrong*! We need the nine-foot tables, not the six-foot rounds. Take those back downstairs and bring up the right ones. Hurry up, go!" His phone rang, and he answered while power walking toward a delivery truck.

"Downstairs." Fury nodded, and they followed the men with the tables. Blending in was easy. Not a person questioned what they were doing, but then again it appeared the only one with a clue was the man currently berating the delivery truck driver on the other side of the warehouse. They waited until the required nine-foot tables were brought up in the elevator before they descended.

As one, they stepped into a jumble of furniture. The six-foot tables were blocking their path forward. Smoke kicked the cart and sent the damn thing wobbling into a stack of chairs.

"We need to find an entrance." Tempest headed to the nearest door.

"Split up. Use the comms if you find something." Fury's words registered but weren't needed as far as he was concerned.

"This fucking basement goes on forever." Smoke's grumble across the comms echoed his sentiments.

He followed a path between boxes of holiday

decorations and opened a door, only to find another door. Steel. "Got something." He whistled sharply bringing everyone to the door as he felt the seams of the construction. With the hinges on the inside, a double thickness of steel was noticeable at the locking mechanism.

"Any alarms?" Fury's flashlight pegged the seam of the door, and they examined it for any wires.

"Wow, now that's a door." Smoke clapped his hands together. "Is someone going to pick the lock or can I play?"

"We don't have time to wait." He glanced at Fury. "Can you open it without alerting the people upstairs?"

"I can." Smoke nodded.

"Seriously?" Tempest grabbed Smoke's arm, stopping him from moving toward the door.

Smoke's brow creased. "I'm damn good at what I do. I know your woman is down there. So kindly get the fuck off my back and watch a master at work." He dropped his backpack and fished around in the interior. Two small packages emerged. "This is co-crystallized HMX and CL-20. I'll need enough to disengage the locking mechanism and compromise the deadbolt."

Smoke carefully opened the smallest package

and removed two tiny grains of crystal, each the size of a piece of rice, and placed them in the keyhole. He sealed the package carefully and produced a small package of Det cord. With practiced ease, he placed the det cord in the lock and used putty to cover the locking mechanism and keep the det cord against the explosives.

Smoke stood and looked at the room. "I'll need one of those six-foot tables. Make it two." Fury and Thanatos hustled back to the cart Smoke had pushed away when they exited the elevator. They were back, each rolling a table beside them. Smoke glanced up from connecting the det wire to the charger. "You two behind that one, and Tempest and me behind this one. There is always a chance this explosive acts funky, but I've used it before. It should behave."

"Safety first." Thanatos and Fury hunkered behind one of the tables, and he and Smoke did the same.

"Three, two, one." The sound of the charge box sending a shot through the det cord was expected. The muffled thump of the lock explosion and the small movement under their feet as the door heaved and then settled, wasn't.

"That was it?" he asked Smoke.

"Yep." Smoke flashed him a smile and took the table as Tempest moved toward the door. He used his hooligan tool from his backpack to pry the steel door away from its lock.

"Check for alarms," Fury whispered near his elbow.

He ground his teeth together and answered, "No shit."

"Too many cooks in this kitchen." Thanatos chuckled.

Smoke snorted, "Stop mentioning cooks and food or Asp will appear."

"The man has seriously bulked up," Thanatos agreed.

"Will you two shut it?" Fury pointed the pen light he carried into the seam, and they slowly pried the door open further.

"Why? You two are taking forever. If there was an alarm on the door they'd have responded by now." Smoke crossed his arms.

"Not necessarily," he grunted, and he and Fury did one more check before they opened the door all the way. A long corridor headed down and sloped to the south. "This has got to be it."

Fury keyed his comms. "We found a way in."

Anubis acknowledged the information and

added, "We'll join you and make sure none of the rats leave the sinking ship."

"Roger that. Take the elevator downstairs to the storage area. The access is all the way to the back behind the holiday decorations.

"Copy all."

Fury nodded down the corridor. "You lead. I've got your back. You two have our six."

Smoke sighed.

"Problems?" Fury hissed.

"Nope, love the view from your six. And a fine six it is, too."

Tempest left them, and felt Fury fall in with him.

"Hey, wait." Smoke had his backpack off and removed one of the tiny packages of explosive crystals, det cord and a charging unit. "In case you need it. You saw what two grains could do. Take cover if you use more."

Tempest pocketed the items. "Got it, thanks." He moved quickly, but not hastily. Every inch of the tunnel was examined. There were no wires other than the electrical cord which provided energy to bare bulbs.

"No dust." He motioned to the metal adjacent to

the walls. If the tunnel was infrequently used, there would be dust at the sides of the walk.

"Cleaned regularly," Fury agreed.

They stopped and waited for Smoke and Thanatos at a bend in the corridor. Tempest leaned forward and glanced around the corner. "Door. Keypad. No camera."

They moved as one, and Thanatos went to work. He attached a small device to the keypad and using a special filter on the device's camera he was able to see the numbers used most often. "28157. These pads have a requirement for six or more numbers. Seventy-eight percent of all numbers used as passwords in these models were dates due to the simplistic nature and six-digit composition."

"What date would the Fates find important?" Fury glanced at him.

"Birthdays? We'll need to go back outside to get those from Jewell, but if we key in the wrong one..." Thanatos shrugged.

"What about important events in history? Their history? Mary, Queen of Scots was executed on February 8, 1587." Tempest glanced from Thanatos to Fury.

Smoke raised his hand like a kid in school.

"Excuse me, teacher, why the hell would some chick getting her head handed to her be important to them?"

He snapped his head around and hissed at Smoke, "The organization the Fates are rumored to belong to was formed by Mary, Queen of Scots, as an attempt to thwart her cousin Elizabeth's reign."

"No shit?" Smoke chuckled. "The things you learn in a tunnel under New York City."

"2-8-1-5-8-7." He nodded to Thanatos to input the numbers.

Thanatos keyed in the numbers and the lock opened. "How the fuck did you know that?"

"Almost three years of researching everything and anything to do with those bitches and Stratus." Tempest pushed the door open and walked through.

The odor was what hit him first. A lemon scented cleaner mingled with a plastic tinted tang of the forced air and, yes, there was still a pungent lingering scent of sweat. His gut rolled but he gulped a chest full of oxygen and forced the physical reaction to abate. There were two hallways. "Split up. One will lead to the holding cells. The other, hopefully to her quarters. Comms won't work down here so once you clear your area, head to the other. Regina is mine."

"Got it." Thanatos started off.

"Wait. If Pilar is down there..." He let the sentence drop in the silence of the corridor.

Smoke cleared his throat. "We'll make sure she's taken care of. We'll take care of her as if she were our own. I swear it."

Tempest nodded and tamped down the sucking black hole of worry which had draped around him the minute he'd discovered Pilar was here with her mother.

He headed down the other corridor and stopped. He motioned to the camera, the red light flashing as it rotated in their location. "She knows we're here."

"I'm ready." Fury pulled his knife and sneered at the camera.

Tempest removed two FN FNX45s from his shoulder holsters. Fifteen rounds in the magazine and one in the chamber gave him thirty-two rounds before he had to reload. He'd mow them down, and Fury would eliminate those still alive by the time they hit the ground.

A thunder of boots echoed down the hall.

"We don't have cover or a fall back," Fury

sneered and then laughed.

"Then we John Wayne it, brother. It is a great day to die." Tempest leveled the gun in his right hand and as soon as he identified his target and saw a weapon, he fired.

Regina's men collided in a crash of bodies. The confusion worked in their favor. Tempest moved forward a pace at a time as he fired through the throng of men sent to stop them. Fury worked at his side taking down those who made it through the initial spate of bullets. Sparks from ricocheting bullets trickled down his shirt, burning his skin and a stinging sear of pain sliced across his shoulder. He lowered his right hand and brought up his left, firing without missing a beat.

The men returned fire, ducking and dodging, trying to find cover, the constant movement preventing them from firing toward Fury or him accurately. Tempest kept walking forward, following those who were retreating. He dropped the magazines from his weapons and reloaded as he stalked the men who'd run for their lives.

"You good?" Fury motioned toward his shoulder.

"I'll live." He rolled his shoulder and nodded toward where the men had fled. "Let's finish this."

CHAPTER 26

Pilar watched her mother pacing back and forth. Her hands and feet were zip tied to a wooden chair in her mother's quarters, such as they were. Her front teeth were loose and her lip swollen from where her bottom teeth had pierced the tender inside skin when the man had punched her in the face. Her left eye was swollen shut and her brain pounded against her skull so hard she was sure the bone would split open.

"Tell me who assisted you." She lifted her head and stared at Regina.

"Assisted me in what?" she mumbled. She had a fat lip. Was her lip why she was having problems speaking?

"Really? Are we going to play this game? I

assure you those men can do more than rough you up a bit. If I give them permission, they'd be happy to make you talk." Regina sat down behind a smaller version of the desk she had in Florida. "If you are honest, I might be lenient."

"Lenient? I didn't do anything wrong. I have no idea what you're talking about. Where are we?" She swallowed nausea back. Her words were slurred even though she tried to enunciate them.

Regina sniffed and examined her nail beds. "Well your response takes lenient off the table. Why was the tracker put in your luggage found on another vessel? Why did the GPS on your phone suddenly not work, and why did you examine your rooms so closely after you returned from your trip?"

Pilar blinked and tried to follow her mother's comments. "You tracked me?"

"I've controlled every aspect of your life since the day they brought you to my doorstep."

"What?"

"Oh, for God's sake, are you truly such a dullard? Let me spell this out for you. You are not my blood. It is why I insisted you call me by my given name. The thought of actually conceiving makes me ill." Regina stared at her and shook her head. "Why I waited for years to see if you'd actually produce fruit is beyond me. I must have temporarily lost my mind."

The words struck like a bullet, exploding the tiny, precious hope the woman in front of her actually loved her. A chime rippled through the air. Regina spun and pointed a remote at one of the large screens on the wall behind her desk. A picture appeared on the monitor.

Oh! God! "Luke!"

Her mother's head whipped her direction. "Ah... now things are starting to make sense. Which one is Luke?" She turned again and moved closer to the monitor. Her mother's hand dropped, and she stepped forward again. She stared at the screen and then slowly turned around, her eyebrows peaked high and a stark look of surprise on her face. Regina stared at her while she pointed toward the screen. "*That* man. He's the one..."

Pilar coughed a humorless laugh. "He is."

Her mother... no, *Regina,* marched to her desk and picked up the phone. "Kill them." The chilling words echoed in the room as she slammed the phone back into the cradle. "Do you know what kind of man your savior is?"

"I do. Do you?" Pilar attempted a smile but only half her mouth responded.

Regina tipped her head back and laughed. "You have no idea. He is an *assassin*."

"No. He is a good man." Every word was an effort.

"Good at killing, yes. A good man? Please. He killed thirteen people in Tahiti. Do you want to know how? He beheaded them and left their heads on spikes on a public beach." The woman sat down and typed furiously on her computer before she hit enter several times and the other screen flashed up a gore-filled depiction of the scene Regina had described.

"Who were they?"

Regina sighed dramatically. "You are missing the point. *He* did this."

Pilar dragged her eyes from the macabre sight and stared at the woman who'd never given her even a modicum of positive attention. No, she'd never believe a word Regina said. Never again. She raised her chin and enunciated as clearly as possible, "If he did this, they deserved... what happened to them."

Several flashes drew her attention to the monitor. Regina's gaze followed hers. She watched Luke and the other man work as a team. Blood splattered the walls of the hall—the same hall she'd been dragged through a short time ago. Luke took aim and... she flinched as the back of a man's head exploded.

Luke and the other man advanced, firing constantly. Outmatched by two men, the majority of her mother's security team was slaughtered, mowed down like extras in a *John Wick* movie. Fixated and unable to look away, she stared at the ruthless precision, the deadly accuracy, and the systematic way Luke and the other man killed.

Then suddenly Luke and the other man were no longer fighting. They stood calmly in the middle of the hallway amidst a slew of dead bodies. Had she blacked out? When did the fighting stop? She could see the men talk as Luke did something to his weapon.

Regina turned off the monitor and swiveled her chair. "It seems the die has been cast." She opened a drawer and produced a gun. Pilar studied the woman in front of her. There was a tightness to her face. Her mouth compressed into a thin line, and her brow wrinkled when she moved the top of the gun back and then slid it forward.

"What have you done, Regina? The things I

discovered were horrendous, but this––" she swallowed hard, trying not to gag, "––sending men to kill, having me beaten and questioned, what you did to Luke for *years*... What kind of person does this?" Pain lanced across her head from temple to temple. She closed her eyes and breathed shallowly.

An eerie, bitter laugh was her only answer. She opened her eyes long enough to watch Regina saunter across the distance. She closed them again, and the woman spit in her face.

"You could never understand. I am the first of three who control the world. By *my* decree wars are fought. *I* determine how countries are run, who lives and who dies. My wealth exceeds that of any person on this planet. *I fear nothing and no one.* Those men, they can kill me, but they will never stop the events I have put into motion which will tear this world apart. Death won't stop my reign. It will ignite a litany of fuses, topple governments, annihilate countries, and destroy civilizations. Maybe next time the world will get it right." Regina pulled the hammer back on the gun and pointed it at her. "Too bad neither of us will be around to see it."

"Don't, please." The agony ravaging her head

marginalized her understanding of the woman's tirade. She did understand one thing. Regina planned on dying and killing her, too. God, Luke shouldn't have to see this. He'd suffered so much already. A tear slipped down her cheek as she begged. Witnessing the unveiled and absolute cruelty of the woman in front of her extinguished any hope of rational argument.

The sound of gunfire outside the metal door drew Regina's attention.

She swallowed back rolling waves of nausea but heard Regina ask herself, "How should this play out?" Regina walked back to her desk and leaned against it. "I could kill you now. A problem eliminated." She placed the gun on the desk and examined her nail beds again. "But I think I want to punish you and your assassin."

Pilar tugged at the plastic zip ties, feebly straining against their hold and trying to fight the pain splitting her skull in half. Regina looked up when the gun fire ceased. "Ah, it is time." Regina picked the gun up again and sauntered behind the chair where she was bound. Pilar felt the muzzle of the weapon lodge at the back of her head. Tears filled her eyes, and she choked on her words. "Please don't do this."

"Shut. Up." The barrel of the weapon smacked into the back of her head. White patches floated, blocking her vision. The pounding of her head reached a shattering pinnacle as the percussion of an explosion pushed her pain past bearable. She lurched as far to the side as she could and vomited.

Tempest and Fury kicked the door open. The moments which followed hit him in stop action snapshots. An empty desk. Swing right. Regina standing behind Pilar. A smirk on her face. Pilar lurching to the side. The weapon in the woman's hand firing. His weapon bucking in his hand. Fury's knife lodging in Regina's eye seconds before the woman's head exploded from his bullets.

He tossed his second weapon to Fury and sprinted to Pilar. She was retching violently. He snatched the knife from what remained of the woman's head and sliced the zip ties holding her.

"I'm here."

He brought her into his arms, carefully.

"She's..."

"Yes, she's dead."

"No... no. She's... she said..." Pilar's eyes rolled into the back of her head, and she passed out.

"Get her above ground. She needs medical. I've got this." Fury's words registered as he moved her gently into his arms. Fury handed him his weapon. He moved from the chamber, holding her in a careful embrace, but one hundred percent ready to kill anyone who got in his way. The damage to Pilar's face sent him into a rage which consumed any humanity he had lingering within.

He heard running and positioned himself to shoot. Smoke skidded to a halt. "Whoa, dude, would you quit trying to put holes in me? Oh, fuck. Is she okay?"

"I don't know." He moved back down the hall. Smoke extracted two handguns, and his head was rotating damn near a three-sixty making sure the coast was clear as the assassin moved beside him.

"Fury?"

"Cleaning up. The threats were eliminated."

"The Fate?"

"Very dead."

"Thanatos found three prisoners. None in as bad a shape as you were, but damn."

Moriah and Asp appeared at the junction. "Where do you need us?"

Smoke directed them to Thanatos' location, and when they encountered Anubis and Lycos rushing down the corridor, he sent them toward Fury before he ran forward and worked the controls on the elevator.

Tempest hit his comms and leaned against the back wall, suddenly exhausted. "We need an ambulance."

"I have three on scene," Jewell said.

"She's hurt."

"I can see that. I've told first responders she's unconscious with facial injuries. We had you on the warehouse's camera system before you got into the elevator. Is that a gunshot wound?" Bengal asked.

"No. Just the facial damage, vomiting, concussion, possible skull fracture." He didn't want to think of the ramifications. He couldn't. Not now. Fuck, those bastards.

"Not her. You," Smoke snapped before he hit his earpiece. "He won't leave her, put them in the same ambulance."

"What?" Tempest snapped his head in Smoke's direction.

The man nodded at his leg. Blood seeped down the outside of his jeans. "A flesh wound."

"Like your shoulder?"

Tempest adjusted Pilar's small frame in his arms. "I think Fury sliced my shoulder when he was wielding his damn knife."

Smoke chuckled and then laughed. "Leave it to Fury to bring a knife to a gunfight."

Tempest pushed himself off the wall and walked through the throng of people in the upper warehouse level. People walked around him, crossed in front of him, and no one, not a single person, stopped to ask if they needed help. Bloody and battered they walked to the sidewalk where the EMTs were waiting. He laid Pilar down on the gurney and hoisted himself into the rig.

"Sir, you can't ride back here. Company policy."

Tempest turned his head and glared at the man. "Make an exception."

The medic swallowed hard and nodded. "Roger that." He jumped into the back of the bus and started his assessment of Pilar.

The ride to the hospital probably only lasted five minutes, but it seemed like it took forever. He followed her into the Emergency Room. There he learned forever was much, much longer.

CHAPTER 27

" **S** it rep." Archangel's voice shattered the tired silence of the hospital room next door to Pilar's which Fury had somehow commandeered. He wasn't leaving the hospital to do a debrief, so Fury brought the debrief to him. Lycos was outside the door, and the connection was secure via some magic from Jewell.

"The target was located, and the mission was accomplished." Tempest said, not giving a shit if Fury was running the show.

"Your woman?" Archangel's voice softened.

"She's still unconscious. They've run all their tests. She has a linear fracture to the skull, but no bleeding or swelling they can see. They're watching her closely."

"I understand you were injured, a knife and bullet wound."

Tempest glared at Fury. The man rolled his eyes. "That is accurate. None of which will slow me down. Was there any useful information in the bunker?"

"Useful. Yes." The man said nothing more for several long seconds. "What are your immediate plans?"

"I'm going to be here for her, for her recovery." Because she was going to recover. There was no other alternative.

"And then?"

"Then I believe I'll talk to her. If there are no lasting ramifications from this incident, she'll want to work, so would I, but perhaps not in my current capacity."

"Explain."

"Sierra team and I work well together."

"Sierra team has a skipper."

"I can cooperate, add my expertise to their missions, make them stronger, but not until I find out if Pilar is all right."

"I copy. I'll run this by Alpha. My gut reaction would be to allow it. Fury, do you have any objections?"

Fury shook his head. "None."

"Copy that. Out-brief him on the rest of the mission. Archangel out."

Fury reached across the table and pocketed his phone. Tempest rose and walked to the adjoining door and opened it a fraction of an inch. Pilar still lay motionless and pale on the hospital bed. He closed the door and walked back to the small blue plastic chair and sat down. The damn thing groaned under his weight. "The rest of the mission?"

"We found information and more leads to others within the Fates' organization. In addition, we've got some solid intel on several Stratus operations. We'll be cleaning up the mess the Fates and Stratus have put into action for years to come. Some of the things we found are extremely concerning, possible connections which need to be verified. We have the best people available, in our organization and others, working to track down members of Stratus. With the exception of a few the Council knew about, and had already sanctioned, the leaders will be brought in. Our timeline and our rules this time. The head has been chopped off, but the limbs are still deadly. It is going to take time to sanitize this mess."

"I meant what I said about working with Sierra team. I like the idea of having down time, of working with a team. I hate to admit it, but having backup when I was in the field made shit easier."

Fury snorted through his nose and nodded. "Yeah. Hurts to admit doesn't it?"

"Like a motherfucker." Tempest chuckled. "I may be getting long in the tooth, but I can show those men on Sierra team a thing or two."

"I've got no objection to you working with them. Travis is a damn good skipper; you'll have to respect his position."

"Not a problem as long as he understands I'll do my own thing when the situation calls for it, without getting in his way too much."

A grunt of agreement was all he got. "What did the doctors say?" Fury nodded toward Pilar's room.

"She needs to wake up." It had been twenty-four hours. He closed his eyes and sent the millionth prayer today up toward the big guy.

"She will."

"I'm not allowing anything else."

Fury nodded and crossed his arms over his chest. "I need to tell you something."

He tightened, the assassin never hedged or beat

around the bush he was about to chop down, so this hesitancy was unusual. "Spit it out."

"Your woman, I've seen her before."

"What, like on a mission?"

"No, like on the ranch in South Dakota."

"She's never been to South Dakota." At least not that she'd told him. Tempest moved so he was between the door and Fury. What the fuck was the guy getting at?

"Yeah, I get it, but dude, she is the spitting image of Tatyana."

"Who?"

"The wife of a friend, he manages the day-to-day operations at the Annex. She's now a Guardian and has been searching for her sister who was taken from their village in Russia when the girl was very young. I haven't seen Pilar without the swelling, but... You know how Smoke gets so much shit because he looks like his younger brother?"

"Yeah."

"She's an exact copy of Taty."

"But she's Regina's daughter."

"Remember what Jewell said about not being able to validate the birth records with a hospital or the State of Florida?"

Tempest rubbed his neck. "Yeah. But how could we know for sure?"

"DNA. Let me take a sample with me. We'll be able to know for sure, but I got to tell you, the resemblance is uncanny. Lycos, Anubis, Moriah and Asp agree. Anubis pulled me aside before I could gather them up individually to confirm my observations."

"Do what you need to do. But I'm not going to get her hopes up. If this woman is related, then we'll deal with it after she wakes up. If she's not... impaired."

"She's got the best docs. There is no swelling in the brain. She'll come out of this." Fury clasped him on the shoulder—the assassin's equivalent of a bear hug.

He extended his hand. "Thanks for the backup here, for the support while I was at the Rose, and for not losing faith in me."

Fury took his hand. "You are the reason the Fates are no more. You're the one person who knew where to start and how to finish it. The *world* owes you a debt of gratitude."

"I'd settle for a drink when she's better."

"Deal. Whatever it takes, my friend."

"As long as it takes."

He watched Fury exit and waved at Lycos as the pair left. He quietly opened the door and went back into Pilar's room. The background was filled with soft beeps and the occasional pumping fill of the automatic blood pressure machine. He moved the plastic chair from beside the window and settled it beside her bed. He'd always heard patients who had someone talk to them when they were in a coma could hear what was said. He didn't know whether or not to believe it, but if there was a chance, he was going to make sure Pilar knew he was there. He glanced at the closed door and chuckled. Like anyone was going to care if he was talking to her. The nurses and doctors here had probably seen it all.

"Well, the meeting didn't last long, but it was good news. Are you ready to hear what happens to your sparkly vampire? We only got to chapter three." He sniggered at the novel Moriah had found in the gift shop downstairs. "Do you like these types of books? My friend said the saleslady downstairs told her women were swooning about this story. It's a prequel and there are three or four more in this series in the hospital bookshop."

Moriah had held the paperback toward him with two fingers and an outstretched arm like it was infected with the plague and had added quite a few F-bombs which he deleted from the conversation he relayed to Pilar.

"You know, I'd rather read surfing magazines, but I don't know if you surf. Do you? Living in Florida, you had to have tried it, right? If not, I'll teach you. There's nothing like it." He opened the book and glanced at her unmoving form. He snaked his hand under hers and let her fingers rest above his. He stared at her smaller hand, so fragile in his larger palm. "You're going to get better. You've got to... you see, you were the reason I held on. Let me be your anchor now. Wake up for me. Come back to me. Please." He drew a shaking breath and opened the damn book and began to read aloud.

Waking up wasn't an instant process. More like pulling herself from a vat of cotton batting. A few seconds of sounds, voices... and then the pull of the softness would wrap around her and tug her back into the silence. She heard him, though. Luke. His voice. He was there. Every time she bobbed to the top of the softness he'd be there. His calm, unhurried voice a reassurance. When she finally opened her eyes, the lights above her were off. She blinked and turned her head.

"Hello. I'm so glad you decided to wake up."

Pilar blinked her eyes several times and frowned. A nurse wearing blue scrubs with white and black kittens smiled at her. A hospital?

She turned, taking in the room. There, lying half on the bed beside her, was Luke. He sat on a chair but rested his head and arms on the side of the hospital bed. The warmth of his skin against hers drew her eyes to the hand which held hers.

The woman whispered, "He hasn't left your side, even though the doctors told him he should get some decent rest. This is the first time he hasn't jumped to his feet as soon as I came in the room. Would you like some water?" Pilar rolled her eyes and nodded. "Thought so. Here." She held a cup with a straw in front of her. The ice-cold water filtered across the parched dryness of her mouth and throat like a rare shower drenches the desert. She emptied the cup.

"Thank you." Her words were a mere croak.

"You're welcome. Do you want me to wake him?" She nodded across the bed toward Luke.

Pilar cupped her hand around his and shook

her head. She closed her eyes and opened them immediately, suddenly terrified of not waking up again.

The nurse smiled at her. "It's okay, honey. You rest. Everything is going to be all right." Her eyes filled with tears as the horror of those last few hours found a home in her consciousness. The words her mother... Regina... She wasn't Regina's child. *Who was she then? Where was she from? Did she have a family? Parents? Did it even matter?* She turned her head toward Luke and squeezed his hand gently, ensuring the connection was there.

He bolted upright, putting himself between her and the door. The nurse chuckled. "That's what I was expecting earlier."

Luke still held her hand, but he swung his attention to the nurse. "Damn. Sorry, I must have fallen asleep––" She squeezed his hand again. He jerked and was next to her in a blink of an eye. "Oh God, Pilar!" He leaned over her and touched her face gently. "Baby, I was so fucking scared."

"You? Never." She smiled, but tears still streamed down her cheeks.

"Are you in pain?" He glanced at the nurse who scurried back toward the bed.

"No. Well, yes, but it isn't bad." She licked her lips and tried to wet the parched skin.

"Why are you crying? Do you want some water?" Almost frantic, he whipped around to the nurse. "Can she have water?"

"She's already had some. Why don't I go get her a fresh pitcher of ice and water and give you a few minutes to talk? I'll be right back. Hit the call button if you need me." The nurse grabbed the small plastic pitcher and promptly spun on her heel, leaving the room.

He cupped her face with his hand and wiped at the tears with his thumbs. Pilar grasped his hand and stilled the motion. "She's dead."

"Yes."

She swallowed hard. She hadn't seen Regina die. "Did *you* kill her?" He paled and tried to pull his hand away. She held as tight as she could. "No! Tell me, tell me she's dead. That you killed her and she can't hurt anyone ever again. If you tell me I can believe it. Please--"

His hands returned to her face. "Shhh... she's gone. I promise. She can't hurt you or anyone else ever again."

"No." She shook her head and winced as her headache thudded through whatever pain killers they'd given her. "She said she'd done something. She was going to kill me, and I think she knew she was going to die. She said neither of us would see the results of her work. Luke, you have to find out what she's done. You have to stop it."

"Pilar, babe, stop for a moment and listen to me."

She gulped air and tried to stop the tears, but the terror of what Regina had done was bone deep and wrapped so tight she couldn't breathe.

"It's okay, she's dead. We have all of her computer systems. The emails were in code, but Guardian has cracked the code and is transcribing the documentation. Guardian will do everything in its power to ensure her plans are stopped."

She stared into those gold-flecked green eyes and begged, "Do you swear?"

"I do, on everything I am, I swear." He leaned down and kissed her forehead.

As he moved away, she whispered, "She said you were an assassin. That you killed those people in Tahiti. Did you?"

"I work for Guardian. What I've done is classified."

"Do you know about those people in Tahiti?"

He nodded, never once letting his eyes drop from their connection.

"What did they do?"

"Rumor has it they were bidding on young men and women."

"What?" Bidding... "You mean they were buying people? For what?" Oh God. *No.* "Sex?"

"That was one of the nicer things. These people were the brokers. They bought from people who gathered the children and sold to those who wanted them. At least that's what I recall the rumors said." He stared at her. "They died for their crimes and a message was sent. The world wasn't going to tolerate their activities any longer."

Her head was heavy and pounding harder. She dropped it back into the pillow. "Did it stop? What they do?"

A sad smile spread across his face. "For a short while."

"But she's gone." She had to be sure.

"Yes. She can never hurt anyone again."

"Will others take her place, like the people in Tahiti?" Her eyes closed, and it was a struggle to open them again. There was still so much swelling.

"No. Guardian will never allow it, nor will I."

She closed her eyes and squeezed his hand. "Don't leave me. Please."

"Never." She felt his lips on her forehead again before she slipped into sleep.

He watched the sun come up while sitting in that damn plastic chair. He'd held her hand all night and rewound their conversation over and over in his mind. When she'd first asked if he'd killed Regina, he was sure she'd be horrified, repulsed. Yet he refused to lie to her. Her reaction surprised him. She didn't seem to be upset that her mother was dead, and her desperation to be sure Regina couldn't hurt anyone again bordered on manic, but the early morning conversation also provided insight into her injury. She could reason, speak, she remembered, which was unfortunate but a blessing nonetheless.

The nurse had left a note for the doctor, and at shift change the day nurse seemed happy to let her sleep until breakfast. So, he sat waiting for the minutes to pass and for her to wake again. He needed to see her wake up again. Needed to know her long sleep was past and she was healing and would again be the Pilar he knew.

He didn't respond to a light tap on the door. The nurses usually knocked lightly as a courtesy, but came in anyway. There was no movement. Finally, the door edged open a crack and then wider.

A tall, broad shouldered man with jet black hair, high cheekbones and dark eyes slipped into the room and closed the door behind him. He was out of the chair and at the end of the bed in seconds. The man stood quietly just inside the door. His eyes snapped to and stayed on Pilar.

The stranger held up his hand and because he posed no immediate danger, or at least none he couldn't handle, he waited. Finally, the man jerked his eyes away from Pilar. In a very quiet voice he said, "I'm Mike White Cloud. My wife is Tatyana."

He relaxed immediately and released the air he had trapped in his lungs. He sent a cautious look back at the bed. Pilar's brow furrowed for a moment before it relaxed, and she sighed into a deeper sleep. He nodded to the adjoining door, and both men left the room.

"There is no way the DNA results are back already." He extended his hand. "Luke Wagner."

"A pleasure to meet a fellow Guardian." Mike shook his hand, the grasp strong, but not overpowering. "No, they aren't back. I couldn't let Taty go on another wild goose chase. We've searched all over the world for her sister, and each disappointment has taken something from her. She's stopped looking. The pain of each successive disappointment was too much."

"Then why are you here?"

"Fury, Anubis, Asp, Lycos and Moriah. They swear the woman is Taty's double. Tatyana's DNA is on file with Guardian. They are running the tests without her knowledge, by my request. I wanted to save her if your woman isn't who they believe she is."

"Having seen her, what do you think?"

"The resemblance is striking. Is she... what is the diagnosis?"

"Guarded, but she woke up last night. She remembered everything, which is a blessing and a curse."

Mike nodded. "Taty thinks we are here in New York for a break. If the results come back positive, I'd like to arrange for them to meet."

"Of course, we'll be here until Pilar is cleared to travel."

"I will let you get back to her. Please call me if you need anything." Mike handed him a card. "We'll be in New York as long as necessary." He extended his hand, and Luke shook it again. The big guy slipped from the room as quietly as he'd come. Luke eased back into Pilar's room and made it to her bedside before she opened her eyes.

"Hi."

To him her smile was brighter than the rise of the sun on the horizon this morning. "Hi back. How are you feeling?" He gently pushed her blonde curls away from her face. He'd memorized the bruising left by those bastards and avoided brushing the tender skin.

"Mmm... I feel like I've been hit by a bus."

"Well, fortunately for you, that didn't happen." Her doctor's voice at the door interrupted their moment. "Most people who get hit by things like buses don't fare as well as you did. Not to say you didn't cause us some worry, but the fact you're awake and talking to us is a good sign. A very good sign. I'm Doctor Anders. Guardian has retained me to make sure you receive the best possible care. Let's take a look at what's happening with you now, shall we?"

Luke stepped back and let the doctor examine

Pilar. He spoke to his nurse and ordered another round of tests, as a precaution, and to ensure there was nothing they'd missed. "How is your pain on a scale of one to ten? One being next to nothing, ten being the worst pain you've ever experienced."

Pilar moved her head and winced. "Four when I don't move, six when I do."

"Can you tell me your full name?"

"Pilar Grantham."

"What is the last thing you remember before waking up here?"

"Being sick and then Luke helping me."

The doctor glanced at him. He nodded confirming what she remembered.

"Any nausea, problems focusing, auras around anything? Follow my finger, please. Don't move your head."

Pilar answered as she tracked the man's finger with her eyes. "No. Just a dull pounding, like I've got a hangover, but I'm not nauseous."

"Good. We can give you something to manage the soft tissue discomfort. I'll check in later today after the tests are done and see where we stand. All in all, I'm comfortable with the progress so far. We'll have some food sent up and see how you do." He tapped away at a laptop before he closed it and picked it up. "Any questions for me?"

"Can I make this bed sit up?"

"Certainly, however, sitting up is the extent of your movements until I get the test results back."

Pilar nodded as the doctor hit the button to lift the bed higher. "Better?"

"Thank you, yes." She carefully pushed her hair back. "When can I go home?"

The doctor chuckled. "Let's see what the tests say. If we don't have any problems, perhaps tomorrow or the next day if you have someone to watch you."

He took her hand in his. "I'll be there. What about air travel?"

"Well, when we get to discharge instructions, we can talk about travel, but frankly, I'd prefer if she kept her feet on the ground for a while and then do some follow ups with us." The doctor gave them a salute as he exited the room.

She glanced at him and extended her hand. "Sit here with me?" He dropped the silver rail and sat next to her, holding her hand. "I remember voices. Who was here this morning?"

"Ah, I didn't mean to wake you." He rubbed the top of her hand with his thumb. "I'm not sure how to tell you this." She stiffened at his comment. He squeezed her hand. "It isn't anything bad, just hell, I don't know... awkward."

Pillar rolled her head on the pillow and stared at him. "My mother had me beaten and then tried to kill me. How much more awkward can my life get?"

He chuckled. "Well, I'd say at least a couple levels more. When you were unconscious..." He drew a deep breath and started at the beginning, explaining his coworkers' observation of her looks and then added the fact there was no proof of her birth other than a birth certificate Guardian had not been able to verify as legitimate.

"Regina told me I wasn't her daughter. Is there actually a chance I could be this woman's sister?"

"I don't know. The man who came by this morning was her husband. She's been searching for her sister for a long time, and it has taken its toll on her. He hasn't told her about this possibility. He didn't want her to go through another disappointment."

"I understand why he'd shield her."

"So do I." Luke cradled her hand and kissed the back of it.

"What's next for us?" Pilar's voice was soft, and her eyes dropped to the blanket.

"First we get you well."

She smiled. "You know what I meant."

"I do. I guess the future is up to you."

She blinked owlishly. "How so?"

"Well, we can go back to Florida so you could practice law, or we could travel, find a new place to live."

She smiled wide and sighed. "We. The word I was looking for. I'd like to work, but I don't have to live in Florida. I can study and take the bar wherever *we* find a place to live."

"Perfect. We'll take our time and find a place for both of us."

"Are you going to continue to work for Guardian?"

"Would it bother you?"

She blinked at him and her brow furrowed. "No. Not at all."

"But you know what I do."

"And?"

"You're okay with it?"

She closed her eyes for a moment. "If you hadn't come for me, I would have been killed by the woman who raised me. If you hadn't been involved in the events in Tahiti, more children would have been sold. I don't know what else you've done, and I don't want to know, but I want you to continue to make a difference, unless you choose not to continue. At that point, I'll make you a house husband and teach you how to cook, clean, and peel grapes for me."

He threw back his head and laughed. The pressures of the last days levitated off his shoulders. No one could make him feel this alive. No one had ever eliminated the dark isolation which had surrounded him. Pilar was his buoyancy, the force which propelled him from the darkness into the light. He leaned forward and kissed her gently. *Savior, comforter, deliverer, beauty*, all the words fit her, but one word now surged to the forefront of his mind. *His.*

CHAPTER 28

Pilar stretched, luxuriating in the warm water pulsing down on her shoulders and neck. The palatial hotel room Luke had moved them to when she was released from the hospital three days ago had a breathtaking view from every room. The Manhattan skyline had twinkled through floor-to-ceiling windows while they'd slept the last two nights. *Slept.* She rolled her shoulders slowly. She'd made it a point to specifically ask the doctor if she could have sex. The answer was yes, as long as it wasn't a wild, hanging from the chandelier, event.

Luke had put the brakes on anything amorous the first night, and she had to admit, she was worn out. Sleeping in a comfortable bed without people coming in and out of the room all night long was what the doctor had ordered. She felt good, except for her sore muscles, and soreness was to be expected. Over the counter meds controlled the dull achy throb which still lingered.

She lathered her hair with shampoo which didn't smell like antiseptic and tipped her head back to rinse the suds. She was going to have sex with her man tonight, come hell or high water. Last night a telephone call sent him into the other room, and she'd fallen asleep waiting for him. Not tonight. Luke had errands to run this afternoon, and she'd taken a nap. She'd be able to stay up all night if necessary.

As she towel-dried and combed out her hair, she inspected the array of bruises on her face. Dang, how she really wished she had her own makeup. The concierge had been accommodating and recommended a drug store nearby that would deliver. The concealer was too oily and a shade lighter than she needed, but she'd be able to cover up the majority of the bruising. She dabbed her concealer on the tender blotching. Her hair dried curly, of course. She slipped into her new clothes, compliments of someone at Guardian, and used the blow dryer and diffuser attachment to finish drying her hair. She added lip balm to her lips and stepped back to assess her reflection. Her blonde hair hung past her shoulders in soft curls. The makeup was noticeably heavier than the natural look she normally went for, but she didn't look horrible. The soft silk tee and black yoga pants fit perfectly and molded to her figure. She laughed when she turned sideways. She'd finally lost the ten pounds she'd been trying to lose. "I guess all it took was a psychotic mother and hospital food."

"Pilar?" Luke's voice in the front room sent her scurrying to the door.

"Here." She stepped into view and watched as his eyes danced up and down her body.

"Daa-yum." Luke swallowed hard and rubbed the back of his neck. "Ah, we've got company."

She peeked past him at the door. "Who?"

"That's a surprise." He walked to her and enfolded her into his arms. "You should have been resting."

"I did. I took a long nap and a longer shower. I wanted to be awake when you came to bed tonight."

His eyes softened. "You needed your sleep."

"I did. I don't tonight." She elevated onto her toes, and he lowered to meet her lips. A soft knock on the door drew a low groan from him. She leaned to the side and looked at the door. "Can you send whoever that is away?"

"Right now, I really wish I could. Just... hold those thoughts. We'll get back to them." He took her hand, and they walked to the door. "Pilar, I want you to meet someone."

He opened the door and her mouth gaped open. She couldn't believe her eyes. "Oh, my God. You look like me."

"We look like our mother." The woman standing in front of her spoke in a Russian accent. "I'm Tatyana, your sister."

"My sister?" She gripped Luke's hand so tight her nails dug into his skin.

"Yes." Tears formed in the woman's eyes. *Her sister's eyes.*

"Would you like to come in?" Luke asked and tugged her hand a bit.

She startled and motioned into the spacious suite. "Please, I'm sorry, I was... am... shocked." She stood back as the woman and a tall man came in. "Come in." She led them into the living area and sat down on the couch facing her sister. "Please, tell me everything. Until a few days ago, I thought my mother was Regina Grantham." She put her hand to her mouth. "Our parents?"

"They are gone, it is only us."

"How?"

"Many years ago, in Russia. When they lost you... it was very hard on them."

"Where were you?"

"At school. You were what my mother called a late life gift. The village we lived in was raided and ten girls were taken. You were among them. I searched for you."

Pilar reached out and took Tatyana's hand. "What is my real name?"

"Karina Annika Petrov."

"I'm Russian? Wow, isn't that a rush!"

Tatyana laughed. "Yes and no. You are American, very American, your talk, your speech, your education. Our parents were born and raised in Russia, yes." Her sister bit her bottom lip before she asked, "Did this woman who raised you treat you... well?"

Pilar drew a deep breath and told the truth, "She didn't treat me *unwell*. I was an annoyance to her when I was small. I was raised primarily by nannies, and when I was old enough, I attended boarding school. I was sent to the best colleges. I'm a lawyer in Florida." She wouldn't disclose any of the atrocities Regina had instigated. "What about you? Did you fare well after our parents passed?"

The woman glanced at the man who stood beside Luke. Her eyes softened and she nodded. "I had some difficult moments, but Mike has been my salvation." She extended the hand which was not holding hers. He walked to her and took her hand. "This is my husband, Mike White Cloud. He and I work for Guardian and live in South Dakota."

"You work for Guardian?" She glanced at Luke who smiled.

"We both do. Taty teaches language proficiency, and I run a training complex for Guardian. It is a very small world, isn't it?" Mike gave her a brilliant smile.

Pilar shook her head in disbelief. "Very small." A realization zinged through her. Her life had really begun the moment she walked into the cell and met Luke. A series of events using that meeting as an impetus culminated in the life she was *always* supposed to have... with her Guardian.

Pilar hadn't taken a breath since her sister and brother-in-law had left the hotel room fifteen minutes ago. He answered her when she paused long enough for him to get a word in edgewise, but his participation wasn't necessary. His lady was floating on a cloud, and he wasn't going to do a thing to make her happiness dissipate. This is what he'd wanted for her. Safety and happiness. Tempest tuned back into the one-sided conversation she was having with herself.

"She's going to send me a picture of her, I mean *our*, mother and father. She looks so much like me. Did you notice her arm? She said while she was working for MI6, she was shot so she doesn't have too much strength, but I mean, she was shot! And MI6! James Bond stuff right there."

Suddenly she twisted around, a slight wince at her sudden movement flashed across her face. "You must think I'm the most boring thing in the world."

What? "Excuse me? I think I missed part of the conversation somewhere. Why in the world would I think that?" He rose from the chair where he'd been watching her bounce from the couch, to the windows, back to the couch and up again, and sat down with her on the couch.

She waved an arm toward the door. "You work

with those types of people. I mean Guardian, MI6. You left alone and came back with a team of men." She glanced down at her tightly clasped hands. "How in the world can I keep your attention?"

He slid closer to her and tipped her chin up so he could see those beautiful blue eyes. "You've had my attention every minute of every day since the moment you walked into my cell. What we have, this connection, it is more than a momentary thrill for me. My job has its excitement, and yes, dangers, but I don't need or want such things at home. I want a partner who is vital and alive, who leads her own life but makes room for me. You keep my attention by being the woman you are."

He searched her eyes and noticed the bruising the makeup she wore didn't quite conceal. As if drawn to a magnet he lowered his lips to hers. Her softness yielded to his sensuous assault, and he carefully moved her into his arms as he explored her mouth, jaw, and chin, in a trail of small kisses.

"Please. I want you." She extended her arm and brushed his hair from his eyes.

"You've got me." He picked her up from the couch, stepped into the bedroom, and carefully laid her down on the bed. He toed off his boots, shucked his jeans and boxers and whipped his shirt over his head. Her eyes traveled down his nude body and back up. She smiled and crooked a finger at him. He smiled in return as he crawled up her body.

"You have too many clothes on, my lady." He pushed up the silk tee and waited as she lifted her arms above her head to slide the material off her arms. Her yoga pants followed the shirt's path to the floor.

The exposed skin was too tempting to resist. He trailed his fingertips down her neck, across her collarbone, and down to the lace covering her breasts. The comparison of the darkness of his tan skin to the silk of her sun kissed skin forced a sad smile. "You are so perfect. Young, beautiful, and far too good for the likes of me."

Her hand covered his, and she brought it up to her mouth and kissed his palm. "We are perfect for each other. We both knew it, even when there was nothing between us but hope."

"You were the reason I survived." He lowered over her, careful not to place too much weight on her.

"And you are the reason I survived." She trailed her fingers across his lips. "We survived because of each other. You saved my life when you opened my eyes to the woman Regina truly was." She tugged him down to her, and he willingly complied.

This woman was the center of his universe. Everything rotated around her. Everything, from the air he drew into his lungs, to the hopeful way he looked at his future and the peace he'd made with his past.

He entered her and felt her wrap around him. She sighed and hugged her arms around his neck. He slowly seated himself inside her and let her body adjust to him.

She pushed his hair away from his face again and stared up at him. "I love you."

Her words drew the air from his lungs. "I don't deserve your love, but I'll try to be worthy of it. I swear I'll be a man you can be proud of."

"You already are." She pulled him down for another kiss.

He lost himself in her warmth. She loved him. An assassin, a blunt object used to strike fear into the vermin of the world was loved. It was new and brilliant, this connection and exhilaration. The intensity of emotion added to the spiraling heights her body spun him toward. The warm grasp of her heat consuming him and the way her breath hitched before she sighed were aphrodisiacs of epic proportions. Her legs wrapped around the back of his legs. She whispered words of love, of need and of desire. He closed his eyes, pushing back memories of other whispered words in a dark room three years ago. He lowered onto one elbow and strained when she scraped her nails across his back and shouted his name. He watched in abject wonder as she crashed into her orgasm and prayed he could be the man she deserved seconds before he followed her over the peak and fell headfirst into a powerful release.

He rolled, pulling her with him. He fanned her long curly hair from her neck. "I love you, too. I think I've loved you since the day you left my cell."

She shifted, looked up at him, and smiled. "Then marry me."

He jumped, planting his elbow on the bed. "What?"

"Ouch! You're on my hair." She grabbed at her hair, and he scrambled to move but succeeded only in tugging on her hair again.

"Stop!" He froze instantaneously. "Ok, let's do this the right way. Lift up into a sitting position."

He contracted his abs and did a crunch, then rolled into a sit up. Her hair stuck to the sweat on his arm. She swiped her hair back and flopped the mass of curls away from her face. "Man, did I scare you or what?"

"Huh?" He watched her pull the sheets to her chest and sit up.

"I asked you to marry me, and you damn near bolted from the bed." She chuckled humorlessly. "Guess I timed that wrong."

"No, no, you didn't." He twisted onto his hands and knees and crawled in front of her. "I never thought... why would... I'm not..." He stumbled into silence.

She shook her head. "Okay, how about we come to an agreement. Lawyers are good at this type of thing. I propose, when it comes to us being a couple, I do the thinking. You'll get it wrong nine times out of ten. So, marry me. Be my husband."

He blinked at her and tried to decipher what part of the puzzle he'd missed. "You realize who I am and what I do, right? You do remember what your mother told you, what I disclosed to you?"

"Yes, you are Luke Wagner, a member of Guardian. Period. As in, end of story. I'm Pilar Grantham, attorney at law. Period. As in, end of story. So, whatcha say? Make me an honest woman. Marry me." She arched an eyebrow in a dare.

A smile spread across his face. "Name the place and time. I'll be there."

She narrowed her eyes at him and shook her head. "Not a binding agreement. Is that a yes?"

"Yes ma'am, I'll marry you." He placed his lips on hers and pushed her back into the bed. The time and place would be after tonight. Tonight, his little lawyer had business to conduct.

EPILOGUE

S moke watched the water from the deck of his ship. The boat was lonely without Sage. Sage's mother had contracted cancer; his mean bastard of a father had dementia, and none of his siblings gave a flying fuck, so Sage had taken a leave of absence from Guardian. He listened to the creak of the ship as it rocked against the waves of the inner harbor. He'd worked alone before, he could do it again.

He cocked the hammer of his .45 magnum and chuckled as the soft padding of someone's foot faltered. "Show yourself or die. Don't really care which at this point."

The stowaway came forward from the shadows

of the main cabin. "You're pretty good for an old man."

"I heard you come aboard. The ship talks if you listen to her. Why are you here?"

"Anubis figured you'd get lonely. Fury agreed."

He released the hammer of his weapon slowly and rode it to a rest. "So, they sent you to what... babysit me?"

"Nah, I don't care much for kids, but I've completed my training at the Rose. Our profiles say we could mesh. You like people; I don't."

She moved with a grace and poise most people tried to acquire but only very few had naturally. Long strong legs encased in tight denim shorts crossed as she sat down in the chair next to him. He sent a side eye glance at the woman he'd met once or twice at the Rose. For the life of him he couldn't remember her name. "I have a partner."

"True, but his parents have long term conditions, and he has requested a leave of absence without a return date."

"Where is your partner?"

"He... he died."

Smoke twisted in his chair. She now had his complete attention. "How?"

"Believe it or not in a vehicular accident. He

went home to visit his parents and was hit head on by a drunk driver going the wrong way up an interstate off ramp. He lingered in a coma for two weeks."

"Fuck. I'm sorry to hear that. You were teamed up with..."

"Carter Paulson."

Smoke nodded. The guy was affable.

"So, you don't have a teammate and neither do I. I'm willing to take care of you in your old age if you're willing to show me some of your tricks." She leaned in toward him. "I like to make things go boom, too."

Smoke turned his head and stared at her dark brown eyes. "What's your name?"

"Charley."

"Just Charley?"

"Yup. Like Ashanti, Enya, Ke$ha..."

"Who?" He'd never heard of those women.

She snorted a very unladylike laugh and slapped her tanned leg. "Right... um... Cher, Madonna, Sting? Any of those people ring a bell, Gramps?"

"Watch it or I'm going to yell at you for walking on my lawn."

She leaned forward and extended her arms,

turning to look at the water. "Hey, Gramps, I hate to tell you this, but you don't have a lawn."

"It's a figure of speech. Call me Gramps again and I'll show you exactly why they sent you to work with me." He arched an eyebrow and glared at the laughing woman.

"Okay, okay. Truce." She extended a hand.

He took it in his and told himself he did not feel a zing of excitement race through him. He did not. Did not happen. Nope, it wasn't there. He cleared his throat. "All right Charley, I'm assuming you have orders for us."

A big bright smile spread across the young woman's face. "I do, and I'm one hell of a first mate. I have my captain's license, and I can tear apart a diesel engine and put it back together again."

"Handy. What is your specialty?"

She shrugged. "I do a lot of things well."

He narrowed his eyes. "What do you do best?"

She stood up and took a deep breath. "If you ask my parents? Get into trouble."

Smoke chuckled and stood also. The young woman was tall, at least five-feet-ten-inches in the flat tennis shoes she wore. Her brown hair was hoisted into a ponytail which fell to her waist.

Yeah, this one looked like she was still in high school. *Calling him Gramps. Talking about her parents. Damn. He was getting fucking old.*

"Please don't tell me you have daddy issues, too."

"Oh hell, yeah. What woman doesn't?"

He cocked his head. He could stand being around this one. She was sassy, irreverent and feisty. Besides, he needed a diversion from his self-inflicted misery.

"Well then, Charley, we might make one hell of a team. Trouble is my middle name."

"Mine's not, but I usually end up stirring up a truckload of the stuff."

"Only a truckload? Woman, I have things to teach you. Let's get this show on the road." He tossed his soda can into the garbage and headed to the bridge. "Cast off and stand-by."

"Aye, aye!" The woman raced to the lines. He was impressed with the way she worked. Smooth fluid motions. She knew what she was doing with the coil and was sturdy and sure-footed. Hell, now he was thinking of her in horse terms. Damn, he was seriously damaged and missing Sage. The two of them would have had one hell of a laugh about it. He needed to call Anubis and Fury and determine why the fuck they'd stuck him with an operative who was so damn young. Hell, she didn't even look *legal*. He shook his head. Maybe that was her specific skill, infiltrating high schools or taking down assholes who had a fetish for teenage girls. Hell, it might actually be a usable skill, still...

He chuckled to himself. Whatever. He'd run her through her paces before he'd allow Fury to give them an assignment. He needed to know *what* and *who* they'd dropped into his lap.

Thank you for reading Tempest's story. If you'd like to preorder Smoke's story, here is the link. Smoke, Guardian Security Shadow World - Book Six

ALSO BY KRIS MICHAELS

Hope City

HOPE CITY DUET - Brock and Sean

HOPE CITY - Brody- Book 3

Hope City - Ryker - Book 5

Kings of the Guardian Series

Jacob: Kings of the Guardian Book 1

Joseph: Kings of the Guardian Book 2

Adam: Kings of the Guardian Book 3

Jason: Kings of the Guardian Book 4

Jared: Kings of the Guardian Book 5

Jasmine: Kings of the Guardian Book 6

Chief: The Kings of Guardian Book 7

Jewell: Kings of the Guardian Book 8

Jade: Kings of the Guardian Book 9

Justin: Kings of the Guardian Book 10

Christmas with the Kings The Kings of Guardian

Drake: Kings of the Guardian Book 11

Dixon: Kings of the Guardian Book 12

ABOUT THE AUTHOR

USA Today and Amazon Bestselling Author, Kris Michaels is the alter ego of a happily married wife and mother. She writes romance, usually with characters from military and law enforcement backgrounds.

Made in the USA
Coppell, TX
21 March 2021

52115901R00236